Bum Lambs
And
Red Tractors

Virginia Babcock

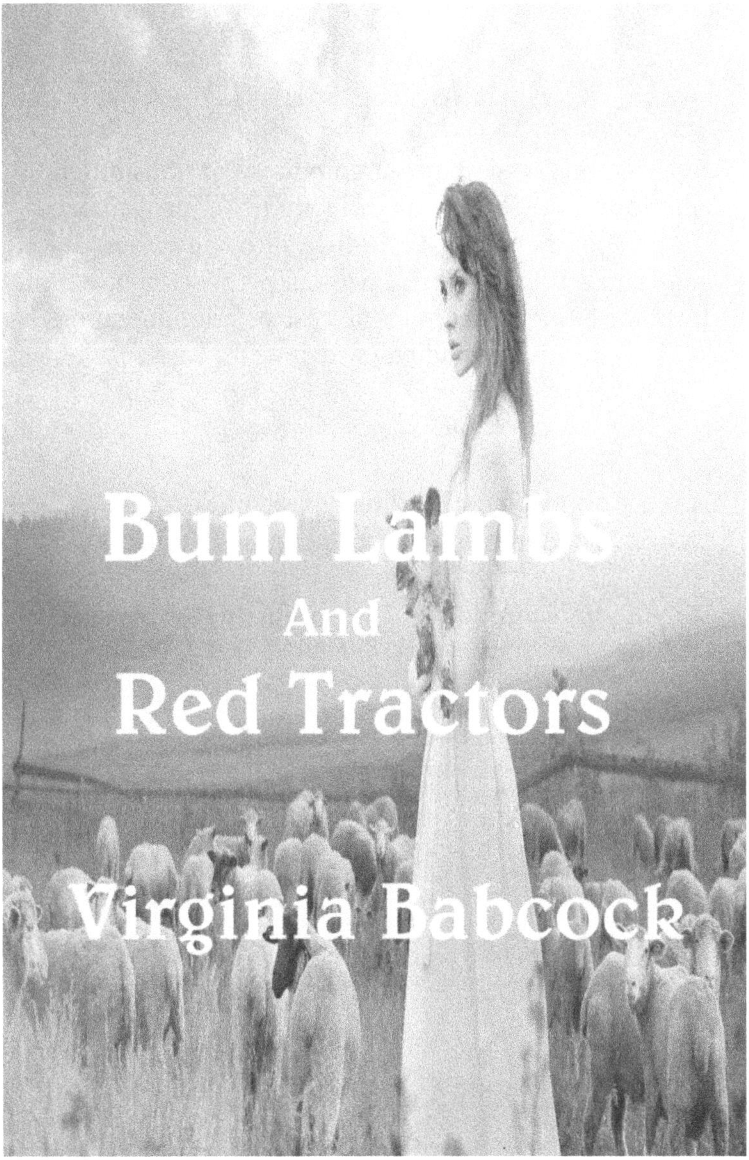

Solstice Publishing - www.solsticepublishing.com

Bum Lambs and Red Tractors
Virginia Babcock

Chapter One

Marion Sullivan wondered, for what seemed like the hundredth time, whether she was crazy. *No one raises sheep here in Utah any more, do they? Can I ever be really profitable?* Gently, but with sufficient force, she held the 1970s glass, Dr. Pepper, pop bottle fitted with a rubber nipple full of lamb milk replacement steady while the tiny bum (orphan) lamb gulped his supper, ravenously. She watched his tiny body strain pushing against her as he suckled, mimicking the motions he would have used against his mother's teat to stimulate the milk he needed to survive.

"I better not name you, little fella," she sighed. "You're destined for the slaughterhouse. I can't afford the risk that your genes would promote single births. I need twins to stay profitable. Of course it was your mom's first time, so this may be her fault, not yours." She considered the baby sheep. "It's really too bad your mom abandoned you, making you an orphan, because you sure are cute."

Marion watched the lamb's long tail, as it wiggled like a snake, as he drank his dinner. She came from a long line of ranchers and farmers, and she pondered once again on the reality of caring for her animals while remaining focused on the fact that she was raising them for meat production.

When he was older, she'd turn this little guy out with the other sheep in her herd, and would dock his genitals and tail with the other male lambs, making him a wether. Then, she'd take all the wethers to be slaughtered in the fall. The female lambs would also lose their long tails, but they'd be kept to have their own lambs to grow her herd.

The tail thought paused her, *I know there's a good reason for docking the tails. What is it?* Ever since her mother had died, leaving the ranch in her and her brother's hands, Marion had worked hard to try to keep it going but, at times like this, she felt very young an inexperienced. *I know we castrate the males to give the meat a milder taste, but I can't remember why we still cut off the tails.*

At that moment, the lamb finished the milk. Marion yanked the nipple out of his mouth so he wouldn't suck in any air and rubbed his textured neck. He bleated for a minute, complaining that he wanted more, but Marion was firm and stood up. The lamb looked at her seeming to understand that she would give no more milk, so he quieted down.

Using his knobby knees, he followed her from the laundry room into the kitchen, his tiny hooves clicking against the vinyl and polished wood floors as she stowed the bottle and nipple in the sink. Turning, she shrugged on the heavy, barn jacket and headed out to feed her other animals. But first, she shut the lamb into the laundry room. "Ok, little guy, hang out here and stay warm while I take care of the rest of the herd."

As she went to feed the sheep, Marion remembered why her mom said they took off the sheep tails. *That's it, maggots. And there are other parasites that the long tails could spread around.* The proximity of a wooly tail to a sheep's anus was a nasty business when sheep feces got in the wool of the tail. Plus, the movement of the tail would spread the manure into the rest of the sheep's wooly coat compromising its quality. Mario could almost hear her mother's voice, *there's no way to keep it clean, and so we cut them off. Besides you can't shear a tail.*

Every morning, before sun up and each night at dusk, Marion went out to the barn next to the main pasture to feed and water her animals or to quote her parents, "feed the sheep." Sheep being the critical animal to her mom. Yip and Mitzy, her two border collies met her on the porch and circled around her as she tramped the two hundred feet from the back porch to the barn. In the barn, two of the many barn cats yowled at her, in a jarring accompaniment, to her flock's noisy baa-ing. The ram was a bit restless too. He wasn't verbalizing, but he alternated ramming his head against the wood slats of his pen with rubbing his horns against the wood, overcome with testosterone poisoning.

Per her habit, Marion turned on the hose and plunked it into the water trough in the outer yard for the dozen or so wethers and her bum lamb's mother in the outside pen. She then went into the barn proper, flipped on the overhead light, and did a circuit of the twenty small pens that held her matriarchs, each with two new, baby lambs. All needed fresh hay and more water in their drinking buckets. *Good, all the lambs and moms look okay. No more bum lambs this year. Thank heavens.* Marion then moved to the ancient, steel gearbox where she stored the large bags of dog and cat food. Grabbing a large, empty, metal, Idaho Potato Flakes can, she scooped out half a can of cat food and spread it in the old, tin, pie plates that served the cats, and then repeated the action on the other side of the open area for the dogs.

Picking up the pitchfork she stabbed a few hay slices from the bales she'd dropped from the stack that morning, and went out to the wethers' pen where she pitched the sweet-smelling, still-green alfalfa hay over the fence to the waiting sheep. Switching the pitchfork to her other hand, she grappled the running hose and pulled it into the barn. Efficiently, she put the hose in the cat's tub as she stashed the pitchfork into the closest bale. Then she systematically filled all the mother sheep's buckets, the ram's tub and then the dogs' tub. Watering done, she pulled the hose back out to the dirt barnyard, flung it away from her walking path, and turned off the water. She went back to her pitchfork and gave all the mommas and the daddy sheep a slice of hay a piece.

Marion paused for a moment to look over her animals. Everyone was busy chowing down. The cacophony of bleats was now replaced with chewing sounds accompanied by the dogs' and cats' teeth clicking as they bit into their dry food with the sounds of falling food pellets echoing off their metal plates.

Satisfied that another round of food and water was successful, Marion exited the barn and went past the home pasture to where the first field started. A mile or so away, she could see the stockyard where her family's cows were mooing for their dinner too. She saw a cloud of dust along the access road and recognized her brother, Gene's, farm truck with a ton hay bale on its flat bed. *Okay, guys, there's your hay. Gene will check your water, and then you, too can quiet down for the night.*

Chapter Two

Leon looked around the old, farmhouse kitchen visually confirming that all of his grandparents' knick-knacks were removed and packed away. He hefted the bushel basket from the counter where he'd packed the last of his grandmother's salt and pepper shakers and iron trivet safely within her hand-embroidered dishtowels. He looked up at the gun rack over the back door, eyeing his grandfather's ancient, red and white, Case IH ball cap. Deftly, he swiped the hat from the now-empty gun rack and placed it on top of the towels in the basket. He then removed the keys from his pocket and left them on the counter.

Down the three steps and past the side of the two-story structure, Leon was off the front porch and to his packed and ready, pickup truck. He opened the driver's side door and slid the basket over to the passenger seat and then lifted himself into the truck. Years of memories of this house, and his grandparents' farm, choked his throat with strong emotion. He breathed deeply resting his hands loosely on the top of the steering wheel as tears welled up. He blinked them away and forced himself to take a long, last look around. The house looked good and well cared for. Before he'd gotten sick, Grandpa had used some of a good year's profit to re-roof the house and paint it. The black shutters still hung neatly, but Grandma's curtains were all down in readiness for the pending demolition.

Leon started the engine and drove around the house back towards the nearby machine shed and hay barn. Both looked sadly empty. Most of the machinery and other equipment had been portioned off amongst the family, or sold, with the remainder waiting at his parents' place. The hay was sold along with the last cows. Grandpa's fences and pens were still standing proud and, while the pastures were empty of stock, they were full of lush and tall, late spring, pasture grass. Four Lombardi poplars remained along the south ditch, and their healthy leaves shone richly green in the sunshine. The blue sky showed a few white, fluffy clouds that would blow by without dropping any rain.

"Grandpa would have cut the first crop of alfalfa about now. He'd have loved doing it on such a beautiful day like today," Leon said aloud.

Leon gathered his thoughts and turned the truck out onto the farm lane that ended a half-mile away at a brand-new road complete with traffic light. For months he'd been resigning himself to the facts. His Grandparents' five-hundred-acre farm, in western Davis County, Utah, was worth thousands in agricultural terms, but worth seven figures to a developer looking to fill it with houses.

All along Utah's Wasatch Front, houses were eating up farmland along the I-15 corridor as more and more people moved into Utah's most populated area and then spread out. This wasn't a new problem, but Leon had hoped his family could have kept farming the land that the first Leon Packer had settled in 1860. As he waited on the twenty feet of new asphalt that joined the farm lane to the busy road that ran from here to Farmington for a green light, Leon thought, *I wonder if the builders will notice great-great Grandpa's one-room adobe house's walls in the center of the 1920s house when they knock it down.*

The light changed and Leon turned left heading to his parents' home in Layton, Utah. He glanced at the clock on the dashboard radio display; it showed 12:10. *Mom said she'd be home by noon. I better call her.* He pushed a button activating his truck's cell phone system.

"Call Mom at home," he commanded. The voice activation system obediently dialed.

"Hello," he heard, after a few rings.

"Hey, Mom. I'm on my way. I should be there in about half an hour."

"Ok, Son. Everyone should be here by then. Are you sure you are okay divvying up the last of Grandpa's things today? I mean everyone has been going through the farm for months. And, with you leaving tomorrow, won't it be too much for you right now?"

Leon felt a tiny bit of exasperation at this reminder of his mother's constant fact-finding, for her neverending feminine plots.

"Mom, I appreciate your concern, but I need to do this now. Tremonton will be a new start for me, and I want to know what bits of the old farm I get to keep for my farm."

"Ok, Son. They're mostly all here and your dad has started the grill. We'll hold the family council after lunch."

"Family council, huh? You're really pulling out the big guns this time," he answered, a smile creeping into his voice.

"Well, there has been talk of you being a grandson, not a son, and I'm hoping by using Grandpa Packer's term for a serious family meeting, I can help your aunts and uncles understand that he made you his executor and gave you a share for a reason."

"And, you'll point out once again to Dad's siblings that none of them wanted the responsibility of the farm, so he didn't choose one of them to execute its dispersal."

"You got me. Your dad's grilling my red-pepper chicken. I figure we'll talk about the Little Red Hen story during dessert."

Leon laughed out loud. "You're going to feed your in-laws your red chicken and then lecture them about familial responsibilities *before* asking them to do a final run-through of the family heirlooms?" Sarcasm tinged his next statement. "Gee, Mom, thanks for helping."

"Well Son, I *am* warning you, now, so you can prepare. But, today isn't to hurt you but to help your dad open a discussion with his brothers and sisters. I'm hoping I'll get tempers stirred enough that Aunt Mary finally agrees to exclude spouses from the final decisions so that your dad and everybody can do this last family meeting like they did when they were younger--when Grandma and Grandpa Packer would assemble the kids around the big dining room table and talk seriously."

"You are one smart cookie, Mom. Getting the spouses out should finally enable everyone to really talk about their parents' passing so they can handle divvying up the final, most contested stuff. No wonder I love you."

"Thanks, Son. Just remember that when you think I won't be able to find you once you bury yourself in the wilds of Box Elder County."

Chapter Three

"Gene, what part do you need me to get while I'm in town?" Marion called out, to her brother in the yard.

Gene came closer, and up the back porch steps, wiping the oil from his hands with a shop cloth.

"I need a new alternator. The mechanic said to check it, and he was right. The bearings are shot."

"Did you call Tremonton Tractor to see if they have one in stock?"

"Sure did, plus they have the new, side mirror Mom ordered months ago. That reminds me, I learned something about the mirror that I forgot to tell you. I guess this new design's been trouble for them. Mom's not the only one who lost a side mirror after a little bump. They've been buried with replacement orders."

"Mom didn't hit a minor bump, she turned too quick and dragged the side of the tractor along the cement wall of the tractor shed," Marion paused after she spoke.

Gene met her eyes and gave her a sad look. "That was harsh."

"Sorry. That just came out. Sometimes I forget the little things that Mom did that we missed were signs that she was getting sick."

Gene came closer and gave her a hug. "Gee, little Sis, don't feel bad. Mom was happy doing what she loved to do to the end. Remember what the doctors said. Mom's tumor was a fast sucker and, even if they'd found it earlier, they couldn't have operated, it reached too deep into her brain."

"Thanks, Gene. Sometimes I feel like I really am rattling around here with just a little bum lamb for company."

"You can always come up to my place. I know Jeanette and the kids would love to have you any time."

"I know. But I need to be sure that I can do this. I need to know for myself that I can hold up my half of the farm. If not, I'll give it all up to you."

"Hey, don't worry. I know Grandpa and Grandma ran it in partnership with Mom and Dad and they proved a two-household partnership still works best. The plan *was* for me and Jeanette to partner with Mom and Dad, but that didn't work out. You know that it's too much for just me, and I need your help."

"Well, if I sold the sheep and you sold one of the houses, you could handle just the cows and fields."

"That's possible, but why sell the sheep or my place, or this place, if we can make it work? You do a great job with the sheep and the fields and you know I'd much rather be in the saddle with the cows than in a tractor cab any day. Besides, look at your mad, farm skills. When you get back from town, you can outfit the new alternator ten times faster than me, and could have the hay cut in the lower field loaded in the barn by bedtime. Who else do you know around here that can do that and is NOT running, or working, on a farm?"

Marion let her doubt creep into her voice. "That's true, but aren't I going to be doing this by my lonesome for the rest of my life? I mean working twenty-hour days, fifty miles west of the nearest, sizable town is not conducive to a productive love life."

"Damn. This is about Nick, isn't it? Did you two break up again?"

"No, unlike what you've heard, Nick and I did NOT get back together last summer despite what his mom says. But, that is my point. Mom intended for me to marry a nice boy to bring back here so he and I could take her and Dad's place in the farm partnership after Dad died. But, I don't meet anybody anymore and I don't know any single guys."

"Yeah, you are right. The Keller boys figured you and Nick were a couple forever back in high school and married those twins, and you hated the Petersons, so you'd never marry into that clan. I guess I never really considered how lucky I was to find Jeanette while we were at Utah State." Gene turned to go back outside. "Well, that's a dilemma I'll have to ponder a while. In the meantime, can you get the tractor parts while you are in town?"

Marion smiled. She could tell by his tone that her big brother was through talking about her love life. "Sure will. And as you so subtly hinted, I'll even install the alternator and take a stab at putting on the new mirror when I get back."

"Well, while you're at TT's, check out the new general manager. Jeanette heard he's real good-looking. He just moved up here from Layton," Gene smirked at her, and ducked out the door.

Marion laughed. *He's trying to fool me, that joker. I bet that the new guy is a white-haired, pot-bellied type who they picked so he could jaw with the farmers as they have their morning coffee.*

Chapter Four

Leon looked around, totally enjoying morning coffee with the old timers who liked to hang out at Tremonton Tractors, LTD, aka TT or TTL, in the mornings. He smiled at the punch line of a joke as he sipped his cold Dr. Pepper from a can. *These old timers have been kind to accept me so quickly, even if I don't drink coffee.* He looked over to the counter as he heard the chime as the cash register opened. His boss, Monte, was filling the till for the day. He met Leon's eyes and nodded.

"Morning, Leon. I'll be in the back if you need me."

"Sounds good, boss, I'll sign in as soon as Baxter finishes his joke about the old maid and the cow." He winked at Baxter as the coffee clutch laughed at his joke. Baxter was a retired farmer and ex-employee at TT. Monte had tasked him to show Leon the ropes, and he'd started by plunking Leon down with his buddies for coffee.

Over the past few weeks, Leon watched spring turn to summer as he got to know his new job. Monte had offered him the full-time position of General Manager so long as he survived a thirty-day trial period. Leon wasn't worried about his skills for this job. Besides the experience he'd gained working on his grandparents' farm, and helping his Grandpa fix his tractors and farm implements since he was a teen, he'd gotten a certificate in both large engine and Diesel engine repair from a local tech school prior to going to Utah State University (USU) in Logan, Utah where he got a degree in Agricultural Machinery Technology. He knew farming, farming in Utah, and tractors inside out, upside down, and backwards. He was grateful to Monte for the job; he was an unknown quantity here in Tremonton and was glad for the chance to prove he could be an asset. *Besides, Monte likes that I can spend part of my time in the shop, saving him from hiring a part-time mechanic. I can really use the salary to grow my ranch/farm fund.*

The sliding of chairs away from the card table jarred Leon from his thoughts.

Baxter spoke for the old-timers as they stood up, "Well, my boy. I think you're ready to tackle this place on your own. We'll leave you to it. Most of these old boys have chores to get back to."

"Yeah Baxter, you promised you'd help me with my alfalfa. That hay ain't gonna bale itself," one of the group chimed in.

With that, the six older gentlemen left the showroom. Leon quickly cleaned up the empty cups, used napkins and stirring straws and scooped them into a garbage can. In the break room, he rinsed out the coffee pot, cleared the filter and slid the coffeemaker back against the wall where it would be ready for the next coffee morning. He then retrieved the cleaning spray and the roll of paper towels from behind the back counter and cleaned the table top out in the showroom. He returned the spray and garbage can to their resting spots then placed the toy tractors on the table and arranged the folding chairs neatly. He took a last look around the showroom checking to ensure it was ready for a busy day.

Monte believed that a clean store was a successful store. Leon agreed and would end his night by dusting the showroom then sweeping and mopping the tile floor. *Monte could hire a cleaning service, but it's soothing for me to do it. He's paying me a good salary so I don't mind being chief gopher and head bottle washer as well as general manager.* He looked at the clock. It showed 7:00. The coffee-clutch farmers usually came in at six and stayed until about six forty-five depending on their daily tasks. Leon understood their work rhythm and knew that most of them had already been up for hours taking care of their animals or water turns before heading into town for a cup of Joe and some company. Monte kept official hours of eight to eight on the door, but usually got to the store at six and left at nine or ten depending on what was happening. He'd told Leon he could work what shift he wanted so long as he was there at either opening or closing each day at least five days a week.

"Work at least forty hours a week, but probably more so you ensure things get done and keep the customers happy," Monte had described of the salary job.

Ok. Got the floor swept and the counter wiped. Break room's clean from last night. I'll double check the till and then open the door. Leon crossed the showroom floor, turned the open/closed sign by the front door to open, and ensured the doors were unlocked. Just then, the side door connecting to the shop opened and their head mechanic, George came in followed by a lady. They were talking and George was carrying a box. Leon recognized the package; it had been sitting in the shop for a week, ever since headquarters had overnighted it to them. George kept talking to the woman as he came up to the counter.

"Miss Marion, I need to get you the invoice for this, but there's no charge for the mirror. Monte pulled your alternator last night so I'll go get it as well."

"Thanks, George. I really appreciate you helping Gene write the letter to headquarters. That busted mirror has been a constant reminder of Mom lately, and I know she felt bad that she couldn't get the part to fix it at the time. Until the day she died, she hated seeing the busted mirror. It made her feel bad that she'd backed into the barn like that," the woman answered.

"I bet. My grandpa got dementia in his eighties and it was hell on him when he realized he was losing his mind, literally. Grandma always said it was a blessing that he was unaware of how bad he was at the end. But, Gene told me the mirror was the first accident that signaled something was wrong and that your mom didn't know she was sick until it happened?"

"Yup. She said the only good thing about her diagnosis was that it caused her accidents and proved that she wasn't just getting clumsy or old."

"Cold comfort at that."

"Definitely."

At that, George looked at Leon and seemed to notice him standing by the front doors.

"Oh, hi, Leon. I was getting Marion the parts she ordered." He then formally introduced the woman. "Leon, meet Marion Sullivan of the Sullivan Ranch just south of Stone." George then addressed Marion. "Marion, this is Leon Packer, our new general manager and part-time mechanic. He's the one who spoke to Gene and helped me diagnose that you guys needed a new alternator."

Leon came over to the counter and watched the lady's face as she stepped closer to him; he was a little shocked when she put out her hand to shake hands formally.

"Leon, good to meet you. I hope our meetings will be few." she laughed, and then continued. "Not that we don't appreciate you guys, but a trip into town for parts usually costs me a lot of money."

"Good to meet you too, Marion. We'll try to keep you from needing more parts best we can. I've spoken to Gene Sullivan a few times, and met him last week, he mentioned a sister Marion. So, I assume that's you?"

"Guilty. Gene was going to come into town today; it's his turn, but he and the boys are working hard to get our bales in before the rain starts."

"Yeah, they've forecasted quite a storm for tomorrow."

"Yup. I'm just glad we finished baling yesterday before the tractor died again. I'm hoping they'll be done by the time I get back, or else I'll have to install these babies." Marion gestured to the second box George had placed next to the first.

George then took back Marion's attention as he worked to open the Sullivan Ranch account in the computer.

Leon picked up the clipboard holding the tractor toy, inventory sheet and went towards the toy display as he thought about Marion Sullivan. *She sure looks like Gene. Tall like him with the same color hair--mahogany brown, with light blue eyes.* Leon wasn't sure yet, but meeting Marion felt like a shock to his system. *But, I don't know her, and I prefer blondes. Why the jolt meeting this brunette?*

George's question pulled Leon out of his thoughts.

"Hey Leon, are you still interested in the old Gorham place?"

"I am, why?"

"Well, remember, Marion and Gene live about ten miles from it, and if you have time later, Marion can show you how to get there."

Leon was forced to look Marion in the eyes. *Damn. She has clear blue eyes that seem to see everything.*

"I don't want to inconvenience you, but I'd really like to see the Gorham spread in person and haven't yet been able to get out there," he told Marion. *Oh great, I sound like a prize idiot who can't find crap. Marion doesn't seem too excited either.* He continued, though, hoping to salvage the conversation. "When I spoke to Gene yesterday, he mentioned that the Gorham place was near yours, and I had played with the idea of delivering your parts on my way out there."

Marion was cool and polite in her response. "Well it's no trouble for you to follow me out there. But, I need to finish my shopping before I head back."

"I can go anytime today. Can you swing by here on your way out?" Leon replied, quickly.

"Sure can. I'll be by in about an hour."

"So, Marion do you want to leave these parts here until you swing back?" George interjected.

"No, better not. I may have to pack groceries around them."

"Okay, I'll load them for you," George said, hefting the boxes.

Leon watched Marion turn and lead George back out the side door. He moved to the windows on that side of the showroom and saw Marion walk up to a late-model, red GMC, crew cab pickup. She lowered the tailgate and lifted a tarp covering the truck bed for George who slid the boxes, in turn, across the lowered tailgate and secured them under the tarp.

George touched Marion on the shoulder, as he appeared to tell her goodbye. Marion smiled and nodded her head, as she seemed to return the goodbye. Then with a graceful movement she slid into the driver's seat and pulled out onto the highway leading into Tremonton proper. Leon enjoyed how sliding up into the truck highlighted the toned shape and curves of her legs. *Dammit, I can never ignore a female who wears real Levi's.*

For the moment, Leon was glad that George had gone back to the shop. He used the quiet moment to gather his thoughts. *Why does she have to be so cute? I don't have time for any romantic entanglements right now. I need to buy my farm and start my legacy.*

Monte came into the showroom and asked a question, jarring Leon out of his thoughts. "Hey, was that Marion Sullivan pulling out?"

"Yes it was. She was picking up that mirror and alternator."

"Good, good. I'm glad the mirror finally came in. They've been back-ordered since before Christmas." Monte shook his head before continuing. "Bad business with their Mom getting sick like that."

Leon couldn't stop his curiosity, "Like what?"

"Oh, cancer. It was a fast brain tumor that caught everyone by surprise. And, it's only been a couple of years since the dad died of a massive heart attack. Their mom had just got things settled again, and was working with both of the kids to keep the ranch going, when she started dropping things and blacking out. I guess in one of these blackouts, back in October, she was backing the tractor into the barn for its winter storage when she had a mini blackout and turned it into the side of the doorway--knocking the mirror off and scraping the hell out of the side of the cab. After that, the kids took her to the doctor who immediately admitted her to the hospital. They ended up sending her down to the Huntsman Cancer Center for more tests. It was too late by then. She ended up dying at the end of January. So, it's just Gene, his wife Jeanette, and Marion running things."

"Wow. That's too bad. That explains what Marion said about the mirror."

"Yeah, well, when the company rep was last out here, Gene happened to come in for something and asked about the backordered mirrors. That's when the rep told him, and me, about the poorly designed, mirror brackets. I guess headquarters had a lot of incidents with the mirrors on that model and traced it to an inferior manufacturing process. They were just getting the replacement parts and mirror assemblies when Gene came in, and Gene's story caught the rep's attention. He promised to personally send a mirror, at no cost, to honor their mother. The rep just asked that Gene write a letter about the incident and send it to headquarters so the rep could share the story with the big wigs."

"That was a nice gesture in their part, and not bad PR either."

"Yup. You're right, there."

Leon absorbed what his boss had said and his plans solidified. He'd done his work time for the week, and Monte was staying closed tomorrow--his monthly Saturday off. His truck should be ready today. He'd first nip over to the house to get his camera and then over to Jacksons to check on the truck, then back here to wait for Marion. Leon finished the toy inventory and began typing the entries into the computer. It's not like he'd have to spend that much time with her. Once she showed him where to go, he could take off to recon the place. He could also keep away from any meal invitations even if they did stop by to see Gene. Resolved, Leon worked to finish his final work tasks for the day.

Chapter Five

Marion hummed to herself, quietly, as she went up and down the aisles in the grocery store. Years of experience made her so familiar with the store that she could grab the ranch's groceries and fill her cart without retracing any steps. Marion's mother started taking her to Jimbo's when she was a tot. Marion was too young to know the history of this independent grocer, but her Mom's mom had started the habit. When Grandma Sullivan was a young bride, newly moved to the northern end of Box Elder County from her home west of Corinne, Utah in the southern end of the county, her new husband showed her where he liked to buy groceries in Tremonton. Back then, it was a Safeway on Main Street, when Safeway still ran stores in Utah. When Safeway pulled out of Tremonton in the early 80s, Grandma Sullivan followed the Safeway baker to the new, tiny Jim & Co.'s, which a couple of young guys opened in an old, brick warehouse a few blocks from Main. The new grocer was next to the railroad tracks, and the elementary school, Marion's parents attended. A few years later, Jim & Co.'s built a new, cinderblock store across town by the Malad River, which became the Jimbo's store Marion grew to love. The baker was now retired, but Marion could still buy the great, white bread that had made Grandma Sullivan stop baking when she got older.

Marion followed the same route each grocery trip. She's start on the west side of the store with the toiletries, then the bulk food and pet food. She'd then cut down the back of the store, past the cold beer and pop, to the canned and baked goods. From there she'd go to the east side for the bakery items, bread, and then produce. She'd end with the cold and frozen foods by swinging from the meat counter, by produce, to the dairy case and then down to the frozen aisles to the checkout stands.

Marion pushed the heavy cart to the checkout stand. Quickly and methodically, she unloaded everything but the fifty pound bag of dog food, the thirty pound bag of cat food, and the industrial-sized box of diapers from the under rack of the cart. As the carousel turned her groceries so they could be scanned, Marion chatted with the checker and bagger as they worked. A swipe of her debit card and she was united with her heavy cart, but everything was now bagged. Marion made her way out the automatic doors and geared herself for her next task.

"Damn, the sun's already hot now. Leon better not hold me up. Even in the cooler, the ice cream won't hold all day under that sun, and the cooler won't fit in the cab where the air conditioning would help," she muttered.

The reasoning for the cart's loading order became clear as Marion unloaded the groceries. She stopped at the rear of the truck and angled the cart so it wouldn't roll down the gentle slope back to the Jimbo's building. Deftly, she lowered the tailgate and flipped up the tarp before tugging the huge cooler back to her. The frozen items went from the top of the cart to the bottom of the cooler. The refrigerated items went on top of them. A bag of ice was emptied over the lot. Marion then pushed the cooler back to the top of the truck bed. She put the diapers next to it, in the empty space next to the tractor part boxes. The cat food went atop the diapers because it wouldn't crush them and wasn't too heavy for Marion to manhandle. It was also just heavy enough to weigh down the lighter diapers. The dog food went next up against the cooler, while the four cases of Gene's Pepsi cans stacked up after it. Marion then closed the tailgate. Hefting the first of her bags of canned and boxed goods; she stood on the rear bumper and placed the bags amongst the larger items in the bed. When all the bags were packed, she secured the tarp and stashed the cart in the return.

Marion breathed deeply to relax once she gained her seat in the truck, and praised herself. *Not bad.* She got three hundred dollars in groceries in thirty minutes. Even stopping to pick up Leon, she should be home in time for lunch; maybe even in time for Jeanette to feed her when she dropped her stuff off. The thought heartened Marion. *By the time I get home, I'll probably be too tired to cook. I think I'll talk Jeanette into feeding me, and then I can mix a batch of bread and start the crockpot for dinner before I work on the tractor.* She finished that thought and looked around for other cars, and people walking, as she started the engine.

The truck started but, as she put it in gear and started pulling out of the parking stall, the entire truck jumped as the engine started running rocky. Marion slammed her foot down on the brakes and watched the check engine light come on as her dashboard's computerized, information display flashed an error message.

"What the hell is safety mode?" Marion asked, as she fished her cell phone out of her pocket. She placed the truck in park as she was only a couple of feet out of the stall, and called her car dealership. Marion's family had been buying their vehicles from Jacksons for more than fifty years. Now called Jackson-Wilber Motors, diehard customers still called them Jacksons though Marion could remember her parents calling them Jackson-Lee for their earlier moniker.

"Yes, can you transfer me to the service department, please?" Marion killed the engine as she waited on hold.

"Hey Joe, this is Marion Sullivan calling about my '10 Sierra."

"Hey Marion. What's happening?"

Marion explained what happened. Joe had her turn the engine on again to see if it was still running rocky and if the message came on again. Marion confirmed both.

"Okay, Marion. It's a problem with the computer control system. There's a recall out for it. You need to bring it in so we can fix it. Until it's fixed, the truck will only run in a very low gear and your max speed will be thirty-five miles per hour."

"I am at Jimbo's right now."

"Great, we have an opening right now, and we'll get on it right after lunch."

Frustrated beyond belief, Marion babied her truck the mile or so to Jacksons. She hoped Jeanette was in the house back at the ranch. She would call her first and then plan from there. *Damn, I don't want to wait an hour for her or Gene to get here. It's really too bad I have a hundred dollars in cold groceries that won't make it if this turns ugly. But, at least I was in town when it happened. I'd hate to do the fifty-mile run into town in first gear*, she thought.

Chapter Six

"Leon, here's the write-up on your truck. You were right; it was the starter. He's bringing it around front in just a few minutes."

"Great, thank you," Leon smiled at the gal who manned Jackson-Wilber's reception desk as he scanned the repair sheet and she scanned his debit card.

Leon pocketed his wallet, folding the service slip neatly as he turned to wait for his truck to be brought around. He passed the time looking at the vehicles up for sale surrounding him. He eyed a brand-new Cadillac Escalade that had a sticker price that was worth half of a nice house in Tremonton. It would be nice to have eighty thousand to lay down for a rig like that. He was glad his old truck was hanging in there. A six hundred dollar starter was a lot better for his wallet than a forty plus thousand dollar new truck. His baby drove up just then. Leon smiled when he saw it. *They even washed it and shined it up*, he thought. He relished a deserved sense of pride in his truck, silver colored with a black body-stripe, it still looked like someone's baby even at nearly fifteen years old. He'd replaced the truck's engine and rebuilt the transmission himself. He'd had it repainted last year, and took it to the dealer for the new starter as a way of testing Jackson's service department.

Leon was capable of most repairs, but was practical about his current situation. Until he had a home shop, or a garage, it was just not feasible to fix it himself. He appreciated the house he was renting in town, but he only had a one-car driveway, no garage or carport and no access to one to borrow. He also didn't feel comfortable working on a personal vehicle in TT's shop. Even if the general manager job worked out and Monte let him, he didn't feel right using his work's shop for personal jobs.

The mechanic who brought his truck around handed him his keys. Leon went out to get his truck and head back to the TT showroom to wait for Marion. He was stashing the service invoice, in his invoice envelope, in the glove box when he looked up and happened to see a red truck pulling into Jacksons and heading back to the service door. *Hey, that looks like Marion*, he thought. Curiosity prompted him to pull around to park his truck over there and investigate Marion's situation.

Leon had just parked in one of the service stalls when he saw Marion flounce out of her truck and forcefully slam the door. Her steps were fast and determined as she opened the service entrance. She looked angry. He followed her into the service shop and caught up behind her at the service desk, where her tone of voice as she consulted with the service manager confirmed her bad mood. He learned two other things as she spoke: she loved her truck and she had a feisty temper,

"Dammit, it's a computer problem?"

"Yes. The system can't tell what's going on and, until we reset it and replace the faulty sensor, it will only run in safety mode."

"So how long will it take?"

"Well, luckily we have the sensor, so we can get started now. Should be done by closing time."

"Five o'clock. Oh no! Will it really take that long?"

"Yes. I'm sorry, but it takes two to three hours, at least, to change that sensor."

"Oh, my groceries, I need to call someone...."

At that point Leon just had to interrupt them. "Um, hey Marion...."

Marion whipped around to face him. Her mouth popped open for a second then she asked, "Leon, what are you doing here?"

"Same thing you are. I just picked up my truck and was on my way over to TT to wait for you. But, from the sounds of things, it's good that I'm here. Can I drive you and your groceries to your place, and then bring you back here to get your truck after you've shown me the Gorham place?"

Marion stood there looking at him for a moment. She was clearly plotting things in her head. Finally, she spoke. First she addressed the service guy.

"You guys will have my truck done by five o'clock no matter what?"

"Yes, ma'am. We'll know as soon as we start whether it will take longer and I'll call you immediately if that happens."

"Ok. I can live with that."

Marion then turned to Leon. "If you're sure about this, I'd like to take the parts too. That will give me something to do while you scope out the Gorham spread."

Leon smiled at the way Marion processed a quick change of plans and seemed calmer now that her groceries were no longer in jeopardy.

"Sure thing. I don't have the cab room you do, but my truck has a bigger bed."

Marion responded to the service guy and Leon before heading out to her truck. "Give me a few minutes to move gear, then you can have my baby. Leon, are you parked out here?"

"Yes, the silver and black truck a couple of stalls down from you," Leon answered.

With that, Marion headed out the door.

Leon turned to look at the service guy before leaving. "I bet the guys are going to gossip over Marion and me like little, old ladies," he said quietly, to himself.

"So Joe, service shuts down at five and closes at five-thirty, right?" Leon spoke.

"That's right, Leon, but if you get delayed, we'll leave Marion's keys and invoice with the sales guys. They're here until six."

"Ok. Sounds good. See ya."

"Bye, and good luck."

Leon realized that Monte was probably serious when he warned him that Tremonton was a classic, small town where everyone knows everybody's business. At least the service guy was professional to his face, heaven knows the stories to come.

When he got out to the parking lot, Leon spotted Marion by his truck. *Well, she's a fast worker, that's certain.* Marion had already opened the tarp on her truck and had lowered his tailgate. She was busy in the back of her truck piling her loose, grocery bags in neat piles away from the boxes and cooler.

Leon went over to her. "Marion, I'll start loading if you want to keep unpacking, okay?"

"Sounds good. I'll have the cooler free in a second."

Leon nodded as he hefted the alternator box and carried it to his truck. They worked together well. He smiled over Marion's take-charge manner. She clearly preferred everything be packed just so, but seemed to accept his placement of items in his slightly larger, truck bed. Together, they filled his truck and covered the load with her tarp to keep the lighter stuff from flying out. They kept up with each other well. Leon noticed Marion finished tightening the last tie-down on her side at the same time he'd done his.

"So, do you need anything from the cab?" he asked.

"Just my sunglasses."

"Can I get them for you while you drop off your keys?"

"Sure can. They're on the center console."

Leon took the few minutes while she was inside to calm himself. *Putting her stuff in my truck is unsettling. Why?* He thought for a moment. He'd always driven a truck and he'd helped people move things countless times. He couldn't figure out if it was because she was a stranger, or maybe because she was female. He'd helped girls move stuff before. Then it hit him. The last time he felt like this was when he helped Shelly. Helping Shelly move into the dorms felt this way. That explained it. Damn. Leon took a deep breath. Shelly had been married for five years. She had broken up with Leon six years ago but, just because she was his first love, didn't mean he had to feel the same way about Marion. *Calm down. Yes, Marion's sexy, but I'm just doing her a favor.* His taking her out and back would more than pay her back for showing him the farm he was considering buying. There was nothing romantic here. He needed to change his thoughts. *You are taking a client parts.* Leon repeated that last thought a few times until it stuck.

Now that he was in the right state of mind, Leon walked around his truck verifying the load was secure, then got in the driver's seat. Marion got in her side soon after. She slid her sunglasses on, and then gave him initial directions to her farm.

Chapter Seven

Marion sat quietly as Leon drove them west and north of Tremonton. Her temper had faded as soon as he 'rescued' her, as was her habit. She had a quick temper that flared hot, but cooled quickly. She watched Leon driving as she alternated between looking around the truck interior and looking out at the scenery. Years of farm life had taught her to roll with the punches when necessary. Marion found that if she kept calm and looked at the situation objectively, she usually could deal with whatever happened. *So, why did I lose my temper over the truck today, then?*

She stared at Leon's hands on the steering wheel. He had nice hands. Clean, with a nice shape and close-cut nails like her grandpa's… she realized she was staring at his hands and quickly turned her head to look out the window to hide her unexpected blush. Geez, she didn't know anything about him, but was blushing noticing his nice hands. *Am I on one today over Gene teasing me about hooking up with Leon only to find out Leon's a looker? Am I a teenager still?* she sighed. What a day, and it wasn't over yet.

Leon must have heard her sigh, because he spoke up. "Hey, why so quiet over there? Are you okay?"

Marion decided she was old enough to talk about a blush if her cheeks were still pink and turned her head to face Leon.

"I was just thinking about what I'd *planned* to do today and how it compares to reality," she answered.

"So you don't buy tractor parts, groceries, and visit the GM dealer every time you come to town?"

"Nope, and I don't move my groceries and parts to a stranger's truck and have him drive me home and back every time either."

"Hey, I'm no stranger, I've talked to your brother plenty of times. But, I agree that your place must be way out there. We've been on the freeway for a half hour and we're not yet to Snowville."

"Well, if you like the Gorham place, you'd best get used to the drive, buddy."

He laughed. "Hey, I'm not complaining. This is half the time it takes to get to Layton with a lot less traffic." Leon expertly passed a slow semi going up the last hill before they reached Snowville. "So we get off on the Snowville exit?"

"Yep, and then continue on North Stone Road."

"So named, because it heads straight north to Stone?"

"You got it. We're a wildly, creative bunch out here. But, you won't go all the way to Stone. You'll turn off after a few miles and head east for a bit. I'll tell you where."

"So why did George say you lived south of Stone if we turn east?"

"I think it's 'cause George's great-grandma lived in Stone. Technically, my house is halfway between Stone, Idaho and Snowville, Utah, north to south, and an equal distance east of them. On Google Maps you can draw an equilateral triangle between the three. However, 'unincorporated Box Elder County' describes a lot of places and, since our land stretches north to the Idaho border, we are technically closer to Stone. So we say Stone usually. But, our mail is delivered to Snowville and we keep a PO Box in Tremonton."

"Equilateral triangle, eh?"

"I was a math geek in school."

"So, where was that? I know Stone is tiny and Snowville is too small for a high school."

"Or a middle school. After elementary they bussed us into Garland, a town next to Tremonton, to attend Bear River High."

"Wow, what time did you get on the bus?"

"Oh, six, and home by five. But we had it easy. The kids in Park Valley usually had to live in the Tremonton area during the week and come home on weekends. They're at least an hour farther out."

"Wow, so no extracurricular activities?"

"Well, we could have done something but neither Gene nor I had our own cars, and Mom and Dad didn't have the money, or time, to chase after us so we made our own fun here."

"Wow. So what are my entertainment options if I move out here?"

"Be busy taking care of the land and your animals. I personally have a lot of books, and Dad bought me an iPod back in the day, so I buy a lot of music and movies from iTunes. We have satellite dishes for TV and the internet, so we stay connected."

"Yeah, but how do you get what you need? I mean what if you need a new pair of jeans?"

"We plan big trips quarterly and take the whole family clothes shopping. We do the same for farm and household items. We also do shopping for whatever we need when we're out for another reason. We go to Tremonton weekly if we can, and every other week if not, if only to buy milk."

"What, no milk cow?"

"No, and no goat's or sheep milk either. Our sheep and beeves are meat, not milk producers."

Marion noticed Leon had exited the freeway at Snowville, and had headed north as instructed. "Hey, you'll turn right at the next intersection."

"Okay."

"But, getting back to what we need, we have a well, a wind-turbine generator to pump it and provide emergency power, phone and power poles to the houses and barns, cellphones and OnStar in the vehicles. We do online statements and bill pay. We grow our own fruit and vegetables as we can, and try to live as best we can with what we have. I buy a lot of things online too, and I pick them up at our PO Box when I'm in town." Marion slapped her forehead.

"Oh, crap. I forgot to get the mail. Damn."

"You are having a heck of a day today, aren't you?"

"I am, I wonder if it's your fault. Maybe I was supposed to take you on a tour today. Oh, well... the *only* good thing about today is that I won't have to pay for the truck repair this time because of the recall. That reminds me, I'm debating on trading in my truck this year or just buying a new one and keeping my old one for around the farm. But, when I'm ready for that, we'll gear up the whole clan and spend a day truck shopping."

"Do you go into Logan or Salt Lake?"

"Why should I? Jacksons has always taken care of us. I have no reason to shop around. Besides, last time Gene did that, he saved a measly three thousand dollars and the engine blew in the first year--a factory defect that Jacksons graciously fixed for us. That's one thing Dad believed, that I'm beginning to, Jacksons doesn't sell lemons."

"Wow. That's interesting."

"How about your rig? I noticed it's older, but in fantastic shape."

"I bought it right after high school from one of my Grandpa's buddies who likes to buy a new truck every three to four years. It became a hobby of sorts to take care of it over the years, that's all."

"Well, seeing it gives me room for thought about maybe keeping my rig a bit longer. Dad always said we were too hard on trucks to keep them forever."

"Well, you guys sure put a lot of miles on them. What's your truck at now?"

"Oh, about one hundred thirty thousand give or take. It doesn't have as much as I put on my last truck, which I traded at two hundred fifty thousand miles, but Gene likes to trade trucks every five years or so, no matter the state of the rig and thinks I should too."

"Well, living in Layton, this baby has a lot of highway miles, but I am at two hundred twenty thousand right now. Of course I redid the engine and transmission at one hundred ninety thousand."

"Yeah, I'd expect that. Oh, here we are; the pavement ends here and we'll go straight for a bit and then dogleg around the fields until you hit Gene's house; mine's past his. Are you okay going to Gene's for lunch?"

"Um, sure, if I'm not imposing."

"You won't be; Jeanette will probably have plenty... she likes to feed me on town days. She also feeds the farm crew; so one more body won't be trouble. I was figuring that we'd go to my place, stash my supplies, take Gene and Jeanette's over there then head to the Gorham spread after lunch. Its road starts after Gene's, anyway, the other way from my place."

"Sounds good. Will you hang out with me at the Gorham place? It'll save me time."

"I can. I don't feel much like working on a tractor right now."

Chapter Eight

Leon looked around Marion's place interestedly. They parked on a cement, double driveway in front of a newer, two-car garage that had been added on to a 1930s one-level, clapboard house. Past the garage, he saw a large, open-sided, hay barn half-full, and past that a sprawling wooden, stock barn with pastures attached to it all around. The pasture that attached to the front of the barn ran next to the house along a gravel drive. Huge Lombardi poplars lined the southern border of the pasture. Stately cottonwoods lined the irrigation ditch at the front of the house, and he spotted a half-dozen fruit trees and a large garden behind the house bordered by a couple more cottonwoods. Fields surrounded the house, barn, and pastures. If he looked straight past the barn, he could see the low ridge of hills that Marion said marked the eastern border of the Sullivan Ranch.

Marion must have noticed him looking around. She came around the back of the truck to stand next to him.

"So what do you think?" she asked.

"I like it. Of course, it's a gorgeous day with a blue sky and just a few white, puffy clouds so far, but I like the set-up. You keep animals in the barn, right?"

"Yup, all my sheep when they're here."

"I see one over in the far pasture."

"That's my ram. He's getting fat and sassy here in his own pasture while his women and lambs graze on the range. His buddy must be over behind the barn."

"Buddy?"

"One of his sons. I keep a wether here with my ram to keep him company. Sheep are herd animals and I don't want Rambo getting bored, cause then he'll get mean, so I keep Howard with him."

"Rambo and Howard?"

"Well, I won't eat these two, and they live here with me except during breeding season, so they have names."

"Here comes Howard. He looks smaller."

"That's 'cause he's a baby. He's only about five months old. In reality, he's a sheep teenager. I got kind of attached to him, and Atzo reminded me that I needed to keep a wether around, so I picked the one I bottle-fed since the day he was born."

"I get naming the ram Rambo, but why Howard?"

"Well, when I was taking care of Howard in the house, I was babysitting the kids, and my nephew found *Howard the Duck* in my movies and noticed that my lamb had a curl of wool on the top of his forehead like Howard's tail, so the kid named the lamb."

"Wow. I don't know whether I'd admit to seeing that movie. But that makes sense."

"Well, my five year old nephew liked the movie. I refuse to state my opinion for fear of incriminating myself."

Leon laughed at that.

Marion's two dogs came up to greet her at that moment. Laughing, she petted them and gently kept them from jumping up on her. She looked at him and introduced them.

"Leon, this is Yip," she said, gesturing to gray, Border collie with a white collar. "And, this is Mitzy, the matriarch of our pack and latest female Mitzy of our line." Mitzy was black with the golden spots above her eyes and four golden feet, the coloring of a Doberman.

The dogs came over and greeted Leon wagging their tails and smelling him as a new human in their midst.

"Atzo must be down here and have brought them down too," Marion said.

"So who is Atzo?" he asked, as she looked around.

"My Basque shepherd. He's had the sheep up in the hills, but probably brought them down to the salt lick earlier. He knew I was getting his supplies today." Marion turned back to the truck and pulled down the tailgate. "Ready to unload?"

He joined her. "Show me where to stash it."

It took about a half hour to unload everything. Marion's house was attached to the side of the much newer garage at what had been a screened, back porch that ran the length of the house. It was now all enclosed and Marion and he placed the large cooler in front of one of two large, chest freezers in this long, narrow space. From the porch, they entered the kitchen. Leon absorbed pine paneling, solid wood floors and sunshine from the many un-curtained windows. He and Marion placed bag after bag on the large, bar counter in the 1980s remodeled kitchen.

They left the Pepsi and diapers in the truck for transfer to Gene's, and Leon unpacked the cooler into the nearest freezer as Marion grabbed a large box, a small box, a smaller cooler, and began separating supplies.

Leon was bending over the chest freezer making room for two huge bags of frozen potatoes when Marion came near to him with the small cooler.

"Thank you for helping me."

"You're welcome."

Marion then took four of the six gallons of milk and the two buckets of ice cream from the big cooler to the little one.

"When you have finished emptying the cooler, do you mind pouring what ice is left into this one?"

"Sure, no problem. Can I pour the water on the grass when done?"

"Yes, please. Thank you."

Leon mused on Marion as he worked. He'd counted at least twenty bags of groceries. It was clear she put a lot of care and planning into the grocery runs. He'd guessed that the smaller cooler and the big box were for Gene and Jeanette, while the little box must be for Atzo.

He watched Marion carry the now full, big box back out to the truck. On the way back into the house she stopped by the big cooler once again and grabbed the two remaining gallons of milk and the quart of Neapolitan ice cream and went into the kitchen. Shortly after, she came back for the quart of heavy cream and five pound brick of yellow cheese. By then, Leon had finished emptying the cooler. He lifted the large cooler over the smaller one and transferred as much ice as possible.

He had turned over the large cooler on the grass next to the garage and was watching the water drain, when he spotted a man walking up the drive towards him. The man had a weathered, leathery face and dark hair. His colorful poncho and large shepherd's hook proclaimed him to be Atzo. The stranger met his gaze and nodded a "Hello" as he walked past Leon, laid the hook against the stairs, and walked into the house, Leon tipped the cooler up and propped open the lid so it could sit in the sun and dry out. Curious he followed Atzo's path into the kitchen.

"Thank you for the apricots, Miss Marion," he heard Atzo say.

"You're welcome, Atzo, they were on sale and I know how much you like dried apricots."

Marion spotted him and introduced him to Atzo. "Atzo, this is Leon. I'm going to take him over to look at the old, Gorham spread. He was nice enough to drive me out here."

Atzo came over and shook Leon's hand. "Nice to meet you. So you are thinking of coming out here to live and work by the Sullivans?"

"Thinking about it. I've always wanted my own spread and I like the country around here."

"Well, there's good water on the Gorham land. Good pastures, too."

"Thank you. I'll keep that in mind."

"Okay, Atzo, here is your box ready to go. Do you want a ride back to the sheep camp?" Marion said.

"No, Miss Marion. Me and the dogs are enjoying a nice walk on a nice day," Atzo addressed Marion and then Leon. "I'll head back, then. Thank you again, Miss Marion. Good luck with your decision, Mr. Leon." Atzo tucked the box under his arm and made his way out the door. Leon looked out Marion's living room following Atzo's progress down to the lane with the dogs at his side.

He looked back to her. "So how far is the sheep camp?"

Marion looked at Leon. "Oh, about a mile to the south. The land dips there where a small creek runs, otherwise you could see the salt lick and sheep camp."

"Do you get your salt from Redmond? My grandpa did. I can remember riding all the way down there with him."

"We do sometimes, but that salt's up with the cows. I've been working with the vet to get special blocks for my ewes. They've weaned the lambs, but I want them as healthy as possible before breeding, so I have a special mineral block just for sheep down there. Gene went to Redmond last. It's a long drive for me."

"Well, that makes sense."

Marion changed the subject. "It's been a long morning, I think. She pointed to her left. "There's a bathroom right down there if needed. I'm going to my room to freshen up a bit."

Leon looked around Marion's house with interest. It was a pleasing mix of the original house with some needed updates. The hall bathroom he'd used was easily identified as half of an old bedroom. He'd peeked behind an adjoining door and saw the other half of the bedroom was now a laundry room.

Back in the kitchen, he could tell that it had spread out into what was probably the front parlor when the adjoining wall was removed. A column on the end of the bar probably hid a post that helped support the ceiling after the wall came down. Part of him was curious to see the rest of the house, but a larger part of him was ready to go. He felt like there were tentacles trying to suck him into Marion's world. It seemed clear that all Marion needed was a good man to make her life picture-perfect. And, something like what she has was all Leon ever wanted, but he also wanted his own place--his own space. If he stayed here he'd be forever, Mr. Marion.

Leon tried to shake off his discomfort, as he felt the weight of Marion's responsibilities press in on him.

"I'm heading outside. It's too pretty of a day to be inside," he hollered to the back of the house.

"Okay, I'll be out shortly," came a muffled reply.

Back at his truck, he consciously took a few deep breaths. Marion had removed her tarp and tie-downs, leaving the box, small cooler, diapers, and the cases of Pepsi in the bed. Leon inspected the large cooler and found it dry. He closed the lid and carried the cooler into the garage. He spotted another cooler just like it on a shelf by some totes and camping gear and noticed an empty, cooler-shaped hole. Placing the cooler on the shelf helped him regain some control. *It's like with each item of hers I put away, I get a chunk of myself back*, he thought.

Marion's arrival interrupted his thoughts.

"Thank you for stashing the cooler. Ready to go?" she asked.

"Sure am," he replied.

Chapter Nine

Marion watched Leon sit at the table and talk to her nephew. He'd seemed genuinely interested in meeting Jeanette and her three kids. Mick, their five year old was regaling Leon with his water snake adventures. Three year old Nancy had a summer cold and was lying on the living room couch asleep. Jeanette was feeding six month old Jeremy in his bounce chair on the table and giving her weird looks. It hit her that she didn't know how to explain Leon to Jeanette. She could almost see the wheels turning in Jeanette's head, but, just because she may need a husband and Leon wanted a farm was NOT proof they were meant to be together. Marion tried not to sigh as she ate Jeanette's delicious sliced beef and dill pickle on homemade bread sandwich.

Thankfully, Leon seemed intent on getting out to the Gorham place, so Marion was able to make a quick lunch. She scarfed down her last bite and noticed Leon's plate was empty. She stood up and gathered her plate and reached for Leon's.

"You done?"

"Yes, thank you."

She turned to Jeanette. "Thank you for feeding us. I'm going to take Leon up to Section 34 and show him the Gorham place. Then we'll probably head back to town to get my truck. I'll put these in the sink."

"Ok. Sounds good, Mare." Jeanette said, then addressed Leon. "Thank you for taking care of Marion today. Gene will be sorry he's missed you, but I hope if you like the Gorham place, you'll become our neighbor."

Leon was the picture of politeness as he stood to leave. "Thank you, Jeanette. It was a fine meal," he smiled at Mick, "It was good talking to you, sport. Keep keeping your little sister and brother safe from those snakes."

"I'll try," Mick responded.

Marion put on her sunglasses and led the way to Leon's truck.

"So, Gene and Jeanette built a new place on the old homestead?" Leon asked, once she was belted in.

"Yup. Over the generations that's what all the Sullivans have done. The original cabin was here and the first son built his own cabin at my place. Then his son lived back here and expanded the first cabin. Then the grandson knocked down the cabin at my place and built my house. His great-grandson, my grandpa, built on to the cabin here, once again, and then Mom and Dad took over my house and updated it. Gene and Jeanette lived in the old place for a summer but it had a lot of problems. Gene was getting ready to gut it, and had moved Jeanette into a camp trailer temporarily when it burned down one night. So, Dad and Gene built this place."

"Wow, so the Sullivan place has always had two houses."

"Yup. And, we hope to continue to swap houses each generation. For us, we've found that overlapping the generations and running it as a partnership work best. Plus it makes it easy to transfer the ranch between the generations."

"So now, with your mom and dad gone, you and Gene are partners?"

Marion wondered how best to answer that; it was a sore subject to her. She was a forthright person, but she'd only met Leon this morning.

"Well... um... our generation is special. I think Mom and Dad wanted more kids, that way they'd have more help until one of us stood out as 'the heir', but that didn't happen. Then, like you said, they both died too early, and Gene wasn't ready yet to do it all on his own, so I stayed on. I guess, though, it worked for the best. Helping to run a farm is all I know, and I'm good at it." And there she went, sharing too much with a stranger.

Leon looked at her and then responded carefully. "I think that you and I are good examples of what often happens to farm kids. I wanted nothing more than to take over Grandpa's farm. I'd worked it with him for years. And, for a while it looked like I might get my wish. None of my aunts or uncles, or my parents wanted it. Then Grandma died and a developer came and offered Grandpa a lot of money for the farm. He waffled over the decision for a year, and never told anyone his decision or if he made one. Then one day last fall, he didn't wake up. We all learned his decision from his will, 'sell the farm and split the proceeds between the kids.' He even made me executor and then bequeathed all the stuff away. So, I wanted the farm, so bad I could taste it, and it slipped away from me. Meanwhile, you maybe could have left yours, but it needs you too bad so you stay."

Marion was touched by Leon's story. He'd matched her truth for truth.

"Thank you for sharing that." She knew the T in the road was coming up, and she wanted to break the tension from the serious turn in conversation. "It sure seems like nothing in farming is ever easy.... oh, look, the turn is coming."

"Turn left, right?"

"Right," then Marion giggled. "I mean yes, left, that's correct."

Leon shook his head at her and smiled, as he turned left where their dirt road ended at another crossing it.

"This is the state line." Marion pointed out.

"You mean between Utah and Idaho? There's a road along it?"

"Yup. Here, there's a road, because a lot of the farms here stop on one side or the other of it. It marks the northern boundary of both our land and the Gorham land." Marion sat up straighter in the truck seat and pointed to her left. "Oh, stop here. We've passed the Adams boundary. This is where the Gorham land starts."

Leon stopped the truck. He shut off the ignition, got out, opened the door to the extended cab on his side, scooped out his digital camera, went to stand on the edge of the Gorham land, and started taking pictures.

Marion sat there quietly. *Well, if I wondered how serious he is about buying a farm, now I know for sure. I bet he had no trouble giving me all the help he did today just so I would bring him here and show him the farm*, she thought.

Leon opened his door and broke her reverie.

"Can you slide over here and drive me around the perimeter so I can video it?" he asked.

"Sure will."

Marion slid across the truck bench and fastened the safety belt. She rolled down the window and watched Leon go back to the truck bed and settle on the wheel well directly behind her. He hit the top of the truck cab with his open hand a couple of times to signal he was ready.

She smiled as she put the truck in gear. He may not say what he wanted, but his actions were sure telling.

Obediently, Marion slowly drove Leon past the Gorham land. It ran mostly east and west in contrast to how her Sullivan land ran from north to south. The Gorham house sat on the northwest corner of the property, and its lane defined the western property line. At the lane, she stopped the truck.

"This lane marks the western boundary. I'll finish the circuit and bring you back here to look at the house," she hollered.

"'Kay, sounds good," she heard him say, over the truck noise.

Soon enough, she reached the southern boundary, also marked with a lane, and they repeated the stop. Then Marion drove to the eastern boundary. This time, she stopped the truck and got out so she could point out the boundary markers to Leon. She stood back by the rear wheel so he could hear her as she pointed out landmarks. "This boundary you'll have to confirm with the real-estate agent, but I believe this ditch runs all the way along the eastern line and defines it, 'cause this side is the side with water. I think a fence starts in the next field up. I think it used to be rangeland, but it's been wheat lately. I can't recall for sure, because it's been years since Dad rented the Gorham land from old Mrs. Gorham. I think Gene's buddy, Bill, is renting it now."

"But, this side's just the short side of the land like the east side, right?"

"I think so, from what I recall. Do you want to walk it? I can pick you up at the other side."

"Nah, that'd take too long. It's a mile, isn't it?"

"I think so, but we can check on the tachometer on the way back. Do you want to drive back to the house?"

Leon looked away from the land and back at her.

"No, you can drive. I recorded as we came down, I'd like to watch as we go back," he answered.

"Okay."

Marion made her way back into the driver's seat, and noticed as she checked the rearview mirror that Leon had switched sides and was sitting on the passenger side wheel-well, with his camera hanging down from its strap around his neck as he watched the land go by. *That man sure knows what he wants. I admire that kind of drive*, she thought.

She watched the tachometer as they retraced their path. Mentally she noted the details. About three miles, so three sections long, and about a mile wide. Not huge, but not a tiny dude ranch either, at least sixteen hundred acres.

At the homestead, Marion parked next to the large, machine shop facing the house. Leon jumped down from the tailgate and met her at the front of the truck.

"So, what do you know about the buildings here?" he asked.

"Well, from what you can see, and what Gene told me, the house is in pretty bad shape but the machine shop is in great shape." Marion walked Leon around showing him the rectangular 1920s house and 1990s era, metal and concrete machine shop.

She pointed out things she thought Leon should know about, like the fact that the electricity had been fully disconnected from the house a few years back, and that no one had lived in it for nearly twenty years.

Marion watched Leon walk entirely around the weather-beaten house photographing it as he went. She answered questions as best as she could when he asked.

Leon joined her at the front of the house.

"I assume it was whitewashed at one time, but why is it all boarded up with new plywood?" he wondered.

"You're right. When I was little, I can remember bits of white paint still in spots. The plywood is to keep squatters out."

"Squatters? Out here in the middle of nowhere?"

Marion snorted. "Scoff if you must, but meth heads like to make their products in empty houses off the beaten path, and there's been trouble with skinheads and militia-types taking over far-flung farms and turning them into compounds."

"You can't be serious, skinheads, really?"

Marion sighed and tried to not lose her temper over his doubting her. "Granted it hasn't happened a lot, and the case I know of personally happened to Dad's buddy out closer to Yost, but it has happened. You can see for yourself how isolated we are."

"Well, that makes sense. Sorry I doubted you."

"Well, it's something you should be aware of if you buy this place. If you're not here to watch over things, undesirables could move in. Otherwise you'll have a heck of a commute to Tremonton and back every day."

Marion looked up and worried whether she'd pricked his temper. Leon's eyes were narrowed and his mouth was tightened, but he didn't say anything.

"You make a good point," he answered, finally, then asked a question, seemingly to deliberately change the subject. "So, what's the story on the shop?"

So, he wants to talk about something else, fine. I can be nice for as long as it takes, answering him.

"When old Mr. Gorham died, Mrs. Gorham stayed here, but their grown son ran the place. He lives in Snowville and would drive out each day." She pointed to a bramble-covered lump of earth beyond the shop. "There used to be a great, old barn there, but it blew down in a big wind storm a season or two after Mr. Gorham died, so the son built this machine shed to replace it. It has all the amenities and he even installed a kitchenette/bathroom area in the back so he wouldn't bother his mom in the house."

Leon had walked over to the shop and was taking more pictures as she talked. He looked to at a cement pad to the left of the machine shed's front door.

"What's this?" he asked.

"Fresh water and electricity hookups and an RV dump. Everything's disconnected right now, but Gene told me the pipes and stuff are in the shop ready to be reconnected. The son would park an RV here during harvesting, or when he and his buddies were hunting around here."

"Deer?"

"Sometimes, but mostly pheasant and geese."

"Interesting." Leon began walking around the homestead plot taking still more pictures.

Marion stood and looked up at the sun. From its position she decided it was about three o'clock. "Hey, Leon, since we can get a cell signal here, I'm gonna get my cell phone and call Jacksons. I'll be over by the truck when you're done."

"Okay."

Chapter Ten

Leon felt a sense of 'rightness' come over him the more he saw of the Gorham place. He really liked it. The fields looked good and the well water tasted sweet. Atzo was right. The smaller pastures would be great for a milk cow or two. He also loved the shop. The rangeland looked good, and dry farming was working. The pictures of the farm online, plus Marion's descriptions made the farm, seem perfect for him. Maybe he could even use it to house a tractor-repair shop one day. Thanks to his grandpa giving him a share of the Layton farm sale proceeds he could even afford buying such a large spread. He figured he'd keep thinking about what he could do with the place the whole way to Tremonton. He knew he was too distracted to converse with Marion, but she didn't seem to mind.

"Jacksons says it's done. We can head back any time," Marion said, interrupting his thoughts.

"Okay, I'm ready."

They hopped back in the truck with Leon still deep in thought. He needed to talk to his father, he'd have good input. Hitting pavement pulled him out of his thoughts. He glanced over to Marion. "So, how far are we from Snowville here?"

"Oh, about nine miles. As you can see, this road is a straight shot from the highway to the Gorham place. If you do buy it, your commute will be slightly shorter than mine."

"Thank you, again, for showing me around the place. You should get some of the realtor fees; you did more work than the lady I called about it."

"That's funny. I didn't do anything special. I just wanted you to know what you'd be in for if you bought it. I hope my input helped."

"Oh, it did. I was planning to drive around out here and stop anybody I saw out in the fields with my questions, but you made it easy."

"Glad to help."

"I kept you from working on your tractor, though."

"Well, you can see from the clouds that this rain is probably going to start later tonight, so Gene and the crew will have plenty of time to get the hay in before it hits. It's Gene's turn to do the fixes anyway, so he can't use the hay as an excuse to make me do them." Marion paused and continued. "The rain will do my winter barley good so long as it doesn't lay it down."

"I know what you mean. Grandpa always loved the water that summer storms would give his grains, but he hated the loss in yield if the wind or rain or hail laid down too many stalks."

Marion nodded.

That seemed to be all they had to say for a while.

Leon found that if he let her, Marion could distract him from his thoughts about the farm. He looked over her now and then as he drove and wondered what was so captivating about her. *I know part of it is her looks*, he thought to himself. She's got a great head of hair that a man could really sink his hands in, and a great figure. But, he'd known a lot of women just as pretty in his day. *Why is she so fascinating?* From what he'd seen so far, she would make the perfect farmer's wife, though. Maybe that was it. She was restful to be around and would be great on long, road trips. He looked at her again; she looked like she was wrapped up in her own thoughts.

The fast-moving freeway ate up the miles, and they reached Tremonton and Jacksons at four-thirty in the afternoon.

"Oh look, they've got it parked out front, and it's washed," Marion said, as Leon pulled in and parked.

"Do you need me to wait for you?" he asked, turning off the engine.

"No, I should be fine. I've got to get to the post office."

They looked at each other. Leon wasn't sure what to say. They'd spent all afternoon together, but it wasn't a date, or a business meeting and he wasn't sure what words to use. Marion looked to be in the same position. Thankfully, she broke free and spoke first,

"Thank you for rescuing me today. Me, and my groceries, really appreciate it."

"My pleasure. Thank you for going over to the Gorham place with me. You really helped me."

"That was my pleasure," she smiled. "Well, I'll be going. See you around some time."

He got out. "See ya," he replied, as she opened the door and exited.

Leon had been trained by his dad to ensure any other driver he was with got their vehicle on the road before he left them, so, despite what Marion said, he waited at Jacksons and watched until she got into her truck and pulled out into the highway. He then left Jacksons himself. He stopped to get gas in the gas station just down from TT, and noticed Monte's rig was still at TT. Relief settled in as he thought he could stop and talk to Monte about the Gorham place before heading to Layton. As he got into the truck, his truck's cell phone rang.

"This is Leon."

"Hello, Son. How's things?"

"Hey, Dad! Doing well. Went out to see that farm I've had my eye on."

"The one that's near the Idaho border past Snowville?"

"That's the one."

"Well, good to hear… hey, are you coming down tonight? Do you have a day off tomorrow?"

"Yes to both. What's up?"

"Nothing, but your sister is up from school this weekend and we wanted to have a family dinner tonight and maybe go hiking tomorrow."

"That sounds great. Let me swing by my place to get some gear and I'll be down directly. I should be there between seven and eight."

"Sounds good, Son. See you then. Did you get any pictures?"

"You know I did, I'll share them too."

"Ok. Love you, Son, travel safe."

"Will do, Dad. Love you."

"Bye."

"G'bye."

Three hours later, Leon was sitting in the basement family room of his parents' house. Everyone was sprawled on the huge, leather sectional eating popcorn and watching everyone's pictures run across the huge TV Leon's dad bought to watch Utah Jazz basketball games on.

Sharing pictures was a Packer family tradition. Leon's mom had been a professional photographer and had passed her love of photography on to to all her kids. Everybody had cameras as children, and the usual high school graduation, or sweet-sixteen present, included a nice camera. Also, everyone received a cell phone as a teenager to help keep track of each other, and those phones had cameras too. When Leon was about ten years of age, his parents started making Friday night a family picture night. The times later varied based on schedules and whether or not anybody had a date but, on Friday after school, everyone would congregate in the family room and show each other any pictures taken during the week and talk about it.

For the past few years, everyone had good digital cameras, most as part of a smartphone, so Leon's dad had begun showing the pictures on the big TV through the Audio-Visual or HDMI cables.

Leon's sister started the round tonight.

"Well, everybody, I had a big project due this week in my landscape architecture class. So, I don't have too many shots, but here's my completed project." She continued scrolling through a sunset she'd caught while parked during rush hour, and some shots of her and her friends at an after-church "linger longer" where folks hang out at the church eating refreshments and socializing after Sunday services.

His brother and sister-in-law went next.

"Baby Packer is twenty weeks this week and is about as long as a banana but here's the sonogram we got from the doctor." They then shared pictures of the nursery paint job and crib assembly. Leon's mom jumped in at this point and shared pictures of the baby-carrier cover she was sewing.

Everyone turned to Leon next.

"Leon, Dad told me you went out to see that farm you're thinking of buying. Did you have your camera?" his sister asked.

"Sure did, Sis. I took some video too, but I worry about showing my pictures right now. I haven't gone through them yet, and I took a *lot* trying to document everything before I put money down."

Everyone clamored for him to show his pictures.

"Hey Leon, go ahead and show them all. None of us has been in that part of the state and, even if it's all sagebrush, we're all interested in seeing your prospective homestead," his brother said.

Leon knew well that his family didn't mind a long slideshow of somebody's vacation. Confident that he could withstand any teasing comments, he plugged his camera into the HDMI port and began showing his pictures as he narrated. When they got to the video tour around the perimeter, his brother spoke up.

"So, Leon, how did you get this video? Did you hold your camera out the window and drive with your other hand?" his brother asked.

"No, actually, I was riding in the back of the truck as Marion drove me around the place."

A chorus of "Marion, who's he?" met that statement.

"Marion is one of my tractor customers who happens to live near the farm. *She* graciously agreed to show me around the farm, because I didn't know exactly where it was," Leon responded, trying to sound nonchalant.

He noticed both his mother and sister looked at him with the look they had when they were matchmaking. He paused the video and held up his hands.

"Hey, you two. Don't go matchmaking on me. Marion's just a customer who may become a neighbor if the sale goes through."

"Okay, okay. Don't get huffy," his mom answered, winking at him. "Though I could say that you responded to us a little quickly, don't you think? Do I smell interest?"

"Yeah. He seems a little touchy. Did you get a picture of this Marion?" his sister chimed in.

Leon sighed and resigned himself to talking about Marion. "I was a bit focused on documenting the farm, but I may have. If you see a brunette with long hair in any of the shots, that's Marion." He gave everyone a look that meant "Don't push me."

The narration continued through the end of the video. The video ended when he and Marion had reached the eastern border where she had stopped the truck and showed him the ditch that marked the boundary. The next pictures after the video showed Marion pointing to the ditch. Leon's mom spoke first,

"Hey, Leon, she's cute."

"And young. With the name 'Marion' I was picturing a middle-aged lady," his sister-in-law added.

"She looks like she'd be fun to come home to each night. Is she single?" his brother said.

Leon met everyone's looks and shook his head. "Look, here's what I know about Marion. She's single, but she and her brother are partners in their parents' farm. Her brother is married with three little kids and between them they run cows, a few sheep, and raise hay and grains to feed the lot. Marion came into the shop today to pick up a couple of tractor parts, then went to get the farm's weekly groceries. We'd agreed that I could follow her out to the farm, because it's near hers, and she'd come by the shop after the grocery store. I'd gone to the Tremonton GM dealer to pick up my truck after getting the starter replaced and was leaving as Marion pulled in. Her truck had had an engine sensor problem that set off her check-engine light, and the dealer needed the afternoon to fix it. So, we transferred her supplies to my truck, then I took her to her place to drop everything off, and then she took me around the farm. When done, I took her back to the dealer for her truck, got gas, and came here."

It was Leon's dad who responded to his description. "Wow, Son. You've had an eventful day."

Everyone nodded, but no one seemed to know what to say. His mom broke the tension.

"Well, Leon, we trust your judgment, and I know how you prefer blondes, so we'll let the Marion-thing go." But, she couldn't resist a jibe, "Although I must say, a lot of folks I know have long-lasting love stories that start with a day like you had today. Just warning you."

Everyone laughed, and Leon continued his slide show. He felt really good by the time the pictures turned to the house and shop.

"Wow, that house doesn't seem livable. Where will you live?" his brother remarked.

"Well, I think I can hang out in the shop temporarily, but I budgeted enough that I think I can build a new house." Leon turned to his dad. "Dad, there's an RV hook-up with power, water, and a dump attached to the shop. Could I borrow your RV if needed?"

Leon's dad looked at his mom. "I think so. Honey, what do you think?"

"I don't see a problem. We can certainly plan our camping trips around Leon's schedule this year."

Leon was grateful. "Thank you, you guys. I don't want to be a burden on you."

"No problem. We want you to be happy, Son."

"Yeah, and we can even help you when you are ready to build," his brother chimed in.

Leon felt joy in his family's support. "Thank you, guys, that means a lot. I got a good feeling from the place and you're helping me keep it. It could really happen for me, finally."

Everyone agreed and Leon finished his slide show. By fate, or happy accident, his last picture was of a side of the machine shop, but the other half of the photo captured Marion shielding her eyes as she looked up in the sky at the sun.

"Wow, Leon, can you zoom in on Marion in that shot?" his mother asked.

"Yeah, Leon, that's a great shot of Marion with the sun shining down on her like that," his sister-in-law agreed.

Leon forced himself to look at the shot objectively. The field behind Marion and the shop was full of winter wheat, which was a rich green color. Marion was facing west looking at the sun, and it shown down full on her, but with her face tilted up, there were no weird shadows on her. Her sunglasses reflected the sun just right, and the bright light brought out a variety of colors in her hair. As he zoomed in the shot with his camera, he was compelled to agree with his family's opinion. "You guys are right, that is a great shot."

He turned to look at his mom. "Mom, will you get me a print of this? I'd like to give it to Marion as a thank you for her help today."

"Sure will, Son. That's a great idea. I'm glad I taught you guys how to capture a good image. Though I suspect you were looking at the width of the machine shop, right?"

Everyone laughed as Leon answered, "I sure was."

His brother had to zing him. "Now, I may be happily married, but only a killer man-cave could have turned me away from looking at that female. You've got control, Bro."

Later that night, Leon lay in his old bedroom thinking over his day and trying to go to sleep. He felt really good about buying the farm. But the down payment will take a huge chunk of savings. He'd have to keep working at Tremonton Tractor for at least another year, maybe two if he had to build a house. Other thoughts hit him as he tried to troubleshoot his problem. Of course, he could keep renting the land out for those years, and move out there when he was ready. He'd have to price gas and utilities out there along with wear and tear on the truck to see whether commuting was an option.

Satisfied that he'd thought enough about the farm for a day, Leon went to sleep. He nearly missed his final thought before he succumbed to unconsciousness. It wasn't words, but a picture of Marion that drifted through his mind. *She is beautiful, and she'd be the perfect farm wife. Too bad, I am not interested in a wife right now.*

Chapter Eleven

"No, George, the arm needs to go up and bring the cam to this point." Leon gestured with his hand as he showed George the desired action on their prototype, baler assembly.

"Show me again," George said, moving around the prototype.

"See, if we bring it this high, we can build up a little more momentum we can use to tilt the bale when the arm releases," Leon said.

"I get ya."

Both men flipped down the facemasks of their welder's helmets as George picked up his gas cutter and cut the tack welds he'd used to anchor the hydraulic arm to its current location. Once he had the arm free, Leon shifted the piece slightly and held it.

"Hey George, if I hold it here, can you check the arm to ensure this is the right spot?"

George came around and checked the position, then marked the position of the arm with a grease pencil.

"That's good. Now hold her steady while I tack it into place," he said.

The helmet masks went down again as George worked to reattach the piece.

Leon watched the joint as George welded hoping it worked this time. He'd won the Annual Amateur Prize before, but George hadn't. It'd be a great thing for both him and Monte and this location.

George flipped up his mask, and Leon did the same. George asked, "What do you think?"

"It looks good from here; try it."

George lifted the arm. "That's it!"

"Great. I'll get the upper frame and hold it over the top so you can see how much we need to modify it to fit the new position," Leon replied.

"Good idea. I'll get the notebook."

Leon wheeled the heavy cam frame over on its dolly. "How about here?"

"That should be good. I need to look at it as it comes in so I can ballpark the measurement before we fit it on," George answered.

The two men kept working on the baler assembly. Monte came in as they were sitting side-by-side talking and making notes in George's notebook.

"Hey guys. How's it going?" he asked.

"I think we fixed the hydraulic arm angle. It moves the cam much easier now," George replied.

Leon nodded his head.

"That's great news. I have to say, Leon, I'm glad that you brought up the Annual prize to George and me. It would be great not only for George to have the prize money, but it'd be great for our store to be featured in the annual magazine," Monte answered, enthusiastically.

"You're welcome. I'm just glad that the tractor company rep told us about the Annual prize back in college. There were six teams at Utah State working on projects for the prize the year that my buddy and I won. And, what's neat is that, even if you don't win one of the cash prizes, it's great exposure. One of my classmates ended up getting on at the manufacturing plant because of it. He didn't get his design perfected, but the engineers saw great potential in him and took him back to Racine to work at the factory," Leon said.

"Is that how you got to work with the Troubleshooters?" George asked Leon.

"Sure is. My buddy and I got to tour the facilities in Wisconsin and, while there, we met one of the Troubleshooters. They have this weird test they do to find good problem solvers and my friend and I passed it. Get this, you go into the factory and they have you wait for something. For us, we were going to have lunch with some of the designers in the cafeteria. While you wait, somewhere near, something breaks down and there's a ruckus. Evaluating how you react and how well you do tells the big wigs whether or not you're suited for the Troubleshooters. It's also videoed and shown on the CCTV for the plant workers. It's great entertainment."

"That sounds like a bad email joke," Monte said.

"I know, but it works," Leon laughed.

"What did they do to you?" George asked.

"Well, the plant manager, a cute redhead by the way, who'd been flirting with us all morning, left us in a pseudo break room near the cafeteria. Along one wall was a row of windows looking in on the cafeteria kitchen. As we sat there, we started to get bored. I mean, she left us for nearly forty minutes. So, Eric, my buddy, starts getting fidgety. He's an active guy and a pacer... so, he's sitting there by me, then he stands up and watches the cafeteria crew cooking then he goes and stands and looks at the outside window, and then he sits down. I was just getting ready to tell him to not be so antsy when the huge mixer in the kitchen went berserk. I mean, one minute you can see the arm going round and round, and the next minute, it starts shaking and spitting out some type of yellow batter all over. Smoke starts coming out of the top of the mixer."

"Why didn't they just unplug it?" George interrupted.

"Well, it's not that easy. It was one of those big industrial food mixers. Seriously, it looked like my mom's counter top Kitchen-Aid, but it's over six feet high and sits on the floor. The metal mixing bowls are waist-high and sit in this wheeled ring to get in and out of the mixer. Plus the paddle's huge, like the size of two shovels, and we'd watched the baker pour two hundred-pound bags of flour into the bowl."

Leon continued, "So anyway, I'm sure Eric thought what you did, George, unplug it, right. But, anyway, batter's flying, smoke's everywhere, and the workers are just standing there shouting and staring. Eric sees there's a door by all these windows, so he says, 'Leon let's help them.' So he and I go through this door and make our way to the mixer. He takes one side and I take the other. I spot the power source and it's wired right into the wall, like I could see the conduit, but no plug. Eric looks over my shoulder and says, 'You get the fire extinguisher and I'll get the power.' And, I've known Eric for years and I trust him, so I spot the fire hose and extinguisher behind glass. So, me and Eric go over there. Eric yanks the fire axe off the wall and breaks the glass. He then heads back to the mixer. I grab the fire extinguisher and pull off the lock and spray it a few times to make sure it works. And then I'm on Eric's heels just as he hauls off and axes the power conduit, cutting the power. Then he yanks the bowl out of the arms of the mixer, so I can spray it down."

"Why wasn't he electrocuted?" Monte asked.

"To this day I don't know. I wouldn't have done it, but to ask Eric, he figured the wooden handle ax would protect him," Leon said.

"So, then what happened," George asked.

"So, after I sprayed the heck out of the mixer, I shut down the fire extinguisher and went over to Eric and was checking his hands and arms to see if he had any electrical burns. We were then going to check on the cafeteria staff, when all of sudden we hear applause. The cafeteria was full of factory employees watching the show, and in front of the group is the plant manager, our escort, and the big wigs. We got points for quick action and problem solving for stopping the out of control mixer, and points for asset protection for putting out the fire. Then, after all the accolades, Eric and I spent the rest of the day with the Troubleshooting team and got to know them and their process. We're now on a select mailing list where they send us plans or prototypes or wish list items and ask us to respond. If they like our replies we get a check. The better our stuff, the bigger the check."

"What about the damage you did to the mixer? And what would they have done had you guys not jumped in?" Monte asked.

"Well, they didn't seem to care about the damaged power conduit, because Eric surprised them. No one figured he'd axe the power, and it was so creative that they use it as an object lesson. Last I heard, they moved that mixer and power conduit into the Troubleshooters' lobby, where it's like a big sculpture. And before we left that day, the plant manager took us back into the kitchen, where she pointed to a red, shut-off button about eye-level and six feet away from the mixer. The sign above it said, *Emergency Shut Off.*"

All three men laughed.

"Wow, that's great, Leon. Good for you and your friend," Monte said, looking at George. "You guys are welcome to use the shop as needed so long as we don't hurt any customers, and let me know if you need extra supplies, within reason. I'm heading back out front. I'll holler if I need you."

"Okay, boss," both Leon and George said.

"Do you think they still do practical tests like that today?" George asked Leon, after Monte had left.

"I don't know for sure, but I think it's part of the way the Racine plant works. The plant manager drove Eric and I back to our hotel, and she told us about her test that got her the plant manager job. She and the other candidates were all grouped in a room where they observed a portion of the line for about twenty minutes. They were told the machine they were watching was set to be replaced in a few weeks, as soon as the replacement arrived, and that this machine was producing eighty percent of the desired output. They were tasked to identify the problem and try to solve it. That was it. The room they were in had big tables, computers, operating manuals, factory plans; you name it."

Leon paused to take a drink. "They were then pulled into another room where they sat watching the rest of the floor while each candidate, in turn, went out to the machine, did what they could to identify, and fix, the problem and then were sent home to wait to hear whether they got the job. Our PM had been in the middle of the pack and she identified the problem as an arm that moved parts from one level of the machine to another. She said it would swing too high on about every third rotation and mess up the line. She said the angle was awkward and that the arm wasn't well-placed to span the gap. So, she solved the problem by tying the silk scarf she had around her neck to a bar above the arm and then tying the other end to the arm at a certain distance. She said it only worked because of the setup. A contact point on the upper part of the machine controlled the arm joint. The arm would rise up to that contact point, stop, and then drop the part. The joint needed to be flexible to handle small fluctuations, so her scarf lessened the arm's excess swing. It solved the problem and would last as long as her scarf did."

"Wow."

"Yeah, and she said it wasn't so much what she did that got her the job. Her reasoning and justifications for why she did what she did got her the job."

George looked down at his feet. "I don't know if I can do that."

Leon shook his head. "George, you already do that. Every day when somebody brings in a broken part or machine, you find out what's wrong and fix it. Usually it's a replacement part, but you also do those 'adjustments' and 'quick fixes' for folks who can't afford the handbook repairs. Think of it as your way to think outside the box. I mean, who says it can't work that way or it should work this way? There's always another way and, if it works, you ask 'can it work better?' That's why I asked you about the Annual prize. I truly think you could win it, and why not."

"Thanks, Leon. It's good that you're here. Monte runs the business because his dad and granddad did. But you love the machines like I do."

"You're welcome. I am just grateful that Monte had an opening so I can do what I love and get paid for it."

They went back to their baler prototype design and were discussing the next phase when Monte poked his head into the shop.

"Hey Leon, I need you to come help a customer."

"Will do." Leon stood up and took off the welder's helmet and heavy, leather gloves. He looked down to gauge his cleanliness. *Better leave my apron on. This will probably be quick, but better wash the hands. It's not good to get grease and gunk on the customers.*

Hands clean, he pushed through the shop doors that swung directly into the showroom and was past the counter when he saw the customers Monte must have meant.

Marion Sullivan was standing there holding Mick's hand and a lidded, metal, 9X13 cake pan. Jeanette stood by her with Nancy's hand in hers and Jeremy nestled against her shoulder.

Mick spoke first. "Hey Leon. You've got a welder's apron like Dad's."

"Hey, sport. Sure do." Leon then looked to Marion and Jeanette. "Hello, ladies. What's up?"

"Hey Leon. We're on our way to Ogden for some things, and Mick wanted us to stop by and share the cookies he and Marion made. He said that you loved 'iced cookies', and that we should give you some to thank you for helping Auntie Marion the other day," Jeanette answered.

"Yes, Leon, thank you. We made plenty and there's enough to share with your crew," Marion chimed in, holding the cake pan out to him.

Leon took it and laid it on the counter. *I do love sugar cookies.* He slid off the cake pan lid and saw that Marion had carefully layered three tiers of round sugar cookies with pink icing on sheets of waxed paper. He took one out and took a bite. *Perfect. Soft and sweet with just the right bit of give in the cookie.* He addressed Marion and then Mick. "These are really good cookies. Thank you, Marion for making me some. And you, Mick, thank you for talking your auntie into making cookies for me. I don't have the patience to bake and ice cookies."

Mick showed his mother's teaching. "You're welcome, Leon."

Then little Nancy piped up. "Me and Mick did the sprinkles."

Leon crouched down and smiled at her. "Thank you, Nancy. I love sprinkles." He pinched her nose and she giggled.

He straightened up and addressed the ladies. "So you and the little ones are off to Ogden?"

"Yes. We're going shoe shopping for everybody" Marion answered.

"I need new boots," Mick blurted out.

"Yup. And I need a new pair of tennis shoes, so we're heading south," Marion laughed.

"Good for you."

Monte came over to the group.

"Cookies?" he asked Leon.

"Yes, they're for all of us from the Sullivans," Leon answered.

Monte took one and bit half off in one bite. He looked to Marion. "These are good cookies, Miss Marion. Thank you."

"You're welcome, Monte. It's a small thing we can do to thank you for the good things you've done for us over the years."

Jeremy started squirming, so Marion said, "Well that's our cue. Have a good day, you guys. Bye."

"Bye," Leon and Monte responded.

"Leon, that's an example of why I love doing what I do. The families that use our tractors treat us like family," Monte said, after the Sullivans left.

"You're right. It's neat," Leon said, picking up another cookie. He then picked up the remaining cookies in the cake pan with his other hand. "Are you okay if I take these into the shop for me and George to snack on?"

Monte nodded. "Sure thing. I am pretty sure that Marion brought them just for you, anyway."

Leon let that jibe from his boss slide but a sneaky thought caught him off guard. *Marion sure looked nice today. Her curly hair is amazing. I'm glad she doesn't straighten it like my sister straightens hers.*

Chapter Twelve

"Hey Gene, what did you need? Sure, I'll stop there on my way home. Anything else? Okay. See you soon. Love you too." Marion disconnected the call with her brother and dropped her cell phone into her truck's cup holder. Her brother had amazing timing. How did he know she was just coming up on the last Tremonton exit?

Marion pulled off the freeway and entered the west end of Tremonton and drove to the tractor dealer wondering if Leon was working there today. *Wait, why do I care?* He did her a favor and she showed him some land, but that's it. *It's not like I have a case on him, do I?* She squelched any romantic thoughts and entered TT in full professional farmer mode. It was a bright sunny day, so she pushed her sunglasses up her forehead to sit on her hair as she entered the showroom. Leon was the only one at the counter. *Marion, you can do this*, she thought, to herself.

"Hey Leon!"

"Why, Marion. How are you?"

"Good and you?"

"Pretty good myself. What brings you in today?"

"Well, Gene called me and asked me to pick up a service manual he ordered from you guys."

"He did. We got it yesterday, let me go get it," Leon responded, immediately.

Leon ducked into the back room behind the counter and came back with a thick paperbound book wrapped in plastic. "Here it is. Let me get the invoice. Gene paid for it with a card, but I promised him a receipt."

"Sounds good."

Marion watched Leon's hands as he typed in the computer and retrieved a printout. He smiled at her and then looked over her head.

"Hey, it's just about noon. I have your cake pan at home. Can I take you for lunch and then we can go to my house and get it?" he asked.

Marion felt a bit blind-sided by the invitation. "Well, I...."

"Hey, no pressure here. I called in a lunch order to Lou's and just need to go get it. My place is off Tremont Street, so if you want to give me a half-hour, I can be back here with your pan in no time."

Marion thought about it, then her stomach rumbled loudly.

Leon must have heard it. "I heard that, missy. Come on, can't I tempt you with a shake or some fries?"

She felt her resolve wavering. "Well I've been all the way to Salt Lake and back and could use a bite. Plus, I love Lou's shakes."

"That settles it. I'll drive you with me to Lou's. We'll eat, get your pan, and I'll bring you back here. Okay?" Leon smiled.

"Okay."

He ducked back into the back room and she heard him talking to Monte. He reappeared and ushered her to the front door, which he opened for her then followed her to her truck.

Marion pushed her sunglasses down to shade her eyes then opened her truck door. She tucked the invoice and Gene's service manual under the center console and then reached to get her purse.

"My treat, please," she heard behind her head.

"Okay. You driving too?" she asked, looking over her shoulder.

He nodded.

"Okay then," she replied, shutting her truck door and pushing the lock button on her keychain remote.

Leon led her around to the back of the showroom and shop where she saw his now-familiar, black and silver pickup. He followed her to the passenger door and opened it for her. He would have helped her up into the seat if she'd let him. He shut the door and then moved around to his side. That got Marion wondering if this was a date since he didn't open the door for her out at the Gorham place.

He drove them the mile or so through Tremonton to Lou's Drive-In. Once inside, he walked to the counter and said, "I have a to-go order, Packer, and this lady would like to order as well."

Marion felt shy as he moved over to let her speak to the teeny-bopper running the till.

"I'll have a small strawberry shake and a medium fry, please."

The teen rang up the total and Leon handed her bills from his wallet, which he then pocketed along with the change. They stood, side by side, waiting as their orders were finished. Leon's sack sat on the counter while Marion's fries were dropped and her shake made.

"What, no shake?" she asked him.

"Not today. I couldn't eat it fast enough. I like the big ones, and I like to savor them, and it's too hot today to eat one slow."

"Here you go!" the teen at the counter called out, as she slid Leon's big bag and Marion's small bag, and shake, forward. They each took their order.

"So do you want to eat here, or would you be okay at my kitchen table?" Leon asked.

"Let's go to your place."

"Sounds good to me."

Once again, Leon shepherded her to her side of his truck and, this time, not only did he open and close the door for her, he held her food while she buckled up.

He handed her, her sack and his sack as well.

"Are you okay holding this for me until we get there?" he asked.

"Sure can."

They rode in comfortable silence a few blocks past the Tremonton City library and adjoining park to a well-maintained Cape Cod style house.

"This is my friend Eric's, grandma's house. She's a snowbird who's decided to live in St. George full time. I'm house-sitting for her until she decides whether or not to sell it," he said, pulling into the drive.

"That's a good arrangement."

"I thought so."

He met her outside the truck taking all the food from her as she got out. He gave her back her shake, but kept the two paper sacks as he opened the side door.

"Kitchen's right here." He stood aside so she could precede him.

Marion entered a sunny, 1960s kitchen done in bright yellow and white with black accents. She noticed it was sunny and clean with sparkling chrome and healthy ferns hanging from the ceiling in three macramé baskets.

"I like it. I take it none of this is yours except the maintenance, right?" she inquired.

"Right. Mrs. Jenkins told me that 'good house sitters maintain and do not change, defile, or destroy'. Her words."

They sat at the classic Formica and chrome table with matching chairs.

"Fun for you," she said.

"Hey, I'm used to it. I have one brother and one sister, and all of us know that Dad does what Mom *lets* him do in our house."

Marion laughed. "I wish Jeanette were here. I can tell you that she does what she *can* in Gene's house. Even in the kitchen, she had to fight before he'd let her have painted cabinets."

"Wow. But, what about you?"

"Well, I live in Mom and Dad's house, and it's a mix of Dad's family and what Mom could do to it. It's nearly a hundred years old, and she didn't want to hurt its charm. But you're right. It's definitely her kitchen and it was Grandma Sullivan's before that."

"So would you change it?" Leon asked, as he opened his sack and started on his sandwich and fries.

Marion opened her sack and dipped a fry into her shake.

"Well, it's not my say. I mean, I'm living there, but the house goes with the farm. I am kind of just keeping it going until Mick or Nancy take it over," she replied.

Leon seemed surprised. "You mean, you don't get to make it yours in the meantime?"

"No, not really. Right now, I am in a long-term, temporary situation."

"You mean that you're holding the spot your mom and dad would have held had they lived longer?"

"You got it. I'm the bum lamb who has the run of the pasture until the breeding stock comes in."

"Marion, that's a heck of an analogy. What if you get married and became Sullivan breeding stock?"

"Well, there's little chance of that happening. You've seen my place. Where am I going to meet a husband spending my days a twenty-minute drive from Snowville?"

Leon opened his mouth to say something, but Marion stopped him. "Sorry, Leon, I didn't really mean that. It's just a touchy subject for me, so can we talk about something else?"

"Sure can. So, why did you go to Salt Lake today?" he complied.

"Oh, it's my turn to take the sweaters down."

"That's the best answer I've ever heard that tells me nil. Please elaborate," Leon laughed.

"Well, you know that I have a tiny herd of sheep that I'm thinking of expanding, right?"

"Yes. Hence the bum lamb story and your Rambo and Howard duo."

"Yup. So, each year, we shear them before Atzo and his crew shepherd them out into the hills and dales. We take the wool up to Dubois, Idaho where there's a wool broker who takes the fleeces to Pendleton, Oregon. And, because our sheep are a meat breed, our fleeces don't rate the big bucks so, for years, Mom took payment for the wool in yarn. She then turned the yarn into fantastic, classic cable-knit sweaters like her Norwegian ancestors did. Jeanette and I maintain this tradition. Knitting is a great pastime when watching TV, and we consign the sweaters we make with a specialty boutique in Salt Lake. You may ask why I am selling sweaters in the blistering heat of a Utah summer, and I reply, that the shop stockpiles them for their winter stock and is happy to pay Jeanette and me about fifty dollars per sweater whenever we bring them in. We take trips down every few months and it was my turn today."

"Wow, that's fascinating. I know this is like asking you how much land you two have, but how does the profit work on something like that, I mean is it worth the effort?"

"I don't mind answering that. Yes, we make a profit. Jeanette and I don't get paid for our time, but we make and sell enough sweaters to cover the cost of the shearers and the trips to Dubois and Salt Lake. It's the best way we've found to make the wool profitable. This allows us to use the sale of the meat to pay for the feed, shelter, and shepherding of the sheep, and we usually net a small profit each year from that."

"You just don't get a wage, then."

"Right, but I find knitting can be soothing when I've had a hard day of work outside. And, once I get a pattern down, I can do it practically in my sleep."

"That's a neat thing. Thank you for telling me about it. I am always fascinated to hear how agricultural folks find ways to make more money now a days."

"Then you should ask Gene about his Herefords the next time you see him. The Sullivans have run prized Hereford cows for generations and we fought hard against the Black Angus, because the Angus calves are too big for Hereford mommas. He's been ecstatic that the Hereford meat is coming back on top. He thinks the whole Black Angus thing was genius marketing."

"So that's why I saw more red cows in your herds than black."

"You got it. We like our cows like our tractors. Mostly red with a bit of black and white."

Leon laughed at that. "That's why Gene has the red tractor hat habit, right?"

"Yeah, but Great Granddad started that. Half the pictures we have of him show him with a hat with the red, white, and black tractor logo. Gene will say he wore the hats because Great Granddad liked those tractors, but Grandpa always said he wore the hats 'cause he got them for free."

"That's why I'd wear them except they're part of my uniform. That also reminds me of those old 'What's black and white and red all over?' jokes."

"What's the punch line?"

"Well, they're many. The intended answer is a newspaper—red as in r-e-a-d. But my favorites are the blender ones—you know various animals like penguins and panda bears in a blender—Black and white and red all over." They laughed at his joke.

Marion dipped another fry in her shake, causing Leon to wonder.

"Why do you dip your fries in the shake?" he asked.

"Cause it's good. Here try it." Without considering the intimacy of her impulse, Marion dipped another fry in the strawberry shake and held it over to Leon's lips.

He looked her in the eyes as he obediently opened his mouth and bit off the end of the fry. *Oh no. Now what do I do with the rest of the fry?* she thought.

Leon solved her dilemma by gently grasping her hand and pulling the remaining half of the fry out of her fingers and popping it in his mouth.

"You know, that's good. I'll have to try that. Although I like chocolate shakes more than strawberry," he said.

Marion fought down a blush stemming from the fact that she'd fed a strange man some of her food.

"Well, back in high school, when my best friends showed me the trick, we started trying it with different shake flavors and decided strawberry goes best with fries," she explained.

"I'll keep that in mind." Leon stood up and went to the fridge.

"I'm getting a bottle of water. Want one?" he asked, over the open fridge door.

"Sure, I'll take one."

Leon came back to the table and set down a bottle by her and then opened the other for himself.

She found herself fascinated by his Adam's apple moving as he chugged down the cold water.

When he'd emptied the bottle, he looked at the remains of his food. "I'm done. How 'bout you?"

"I'm done too."

"Okay. I'll clean this up, go get your pan, and then I'll take you back to the store."

"'Kay."

Marion sat, comfortable in the cool kitchen drinking her water as Leon disappeared through a door and came back with her pan.

"Thank you again for the cookies. Sugar cookies are my absolute favorite."

"You're welcome. I'll keep that in mind as they're Mick's favorite too. He was the one who told me and Jeanette about your preference, you know."

Leon smiled. "I remember him saying that. Well, I am glad I told him. I've had a craving for them and don't know really know how to make them. I'd been thinking about calling my mom and begging her for some, and then you guys came into TT."

"Well, me and Jeanette are handy like that."

"I bet. Say, I have a question I wanted to ask you, but it may be too personal, so tell me to shut up if you don't want to answer."

"Ok. Shoot," she said, warily, wondering what could be so personal.

"Well, if I move out by you, I'll be too far away from my parents for a quick visit and I wanted to ask you how you cope without your parents?"

"You mean as an orphan?"

"Oh, I'm sorry... I mean how do you cope when you need your parent and they're not reachable? And you can tell me to let it go."

"No, I can answer that. It's hard. I *am* an orphan, you know. Gene and I are it. But, I have an idea of what you mean. So to answer you, it depends on what's bugging me. Sometimes I try to picture them with me or remember what they did in a certain situation. Other times, I dig out something of theirs that they wrote, or liked, and try to figure out why they wrote it or what they liked about it. I will say that sometimes I feel like they're near. Like they're on the other side so they can be with me more. I just don't always feel them. However, when Mom was alive and I was at Utah State, I had a bad time or two and once she wrote me a letter that I got right when I needed it and another time she had a feeling that I needed her so she called me. I think that that's how it will be with you and your parents. Mom did say, that you always worry about your kids, no matter where they are or how old they are. She said that Grandma worried about her even when she was an old lady too."

"Thank you for sharing that. Sorry to be nosy."

"That's fine. That's one thing you'll find out when your parents pass, hopefully many years from now, that folks will feel weird talking about them to you, like they don't want to hurt you by mentioning them, but it's usually good to speak about them. I appreciate you asking me, because you helped me remember that neither of my parents wanted to leave Gene and me so soon. Dad, especially, felt like he was abandoning us. And you helped me remember how much they loved me."

"You're amazing, Marion." He looked at her and asked, "So you were at Utah State too?"

"Yup."

"Okay, Miss Details, when and what?"

"I only did a year, and I won't tell you when. I'll tell you the size of my spread, but not my age. I did Engineering. And, I suspect you were an Agriculture major like Gene?"

"I was, but technically a tractors major. I graduated, but I'll tell you when I went when you tell me when you went."

"No wonder Monte hired you. He lives tractors, but doesn't really understand them."

"So, why only a year?"

"Dad died."

"Well engineering explains the equilateral triangle remark."

"Nothing gets past you."

That made him laugh. All of a sudden Leon looked behind him.

"Oh crap. My hour's up. I need to get back," he said.

"No problem, I need to get back too. Thank you for lunch."

"My pleasure. We'll have to do it again, sometime.

Chapter Thirteen

"Thank you for meeting me out here, Mrs. Christensen. I know this was a last-minute trip for you," Leon spoke to the real estate agent as they stood by the well at the Gorham farm.

"My pleasure, Mr. Packer. I'm glad you're interested and Mr. Gorham was happy to supply the keys so you can get inside the house and the shop before you make an offer.

"May I?" Leon held out his hand for the keys.

"Yes. Here you go."

"I'd like to start with the house. You said there's no value attached to it as it would need extensive repair before it's habitable, right?"

"Yes. I'm authorized to tell you that the Gorham family is prepared to cut the sale price slightly in order to allow for a demolition budget."

"Okay."

He made his way to the back door. All was as it was when Marion had brought him out here. Leon noted that sheets of plywood were attached with nails and screws to cover all the windows and the front door. Mrs. Christensen had told him that the back door was also covered in plywood, but it wasn't nailed shut. Instead, Mrs. Gorham's son had installed a padlock so it could open and close if needed.

He'd been told that the padlock on the back of the house matched the one on the shop's garage door, so he knew which of the two keys on this ring would open the house. The large, and tough, brass padlock's lock protested a bit, but Leon was able to force it to open once the key had turned. He pulled the lock's loop out of the brass bracket and yanked on the plywood to open the door. The door opened easily as the plywood was heavier than the sixty year old wooden screen door that it was nailed to. The 1920s inner door looked weather-beaten, but solid. Leon liked its solid wood construction and noted that the upper glass window, though single-paned, was still intact. He turned back to Mrs. Christensen.

"How long has it been since someone's lived here?"

Mrs. Christensen checked her notes.

"About twenty years, and even then, only Mr. Gorham's elderly mother lived here. At the end, she only used the downstairs. I believe that the kitchen and bathroom were updated in the 1980s, and were still functioning, but the upstairs bath needs a total gut. Its 1960s shower pipes are totally corroded."

"That makes sense." He looked over at her in her nice slacks and dress pumps. "You don't need to come in here with me unless you like. You've been in here, right?"

"I have, but I can come with you to answer any questions you have."

"There's no need, I'll look around and then I'll ask you any questions I have after."

Leon made his way into the dark interior. As he went through the house, he noted what he saw in his quest to determine whether the old place could be salvaged. The back door was centered in the kitchen area. The kitchen took up the entire rear of the house. A large, cast-iron woodstove sat in the center of the far wall, facing the back door, with the door to the hallway offset to one side. The stove was clearly big enough to cook on and help heat the place. It probably warmed the hall and the rooms behind the kitchen too.

He pulled out the tiny, metal flashlight he kept in his glove box and shined it around the floors, walls, and ceilings. He observed a lot of solid wood construction. It looked good, but could have termites and dry rot. He looked at the windows from the inside. All in the kitchen were multi-paned, double-hung with wooden frames and old-fashioned sashes. He would need to check them to see if they were painted shut and whether the counter weights still functioned. He looked at the door to the hallway. It was hanging open, but it too had an upper window probably to let in light.

Leon continued through the downstairs. The room behind the wood stove was a sizable bedroom. It was empty of furniture, but he could see sun fading in the wooden floor showing where a large bureau and the bed, had stood. A closet had been added to the room and it looked good, if a bit cramped. Opposite the hall was another tiny bedroom. Maybe a twin-sized bed could fit in there. It had no closet, but did have a nice window to the north. He noticed the window was offset in the wall and decided that the bedroom was cut down for whatever was next door. He confirmed the downstairs bathroom took up the missing space from the bedroom. In the hall, he could tell that the two rooms were originally the same length.

The bathroom looked pretty good at first glance. It was 1980s, all right, but the tub looked older. Leon looked around, at the walls and the shower insert, which confirmed this bathroom was definitely the missing half of the small bedroom. But he liked how they had put a linen closet in the extra space.

The hallway ended with the walls of the bathroom and big bedroom and opened onto the front room. It was pretty dark in there. The only light came from the back door that shown off-center into the room. Like the kitchen, the front room was long and narrow and ran along the front of the house. He turned off his flashlight and looked at the front door. It had a transept window that was covered, but he could still see light, around the frame, under the plywood. *Maybe it's missing some structure up there.* To his left, on the south side of the room, stairs took up part of the room. The banister and rail looked tough, but the spindles were mostly all busted. He better be careful making his way upstairs.

At the top of the stairs he could see pretty well, but that didn't surprise him. There was no plywood on the upper windows. The upstairs was smaller than the downstairs. It consisted of two bedrooms with a Jack and Jill bathroom in the middle. The stairs opened on a small landing that cut into the square shape of the first bedroom with a door. Leon went into the door and saw that he had to go through this room to get to the bathroom and then go through it to the back bedroom. Both bedrooms had gabled windows on the east and west sides, but the back bedroom also had a set of twin windows in the center of the wall facing north. *They must be directly over the back door*, he thought. He turned around and confirmed his reasoning when he spotted the galvanized chimney pipe running up the side of the bedroom door.

He looked at the ceilings upstairs and noted quite a few water spots, a sure indication of a leaky roof. That didn't surprise him. What did he expect? He'd noted outside that there was a layer of asphalt shingles over the old wooden ones, and some had blown away. Back in the upstairs bathroom, he could see what Mrs. Christensen had meant about its pipes. The plaster and lathe had crumbled all around the shower/tub. And, the floor felt springy and spongy. Back in the front bedroom he noticed an antique coal stove. He realized that the kitchen stovepipe must have heated the back room and this stove had heated this room. He peeked back in the bathroom and saw the spot where another stove and water heater would have stood by the marks on the floor and the holes in the ceiling where the chimney vents would have been.

He went back downstairs stomping, and bending, his knees up and down testing each tread. *If there were stoves up here, where were the others downstairs?* he wondered. He looked carefully around the front room. He then spotted the floor heaters. When they electrified the place they put in electric heaters in here. But, he wondered where they stored the coal, and where the water heater was. He turned back around and saw an access door in the stairway that he'd missed before. Leon pictured the outside of the house and thought about what could be under his feet. He opened the panel and saw stairs leading down into what could be a crawlspace, cellar, or basement. *Hopefully, it's tall enough to stand in*, he thought to himself.

It was totally dark down there. He gingerly stepped on the first step as he turned on his flashlight. At the bottom, he crouched down to see what he could. The floorboards were about at his chin. He guessed the ceiling was about five and half feet tall. Crouching made it hard to see everything, so Leon sat on the stairs gingerly and shone the flashlight around.

It could be worse. At least he could mostly stand up. Plus, maybe he could dig down a bit. He covered the light momentarily. It was not totally dark in the crawlspace/basement. Leon could see that the floor was dirt but it was tightly packed and looked good. If he did dig it down, he could cement it and use the space for storage. A few feet away, he spotted the 1960s era water heater with pipes going over to what must be the kitchen sink and the functional bathroom. He also spotted copper water lines snaking around, enough to run the sinks, toilets, and showers he'd counted. He could now see that the light down here came from the front wall behind his back and, when he shown his flashlight in that direction, he spotted the coal chute. He not only found where the coal was stored, but found the water heater and water lines. All of which need updating.

Leon shone the light on the floorboards above his head. The structure looked good. But, again, he couldn't tell if there were dry rot or pests. The stone and cement foundation looked good from inside and outside, but again, he would need a professional opinion.

He stood up carefully and made his way back upstairs and out the back door from the kitchen. Mrs. Christensen had moved under the shade of the cottonwood tree. She looked up and saw him and came over as he was locking the back door.

"So do you have any questions?" she asked.

"Not really. It matches your description. It's an old house that would take a lot of work to make livable. I can definitely handle it as is. Having it sit here until I can knock it down or update it won't bother me either way." He handed her the keys.

Mrs. Christensen was too professional to show her relief, but Leon figured he saw it shining in her eyes.

"That's good to hear, Mr. Packer, so long as you remember, that like the shop, the house comes 'as is' as part of the sale," she said.

"Understood. Though I estimate it would take me about ten grand to knock it down and haul the stuff to the dump."

"I'll confer with Mr. Gorham and see if he will agree to knock ten thousand off the price accordingly."

"Thank you. Now will you show me around the shop? I'd like to see its living conditions as I clearly won't be able to live in the house."

"My pleasure."

They spent the next hour going through the machine shop and driving around the property.

At her office in Tremonton a few hours later, Leon told Mrs. Christensen as he left, "Thank you for going out there with me today. I'll look over everything and bring over an offer tomorrow. Will that suit?"

"Yes. I'll meet with Mr. Gorham later today and have the final paperwork ready. You have financing started?"

"Yes, I have a mortgage broker and bank ready to go. If the Gorhams accept my offer, I've been told the bank will need a week or two to secure the additional financing, but that we can start the closing in the next month."

"Good. I'll see you tomorrow. Goodbye, and good luck!"

"Thanks. 'Til tomorrow."

Chapter Fourteen

Marion pulled into Jeanette's driveway and parked. She'd been to Tremonton to pick up some workbooks Jeanette and she had ordered for Mick to complete during the summer prior to him starting kindergarten in the fall. After hitting the post office, Marion had picked up some milk, ice cream, and soda pop as usual.

She lifted the smaller, rolling cooler from the back seat of her truck down to the cement driveway at the side of Jeanette and Gene's house, then hefted the stack of large envelopes from the post office to carry with her as she pulled the cooler into Jeanette's kitchen.

"Hey, Jeanette! I'm back. I'll drop off the packages on the table and then load your fridge and freezer."

Marion heard Jeanette's voice faintly from the back of the house, "Ok. Sounds good. I'll be in once I've changed Jeremy's diaper."

The other kids must have heard her entry, because Mick and Nancy came running into the mudroom.

"Wuv you Aunt Mare," Nancy said, hugging Marion's knees.

"Love you too, baby," Marion said, dropping the cooler handle and reaching down with one hand hugging her shoulders.

Mick was jumping up and down pointing at the packages in her hands. "What did you bring me? Momma said she ordered me some workbooks. Can I have them?"

"She did. Settle down and your Mom will get them for you once she's got Jeremy ready. There's also some packages for your Mom, Nancy and me. Can you be a big boy and put all the packages on the table while Nancy and I put the ice cream in the freezer?"

"I will." Mick reached up and pulled the packages from her hands and sped off into the kitchen.

Marion then nudged Nancy behind her as she prepared to carry the cooler down the basement stairs to the freezer. "Nancy, follow me down to the freezer and you can help me put the ice cream away."

In the basement, Marion held the freezer door open as Nancy worked hard to put the boxes of ice cream sandwiches in the basket in the bottom of the upright freezer. When she was done, Marion loaded the ice cream buckets on the shelves and nudged Nancy back up the stairs.

"Thank you, sweetie, now let's go back upstairs to put the milk in the fridge and then your mom will give you a treat."

Nancy laughed as she trundled up the stairs. Marion followed slowly carrying the cooler in front of her.

In the kitchen, she'd settled both kids at the table, had loaded the milk into the fridge, stashed the cooler back in the mudroom, and had arranged the packages on the table near her when Jeanette came in carrying Jeremy. Jeremy held out his arms to Marion cooing when he saw her, so Jeanette handed him to her and then sat down between her and Nancy facing Mick.

Jeanette looked at all the packages. "Ooh, Marion, there's more here than I thought."

"Well, I did order a couple of books myself. I figure I can do some adult coloring books while those two color in theirs," Marion smiled, and cooed back at Jeremy then looked at Jeanette worriedly. "There is one that's a surprise. I need you to open it for me. I'm not sure what it is."

"Which one?"

"The thin one from Packer Photography in Layton."

"Not Packer as in Leon?"

"I hope not, but who else do you know who's named Packer and hails from Layton."

Jeanette reached for the sharp pocketknife she used on packages, and went to open the cardboard envelope. "It's been over a month since you brought him to look over the Gorham place, right?"

And it's been just a week or so since our lunch that I didn't tell her and Gene about, Marion thought. "Yeah. But, look at the insignia on the envelope. It looks professional."

"It says 'careful: photographic material' on the outside too. Okay, let's get it open."

"Mommy, whose package is that?" Mick piped up.

"It's for Auntie Marion. We think it's a picture," Jeanette answered.

"A picture to color?" he asked.

"Probably not, but let's see," his mom replied.

Jeanette got the envelope open and pulled out two thin pieces of cardboard sandwiched together. Carefully, she laid the envelope on the table and then set the cardboard sandwich on top of it. Marion watched as she picked up the top piece of cardboard. Underneath it was a typed letter on cream-colored paper, and below that was a nice eight by ten photograph.

Jeanette picked up the photograph and showed it to Marion.

"Wow, Marion, that's a great shot of you. Can you tell where it was taken?"

"Oh my heavens, Jeannie... that's the day I brought Leon out here. Can you put it a little closer so I can look at the surroundings?

Jeanette held it up closer to Marion as Mick cried out, "Mommy I wanna see!"

"Me see, too. Me see!" Nancy chimed in.

Jeanette addressed both kids. "Yes, you can see it, but wait until Auntie Mare has had her turn."

Marion was shocked looking at the picture. "Jeanette, this is over by the Gorham machine shop. As Leon was taking pictures of it, he must have snapped this one of me."

"Marion, hold on, don't freak out. You've gone pale."

"I need a minute."

"Hey, wait, you're forgetting the letter."

"Oh Jeannie, can you read it to me?"

"Are you sure? It's signed by Leon."

"Go ahead, I don't know what to think and I'm not sure if I dare read it."

"Let me read it first to see if little ears can hear it."

Jeanette scanned the letter reading it quickly. She slid it over closer to Marion so she could read it herself. "It's nothing, dear. Just a nice note from a nice guy."

Jeanette then held up the picture to Mick and Nancy. "See Auntie Marion... no, don't touch, you'll smudge the picture and Mommy needs to frame it for Aunt Marion."

Meanwhile, Marion read the letter, which was dated the day after her lunch with Leon:

Marion,

When I was going through my pictures, I found that I'd caught you in one, while you were looking at the sun, while we were down by the Gorham shop. My mother's a professional photographer and, when I showed the picture to her, she said I had to print it for you. Although accidental, I agreed with her that it was great picture of you and we wanted you to have it.

Please accept this picture as thanks again for showing me around your neck of the woods. I've decided to buy the Gorham place, but I'll have to wait to hear whether my offer was accepted and my financing approved.

I look forward to being neighbors with you and your family in the near future.

Leon

Marion finished reading the letter as Jeanette placed the picture back on the table. "You were right, Jeannie. It's a nice note from a nice guy. I shouldn't read anything more into it."

"Well, Mare, I think Leon is one tall drink of water, and very sexy, but I also noticed that he was most polite to everybody that day. That's why I think he was just being kind. And, unless he asks you out on a date or grabs you to plant one on you, I think that you write him off as just a neighbor, not a love-interest."

"I think you're right. I think for a minute I was hopeful though," Marion said, wondering if she should mention that they'd already had a pseudo-date.

"I totally understand. If I hadn't found Gene at school, I don't know how we would have found each other. It's hard to meet single guys when you live in the middle of nowhere, and it's a rare person who can live so far out in the country."

"Like us," Marion sighed.

"Yup, just like us."

Marion and Jeanette spent the next hour coloring and doing workbook exercises with the larger kids and taking turns entertaining the baby until lunchtime.

At lunch, Gene came in from working on the main irrigation point's pump to eat with his family.

Hey Sis, good to see you. How's things?" he greeted Marion.

"Just fine. We got new activity books for your brood," Marion answered.

Gene moved around the table to ruffle Mick's hair and then gave Nancy a kiss, before moving over to his wife and baby son.

"Hey baby, good morning, late," he told Jeanette, planting a wet one on her.

Jeanette kissed him back.

"Look on top the fridge at what Leon sent your sister," Jeanette told him.

Gene walked over to the fridge, asking with interest. "Tall, blond, and handsome Leon Packer?"

"The very same," Jeanette answered.

Marion gave Jeanette a dirty look.

"Thanks for telling the family, big mouth," she hissed.

"He'd see it eventually. I was going to hang it in your front room," Jeanette laughed.

Gene whistled through his teeth. "Gee, Marion, did you pose or something?"

Marion stood up and snatched the picture out of his hands, hoping to keep the letter from him too.

She got the picture, but missed the letter. Gene took a few seconds to read it. He looked at Jeanette and then Marion.

"Well, it seems Leon was just being nice. Interesting, though," he said.

"Why interesting?" Jeanette asked.

Gene raised an eyebrow at his sister. "How my little sister is acting a bit ruffled over Leon. That's what's interesting."

Her anxiety caused Marion to lose her temper at that point. "That's it. I'm done for today." She stood up, hugged Mick, Nancy, and Jeanette, before coming to stand in front of Gene. "You know that Leon is more interested in land than any female. You also know that there's precious, little chance of me finding any male who'll want to come and live out here. I love you, Bro, but you are heartless sometimes."

Marion stifled the tears that surprised her, and took off through the mudroom to leave, grabbing her cooler on the way. *That was stupid. Now, you'll not only have to make your own lunch, but your brother is going to be sure that you do have a case on Leon, when that's not really the problem*, she thought. She had made it to her driver's seat after stashed the cooler in the back when her cell phone rang. She looked at the display; it was Gene. She sighed and answered, "What?"

Gene's voice came into her ear. "Sorry, Sis. I didn't mean to hurt your feelings. Won't you come back in?"

"No, I won't. I've got things to do today. You know I should have the barn mucked out by week's end so you can haul in some gravel."

"That can wait you know. What's really wrong?"

"I don't want to talk about it."

"You need to talk about it. Do you want me to send Jeanette down later?"

"No. I don't want to talk to anybody about it."

"Will you at least tell me what 'it' is?"

"Fine. It's you... you and Jeanette and me. You have your soul mate, Gene. I don't... and, I am not sure I'll ever find one."

"I'm sorry, you know."

"I know. But, not all of us are as lucky in love as you are."

"Do you want me to ask around?"

Horror filled Marion and colored her response. "Hell, no, Gene! It's just got me thinking. And, my thoughts are going in some different directions this time."

"Well, let me know when you want to talk about it. I'll support you, you know."

"I know."

"Sorry, Sis, I have to change the subject... Atzo was looking for you. He may be to your house before dinner. Also, I may be down there later myself to see if Dad stashed any spare couplings in his supplies... I can't seem to get the spare one I have to fit."

"Ok. Fine. I'll talk to Atzo if he's around and I'll be in the barn mucking otherwise. I need to warn you, my thoughts may require an official 'family meeting'."

"Okay. I have tomorrow morning free. I'll be around at breakfast if that suits you."

"That works. Just you and I until we've decided, then you can pull in Jeanette."

"Okay. Love you, Sis."

"Love you, too."

Marion reached her house without incident, and couldn't see Atzo. Mucking out manure was a job she could only do on an empty stomach, so she stashed the cooler and her cell phone, found a facemask and the keys to the little tractor with a bucket she used for the task.

Marion had dismantled the lambing stalls and removed all the remaining hay in the barn earlier that week. She'd closed Rambo and Howard out the barn temporarily, and had dragged their water trough over by the pasture fence. She'd also moved the cat food and cats' dishes to the little machine shed at the side of the barn. The cats were hanging out there in the shade, but started hissing and ran off when the tractor came close.

She did a last, quick check to ensure there were no obstructions in the barn and then got started.

Back and forth she went. Into the barn scraping the bucket against the ground. When full, back out, turn, and drive the one hundred yards to the manure pit. Dump. Repeat. The heat of the day made it a nasty job due to the indescribable smell of rotten, sheep manure mixed with bits of old hay and straw, but the sunshine helped Marion stay positive. She focused on looking at the clear blue sky, green pasture grass, and golden grain and feeling the fitful breeze, as she breathed through her mouth, trying not to smell the stench. The sunshine felt comfortable warming her through her thin cotton shirt. Her tattered, old, cowboy hat kept the sun off her nose and her loosened hairs out of her face. Each trip freed more and more of the barn. Plus the heat would help the stuff break down so it would be safe to spread on the fields as soon as the snow melted after the next winter.

It was good work, a job that needed doing. A clean barn was a satisfying sight and a worthy goal. It had been years since Marion's dad laid the last gravel bed on the dirt floor of the barn and, when the next load showed some rocks, Marion rejoiced in the obvious sign of progress. For the past few years, she and her Mom had done all they could to just keep the manure to a manageable level. Gone was the last sign of how things had slipped when Dad died. "We've now got down to the gravel in the barn, Mom. No more 'maybe we'll get it next year,'" she said, to herself. A cleaner barn and the big tractor's new mirror erased the last signs that the Sullivans had hit a bad patch recently.

Over the afternoon, as things got hotter, Marion made more progress. When she was about three-quarters through, she felt like she needed a break. *I am too hot, and have sweated buckets. I'm thirsty*, she thought. In a reckless overuse of fuel, she drove the tractor up to the old well behind the house in order to get as far away from the stench as fast as she could. She was grateful the old, water well didn't go dry when they dug the new one deeper on the other side of the house. Marion gulped down dippers full of the cool, sweet well water to slake her thirst. She could barely see it, but could make out the thermostat in the shade of the garage's side door. It showed ninety-five degrees in the shade. No wonder she was so hot today. A few more trips and she could jump in the pond and cool off.

Marion replaced the antique, enameled dipper that her great-grandma had bought for the well in the 1930s on its hook, and then dropped the well's bucket down the hole again and pulled it back. She took off her old Stetson and doused it in the bucket to soak it, then lifted the bucket and upended it over her head, then repeated the dousing once more. The cold water got a shivering "OOOH, that's cold" out of her. But, she was glad the water washed off the gritty manure dust that had stuck to her sweaty skin.

She re-tied her facemask and plopped her wet hat on her soaked, braided hair and turned to get on the tractor. She looked over to the western hills and noticed clouds were moving in and they were turning grey. Excellent. It would take her about an hour to finish, and she should be done before any rain or wind starts. Much cooler now, Marion experienced her second wind and looked forward to finishing the final bit of the nasty job, knowing that the sun wouldn't dry her off for some minutes.

She'd made it over to the tractor, and was just starting it when she heard a car horn beep. She hadn't seen anyone come in but, then, she wouldn't have standing by the well behind the garage like that. She backed the tractor up so she could see the entire driveway and was shocked to see Leon's silver and black truck sitting there. He waved at her. Extremely conscious of her wet and smelly self, the last thing Marion wanted to do was to go over and talk to him. She was nearly done and, if he interrupted her, she'd have to finish in the rain. Damn.

Good manners won and Marion turned off the tractor's engine and walked over to Leon's truck praying her soaked shirt and jeans were not too flagrantly showing her naked body.

Leon opened the truck door and met her halfway. They stopped in the shade of the eaves over the garage door. He spoke first.

"Hey Marion. Sorry to just drop in on you like this. You're hauling manure?"

Marion knew she was pink and just prayed he'd think she was sunburned. She pursed her lips.

"Yup. Trying to get done before the wind brings the rain. Got about an hour left to go," she said.

"Well, I won't keep you, but I wanted to tell you that I got the Gorham place. I came out here today to change locks and stash the first load of gear. I didn't know if you'd be around, so I took a chance and drove over here."

Marion was genuinely happy for him. "That's great news. Congratulations! So, are you going to live out here?"

"Not sure yet, but will definitely stay the night now and then."

Oh man, he looks a little down, like I should be more excited, she thought. Marion felt an illogical urge to give him a hug or something. Better not, being all wet and all. She felt bad that she couldn't help him celebrate better. "Hey, I am really excited for you, but I am killer busy right this minute. Would you be willing to let me cook you a celebratory dinner later tonight? I really will be done in an hour and can be cleaned up and cooking in two."

That brought a smile to Leon's face. "I'd really like that. Is Gene or Jeanette home, can they come too?"

"I think Jeanette is, Gene was working on the big well pump, so he may be in and out. Tell you what. If you head over there, tell them to come over here in a couple of hours and I'll feed everyone. That should give you time to stash what you need to in your new digs, and me time to thaw some steaks."

"Sounds good. I'll see ya in a couple of hours. Good luck. By the way, that's a noxious smell."

Marion laughed. "It sure is. Sheep shit's the worst, I've been told. I'd consider that if you're considering raising animals on your new farm. Stick to the smells you can stand. I can stand horse, cow, and sheep, but not pig, and that's a viable concern if you get to muck it."

That made Leon laugh. "Good advice. I'll leave you to it."

"See ya."

Marion walked back to the tractor and was glad to get back to her task. Back and forth, more buckets of manure left the barn. Periodically, she checked the status of the storm front in the west. There was still time. She kept working. At the worst, she'd have only a couple of buckets to go when the storm hit... she was actually glad that Leon didn't offer to help... not that she expected him to. She needed to think. Marion smiled, picturing what Leon must have thought when he came by. *I am sure he didn't expect to see me mucking shit*, she thought. She decided she sure knew how to turn a guy off. Then she remembered that she'd forgotten to thank him for the picture. She resolved to try to remember to thank him at dinner. Her thoughts kept roaming as she worked.

The worries of her earlier conversation with Gene came over her, intensified by Leon's visit. She wasn't sure of her feelings about Leon. On one hand, he came to the house just say he bought the farm down the road. On the other, he invited her brother, sister-in-law and family to the celebratory dinner she offered. Marion thought about her single state and wondered if she should do something to start up a romance with Leon. She was concerned that, if she didn't do something assertive with Leon, she wouldn't have another chance. Thoughts of whether she could really live in her parents' house, doing farm stuff year after year with no hope of a husband or kids, to help swamped her.

Marion pictured herself as a forty-ish farm matron in her mother's kitchen as a grown-up Mick came to announce that he'd found a bride and was ready to take over. *Where will I go then? Is Leon coming out here a sign?* she wondered. She hoped that, if not, he was at least a sign that she needed to move on, finally. She had to face that she had spent the last few years doing what her Mom needed, and then expected her to do. She couldn't remember the last time she did something she wanted to do. Marion felt the questions stirring her up horribly. She wasn't sure of what to do but, while she was worried that she'd finally identified the problem, she wasn't sure she wanted to keep doing what she'd been doing, and if not that, what was she to do?

Chapter Fifteen

Leon felt incredible happiness wash over him as he drove from Marion's house to Gene's. He recalled his day so far as he drove.

He'd awoke this fine Friday in a good mood and got the call from his bank about the loan's approval and the farm sale's closing after lunch. His family members were all out at work, and Leon had found himself without anyone to share his good news with. Monte had been excited for him and told him to take the afternoon off. Leon had debated on what to do, but couldn't keep himself from going out to *his* place. He liked the sound of that. Maybe he'd make a sign saying the "Packer Place" or "The Double P" or something to show it was no longer the Gorham place.

Near Snowville, he realized he was still too excited and needed to share with someone, anyone. He thought immediately of Marion. She'd understand. Even his parents wouldn't get it, totally. They were not farmers and never wanted to be. But, he knew Marion would understand.

He'd gone to his place first and couldn't hold back the thrill he'd felt putting the "Sold" placard on the "For Sale" sign. He was really glad Mrs. Christensen agreed to let him do that part.

He looked around and couldn't decide what to do first. Leon bowed to the need to place some sort of stamp of ownership on this place, so he took out the familiar key ring he'd received with the farm's papers and deeds, and went over to the shop. He used the key to remove the rusty padlock on the shop's garage door and replaced it with his new lock. He then opened the shop's regular door and went inside. The Gorham heirs agreed that he could have any tools and equipment left in the shop; his contract included its contents. He flipped on the light switch and then watched to see if it worked. An ancient set of fluorescents slowly flickered to life, but functioned. Immediately on his left he spotted a workbench. He checked the drawers and found the basic tools he expected including a Philips head screwdriver. He returned to the door and removed both the door handle and the deadbolt and dropped them in a scrap bucket he'd found. He then went to his truck and cut open the package of the new handle and deadbolt he'd bought in town that morning and installed them. When done, Leon added the two keys, one to the padlock and the other to the door/deadbolt, to his truck key ring. He had a lot more to do around here but he'd made a start.

He went back to the shop, undid the new padlock and then pushed on the garage door to open it. It protested, but eventually rose up on its runners. The lights were still on. Leon turned them off because, with that door open, the sun made it bright enough inside, and then backed his truck into the shop. He would need to inventory everything and organize it before doing too much, but he could definitely stash his gear here in the meantime. He emptied his 'essential tools' bag, small duffle, Shop-Vac and other items from his truck. The last thing he took out of the truck was a five gallon bucket of cleaning supplies he'd brought from his house.

Leon was curious to look at the little, living area at the rear of the shop again. He'd seen it, briefly, during his official inspection of the house and shop with the realtor, but he needed to know whether it was livable. If not, he was driving to Layton tonight to get his mom and dad's RV. He ducked into the walled-in box that enclosed the living quarters.

The kitchenette consisted of a two-door cabinet and counter with shelf above it and a single cabinet with a small, metal sink. A Dutch door with a grimy window in the upper half was between the two cabinets. A wall opposite the door had a small table with a chair. On his right, an old-fashioned cast iron wood stove stood against the outside wall where it vented out. To the left, a doorway without a door allowed access to the bedroom and bathroom in the other half of the space. The bedroom area was the bigger half of the square box, but had a corner cut out for the tiny bathroom with an acrylic shower insert, tiny sink and serviceable toilet. Everything looked tough and suited the space. The person who'd planned this space focused on utility, but hadn't slopped things off. The cement floor in the bedroom was covered with a tough vinyl and the kitchen area was tiled with ceramic. Leon had confirmed the apartment was insulated, and the stove would heat it, but there was no air conditioner or other ventilation than the Dutch door. He tried the sinks' taps and toilet and confirmed the water was now on but he'd have to run it a while to check the pipes.

Leon already had an appointment with an old high school buddy to come out and check the stove and chimney. His friend was also going tell him whether he could salvage the stoves in the house. For now, all the shop apartment needed was a good cleaning. His old army cot will fit just fine in the bedroom, and leaving the door open would allow him to feel the breeze at night. Leon left the cleaning bucket by the kitchen sink as he inspected the locks on the Dutch door. It had the same lock and deadbolt configuration as the front door but the door handle was in the lower door and the deadbolt was in the upper. He went back out to his truck and grabbed another door handle and deadbolt package.

Once he'd changed the Dutch door's locks, he returned to the main shop area and looked up at the windows. The shop had three, factory-style windows along the upper roof area of the walls on the north and south sides. Leon found the old-fashioned handles for each fastened to the wall below them. He went and pulled out each handle to open them. The windows hinged out and the winch handle operated a metal arm that pushed the glass frame out and then held it out. Leon resolved to muck out this place seriously before he slept here. He also wondered whether it might be better to sleep outside on a cot, in his sleeping bag for the night. Who knew what critters were in the place? He looked at his watch and noticed it was nearly four in the afternoon. Realizing he'd run out of time, he decided to run over and see Marion.

He'd reached Gene's house by the time his reverie had caught up to his visit to Marion. He saw a truck coming down the lane from the other direction. Leon pulled into Gene's driveway and waited for the truck to reach him. It pulled in right next to him; it was Gene. Leon got out of truck and met Gene getting out of his. They shook hands.

Gene spoke first. "Hey, Leon. Good to see ya. What brings you out here today?"

"I bought the farm. I got the Gorham place!" he announced, not hiding the big smile on his face.

Gene's smile matched his. Here was the happy reaction Leon had been hoping for,

"That's great, man. Congratulations! I am so happy for you. What are you doing to celebrate?"

"Thanks, Gene. I figured you'd understand. As for celebrating, that's what I came over to your house to talk about. I've been out at my new place changing locks and taking stock, and happened to catch Marion mucking out her barn. She offered to make me a celebratory dinner and I want you guys to come, too."

"We'd love to. We're going down to Marion's, right? When?"

"In about two hours. She was on the final push to get the barn cleaned by the time the storm moves in and needs time to clean up."

"Sounds good. What are you going to do for the next couple of hours? You can't stay in the Gorham house and I imagine the shop is full of years of dirt."

"Well, I was thinking of starting my cleaning."

Gene shook his head. "That will take at least a day. Don't worry about trying to make the shop livable today. Today's a day of celebration." Gene seemed to consider Leon's sleeping situation. "Wait, you're not planning to sleep over there tonight?"

"Actually, I was. I figure I can drop my cot and bag under the large cottonwood by the well until the shop's ready."

"Hell, no you won't. Even if it wasn't going to rain tonight, I can't allow that. You can bunk with us until you have it livable. We have a huge rec room downstairs that you can take over for the duration. Both Jeanette and Marion would skin me alive if I let you sleep at the Gorham place as is or made you commute back and forth to Tremonton each day. No. I won't have it; you'll stay here. Got it?"

Leon laughed at Gene's high-handedness. "Yes, sir. I must confess I was worried about cleaning up at a well in the dirt each day."

"Good. Then it's settled. Come in and tell Jeanette your good news. She'll be tickled pink."

"I'll do that in a bit. If I'm gonna stay at your place, I need to get my gear. I'll swing back to my place and be back here, shortly."

"That works. I am so happy for you. See you soon. Congratulations again, man. You've got your own farm. Finally. Good for you!" he said, clapping Leon on the shoulder. He couldn't contain his enthusiasm.

"Thanks, Gene. Appreciate that."

"We're here for you, buddy. We farm boys need to stick together."

Leon felt great as he drove back to his farm homestead. Coming out and celebrating with the Sullivans WAS the right thing to do. They were so supportive and he really needed their help right now. Leon felt blessed and fulfilled. He couldn't believe it finally happened. He had his very own farm. His very own place to do with what he wanted and could. He couldn't wait to get started and was so grateful Gene offered him the bunk. He had to admit he hadn't thought his nighttime plans through realizing he better call his dad tomorrow and get the trailer. It would be a lot easier to live in the RV and spruce up things at his leisure. He knew couldn't stay with Gene for too long.

He went into the shop and worked to close all the windows. The storm was closer now and he didn't want the havoc a windstorm would cause in the shop. He picked up his army cot and small duffel from the pile of gear and took them back out to the truck.

As he got into the truck, Leon was blindsided by a thought he'd been trying not to have for the past hour. For a minute, it controlled him.

He looked out the windshield but all he saw was a dripping wet, and incredibly sexy, Marion standing there looking at him. The shirt. The jeans. That hat. Never in his wildest dreams had Leon imagined such a sexy woman. None of his wildest fantasies could compete with Marion today, he realized. It was like a bad, country-music video except that she wasn't wearing a white T-shirt and cut-offs.

At the time, the male animal inside him had devoured the picture Marion made, while Leon exerted all his control to remain cool and aloof as he'd talked to her. He knew she was embarrassed; she was blushing like crazy and why not. That tan colored shirt looked like skin and was see-through and plastered to her everywhere. Even her breasts were showing through her tan bra, because it was soaked too. And those jeans, man. Every farm girl he'd ever known has worn tight jeans, but Marion's must be her oldest pair. Faded so bad that they were barely blue even wet, and plastered to her legs and hips. She might as well have been naked. And that awful, old Stetson sat crammed on her head as if its only purpose was to emphasize that incredible braid. All that hair braided into a rope that hangs at her hips and was as thick as his wrist. *Heaven help me. I am going to see her wearing just that hat, those boots, and that braid all my days*, he thought to himself.

Leon replayed the scene he'd driven into at Marion's. She clearly hadn't seen him when he'd first arrived. He'd been fascinated to watch her gulp down water over and over from an old, tin dipper. But when she dumped the buckets over her head, he'd nearly passed out. The look of joy and happiness at what must have been very cold water amazed him. He'd been embarrassed and had started to back out of her driveway, uncomfortable that he'd witnessed such a private moment. He'd made it back to where the driveway met the lane at the cottonwoods, but had to go back. He'd pulled back up as Marion was putting her hat on. He'd felt compelled to tell her about buying the farm, so he'd beeped the horn to announce his presence.

Leon felt his hands clenching and unclenching against his steering wheel and realized he was wishing he'd grabbed her and at least took out that braid and played with that hair. That thought didn't help calm him down. He had an image in his head of an all-wet, and naked, Marion lying on soft pasture grass in the shade of an old tree with her wet curls spread out all around her. He had no idea how he would face her again seeing *that* in his head.

There was no hope for it. He was more than turned on. Leon sighed as he got out and painfully walked over to his new, old well. Heedless of the sad state of the old, tin bucket on the rope, he opened the galvanized well cover and dropped the bucket down. When it hit the water, he waited until he felt the slight pull on the rope indicating the bucket had sunk down into the water. He pulled it quickly up and then dumped the dripping bucket over his head, mimicking Marion's earlier action.

On such a hot day the cold water did the trick and the resulting shock cooled him down. He then moved to stand in the sun and the freshening breeze to dry off a bit before heading back to Gene's.

Chapter Sixteen

Marion dumped the last bucket of manure into the pit about five o'clock with satisfaction. The barn was mucked out. Gene could bring in the four yards of gravel to give the barn a new foundation any day. Marion parked the tiny tractor in the newly cleared barn to protect it from the coming storm. The residual manure in the bucket could dry overnight and she would clean it off there, before putting that baby away in the equipment shed tomorrow.

Marion stood and stretched. She then went to the auxiliary shed by the barn and checked the cats' water dish. They needed some more, so she went to the hose, grabbed an empty grain bucket nearby, filled it with water, and used it to refill the cats' water pan. She then topped off the sheep trough. A scoop of cat food, and she'd fed the animals for the night.

At the house, she stopped by the far freezer and rifled the packages for enough steaks then went into the house and hung her hat on its peg by the back door before plunking the steaks into the fridge. Going into the laundry room she stripped down to bare skin. She threw the clothes she'd had on into the washer and loaded the soap and fabric softener dispensers. She decided to turn it on after her shower to save as much hot water as possible. She then streaked down the hall to her room.

When her mother had died, Marion had moved into the master bedroom, which, in reality, was just the largest bedroom in the house that happened to have an attached, three-piece bathroom. She checked the clock and saw that she had about forty-five minutes until everyone was supposed to be here. That was perfect, just enough time for her to get cleaned up and start prepping the salad and potatoes.

Marion didn't rush her shower, but she didn't waste any time either. She toweled off and wrapped another towel around her wet hair in a kind of towel-turban. After applying lotion, she stood in front of her closet deciding what to wear. The sunlight in her room dimmed for a moment, and a quick look out the windows showed the grey clouds were closer and darker. The storm had arrived. She decided to put out some candles in case of a power outage. She dressed in some clean jeans and a new, pink blouse she'd found in a boutique in Ogden, Utah. It was made in a vintage, Western style and had a curved yoke trimmed with lace and puffed short sleeves. Marion rifled her jewelry box and found some pink, opal earrings her dad had bought her as a teenager. They should go perfect, because they matched the pink pearl buttons on the blouse. She went back into her bathroom bending over with a brush and a blow dryer to partially dry her hair. There was no time to let it air-dry. She got it mostly dry and then braided it to keep it out of the way. She skipped the make-up, but applied a little of her light cologne behind her ears. She tidied her bathroom and went to the laundry room to start the clothes washing.

She was in the kitchen, with the oven pre-heating, scrubbing brown and sweet potatoes for baking when the herd arrived.

Jeanette came in the back door carrying Jeremy and holding Nancy's hand. At the hooks, by the back door, she stopped.

"Sweetie, take off your hoodie," she told Nancy, as she pulled Jeremy's little arms out of the miniature hoodie that had kept him warm. She then hung both her kids' jackets on a hook and turned to Marion. "Hey, Mare! That storm's really cooled things down. How's it going? Need help?"

"Not really. Once I get these potatoes in the oven, I'll make the salad. The steaks are defrosting and I figure I'll pull out the grill pan for them when the potatoes are about half done. Do you need a hamburger or two for Nancy and Jeremy?"

"No. Nancy can do a little steak if I cut it real small, and Jeremy can have potatoes and some veggies today."

"Okay, sounds good. Oh, can you guys put the leaf in the table and set it maybe?"

"Sure can. I'll have Mick help Nancy and me when he gets here. I'll plop Jeremy on the rug by the window with a few toys in the meantime."

Jeanette sat Jeremy down on the rug with his favorite stuffed train toy and set the diaper bag near him. She perched on the adjacent couch watching him.

"Come here, sweetie, and we'll see whether Aunt Marion still has her books you like so much." Marion heard her address Nancy. She watched as Jeanette pointed out the old wooden, apple crate by the TV that contained Marion's stash of kids' books. Nancy sat down in front of this crate happily pulling out a handful of books to play with and look at.

Marion finished scrubbing the last potato and drained the sink where she'd soaked the dirt loose. She pulled out a couple of fluffy dishtowels laying the wet potatoes on one as she began drying each spud. When they were all dry, she pulled out a large package of tin foil, wrapped each potato for baking, placed them on the oven rack and set the timer.

Marion pulled out the vegetables for a tossed salad.

"Jeanette, did you bring any tomatoes today?" she called over to Jeanette.

Jeanette was now sitting crossed legged between Jeremy and Nancy. "Oh, I forgot. I brought you a half-bushel, but I left them in the truck. I'll go get them."

"Don't worry, I'll go get them."

Marion left the iceberg lettuce she was unwrapping on the counter and went out the back door. She skipped down the few steps that went from the back porch to ground level in the garage. She made a beeline to the bed of Gene and Jeanette's truck, where she snatched the basket of tomatoes and spun around to head back in the house. Gene's voice stopped her.

"Hey Marion, the barn looks good. You did a great job."

She turned to look at him. He, Leon, and Mick were coming towards the house from the barn.

"Well, I learned how to shovel manure from the best," she answered, going back into the house without waiting for the boys. She did hear Gene laughing at her joke.

She sat the tomato basket down on the utility counter in the mudroom off the kitchen, grabbing three big ones for her salad. She placed these tomatoes on the kitchen counter as she went back to making her salad. She washed her hands and then began washing veggies and greens from the garden.

"The boys were out at the barn checking out my mucking job," she told Jeanette.

"Gene told me he wanted to see it. It's been a long time since you guys got it down to the gravel, right?"

"Yup. But, we were close. When I got down to it, I measured and we'd only been six inches or so away. Mom worried over it awful and I felt better knowing that we hadn't slacked off too much. I just wish I could have done it in the spring before we sheared."

"I hear ya. Gene can't wait until you've guys have cut the last hay crop in the upper field so he can turn the bulls loose in it so he can muck out the sheds up high."

"I bet. I'm also hoping this storm doesn't lay down the barley badly. It's starting really yellowed up and I'd like a good yield this year."

"I agree."

At that moment Gene opened the back door squiring in Mick with Leon following behind.

"Now, Mick, check your boots before you come in," Gene told his son. Marion smiled watching her nephew checking the bottom of each of his new, miniature cowboy boots before coming in the kitchen. Gene helped Mick hang up his jacket, then Mick dashed into the front room and went straight for the cupboard where the TV sat. He opened the doors and pulled out a miniature, red tractor with matching plow and manure spreader. Soon, he was sitting behind his mom plowing the carpet.

Gene and Leon were watching him, and Leon remarked, "That's a neat toy tractor, Gene. You guys have it a while?"

"Grandpa got it when he bought his last new tractor in what, '85, Sis?" Gene nodded, looking to Marion.

Marion nodded. "I think so. Mom and Dad were newlyweds when Grandpa bought the tractor, and the toys came with it. When we came along, Grandma and Grandpa would let Gene and me play with it. Grandpa would even joke that he had a real one that looked just like it, but we didn't believe him until we were old enough to ride with him in it."

"I was always fascinated by the real, rubber tires and metal body that matched the real tractor, while Marion would spend hours lining up the plow marks in the carpet like Grandpa taught her—in fact, just like Mick does," Gene remarked.

"Which is why you make me run the cultivator—you still tell me you can't make straight rows, but I can," Marion laughed.

Gene and Leon made their way into the living room and sat on the couch watching Jeanette and the kids. Marion stayed in the kitchen chopping vegetables. She arranged the chopped cucumbers, tomatoes, green onions, green peppers, dandelion and other greens, and carrots on a large cutting board, and then dipped down into her cupboard for a large salad bowl. She placed it on the counter then grabbed the head of lettuce. She held it steady in the palm of her hand and whacked it, stem-side down on the counter. She turned the lettuce head over her palm checking to see whether she'd successfully knocked the core loose. She banged it lightly on the counter a couple of more times before extracting the core, leaving a perfect cone-shaped hole in the center of the lettuce. She was surprised to hear Leon.

"Wow, Gene, your sister must really hate lettuce banging it around like that."

The living room group laughed at her. Marion responded and showed him the underside of the lettuce. "I was banging it to break the core loose. See, the whole lettuce head is ready to go in the bowl, I just have to rip it apart now that I tore out its core."

"Wow, woman, I am impressed," Leon responded.

"You should be," Gene answered, joining in. He gestured to Jeanette. "The Sullivan women really know how to kill vegetables."

Marion started assembling the salad. Jeanette looked to her and stood up. "Hey Marion, me and the kids will get the leaf and set the table now."

Gene stood up. "No, Jeannie. I'll get the leaf and set it. The kids are having too much fun."

Leon stood up too. "Hey, Gene, I'll help you. After all, the girls are busy with cooking and childcare, the least we can do is set the table."

Marion pulled out her combination grill pan and griddle and placed it on her stovetop grill side up. It covered two of her four burners. She crouched down as she turned them on so she could ensure both burners spewed the same level of flame. She'd got them matched just right and was about to straighten up when a hand touching her shoulder startled her. She let out a squeal and stood up quickly.

"My heavens." She looked to identify the offending hand and saw Leon trying not to smile at her.

He spoke quickly. "Sorry to scare you, Marion. Gene sent me in here for the dishes and silverware and I don't know where they are. By the way, you could match the gas levels on the two burners by using the little numbers on the dials."

"Ha, ha," she replied, and let out a breath to calm down. "Ok, I'll forgive you this time." She opened a drawer. "Here's the silverware." She then gestured to the upper cupboards in the corner nearest the kitchen sink. "The plates are in that cabinet facing this way and the glasses are in the one abutting it."

"You use great words, Marion. Abutting. Two 'Bs' and two 'Ts', right?"

"Close. One 'B' and two 'Ts'. It seemed easier than saying 'the one at right-angles to it' and don't be a butt about it."

"You do good puns, too."

Marion reached into the microwave to get the thawed steaks. She and Leon danced around each other trying to do different things in the same space. She successfully got the steaks on the grill pan and seasoned while Leon, loaded up with plates and flatware, ducked past her as he got out of the kitchen.

A short time later, Jeanette handed Jeremy to his dad and helped Marion load the food on the table. Marion eyed the table setup. The food and plates were arranged just fine but the seating arrangement made her cringe inwardly. *I don't even want to know whose idea, or plan, it was*, she thought. *I just hope I can survive it.* The table held eight with the leaf--three chairs on each side and two chairs on the ends but there were only six chairs and a high chair tonight. While they were getting the food from the kitchen, Gene had placed Jeremy at the foot of the table in the spare high chair that lived at Marion's and then took the middle chair to the left of him. He placed Nancy in the chair between him and Jeremy and had Mick on his other side so that Gene was bracketed by his two older kids.

"This way, Daddy can cut you guys' steaks while Mommy takes care of Jeremy," Marion heard him telling the kids.

This seating arrangement also meant that Marion didn't have to worry about where to sit; she would have to sit beside Leon no matter where he sat. Leon had chosen to sit on the end on his side so he faced Mick. There were only two chairs and if she chose to sit by Jeremy, Gene would know something was up. Resolved not to worry about sitting next to Leon, Marion made her way with Jeanette to the far end of the table. Jeanette held back and allowed her to reach the middle chair, which Leon pulled back for her from where he sat. She was grateful he didn't stand up and pull it out for her and then wait so he could have pushed it back in. But, then, if he'd done that, she'd have better idea of his intentions. *How can the man have such sexy thighs and why do I have sit right next to one?* she wondered to herself.

"Daddy, I wanna say the prayer. Please, can I?" Mick piped up as soon as Marion and his mom sat down.

"Sure can, Son. Do you need help?"

"No. I can do it."

Marion folded her arms across her chest to pray as Gene, Jeanette, and the kids did too. She noticed that Leon followed suit.

Mick prayed. "Dear Heavenly Father, thanks for giving us such a pretty day, for this good food, and for helping Mr. Leon get a farm. Thanks also for helping Auntie Marion muck out her barn today so I don't have to help her tomorrow. Please bless the food so it makes us strong and healthy. 'Name of Jesus Christ, Amen."

Everyone smiled after echoing amen.

"Mick, who told you that you would have to help Auntie Marion in the barn tomorrow?" Gene asked.

"Mom did when I sassed her today. She said that if I didn't behave today, I'd have to help muck out the barn. But, now I don't have to, 'cause it's all mucked out."

The adults smiled, but none laughed.

"I think he should muck out Daddy's barn, 'cause he was mean to me and sassed Mom too," Nancy said.

Gene hugged his daughter. "I'll talk to you and him about that tonight before bed, okay?"

Nancy shrugged.

"Busy morning?" Gene looked to Jeanette.

"I was going to talk to you about it later," Jeanette then addressed Mick, "Mick pulled Nancy's hair and made her cry, so he'll have to make it up to her tonight before bed."

Mick looked down at his plate. "Okay, Momma."

"Well now that's settled, let's eat," Gene said.

Marion and Gene each picked up a food item, served themselves and passed it on. Leon followed suit and each plate was filled family style.

The meal was a great success both in the goodness of the food and the quality of conversation. Marion relaxed and began enjoying herself. As she looked around the table, she saw laughing and happy faces.

Everyone finished eating after about an hour. The antique clock in the living room chimed eight o'clock. Gene looked to his wife, who was wiping down Jeremy's face as he was yawning and squirming, fighting against his tiredness and the cold washrag.

Then Mick spoke up. "Daddy, I cleaned my plate, can I have some of Auntie Mare's chocolate, peanut butter ice cream?"

Gene looked to Marion and she nodded.

"Sure can, sport. Mom, Nancy, do my girls want some too?" he asked.

"Please, Daddy," Nancy said.

"Yes, please," Jeanette nodded.

Marion stood up. "Okay, I'll clear the table and bring out the ice cream."

Leon made as if to stand, and said, "I can help."

But Marion halted him with a hand on his arm. "No, you're a guest and this party is to celebrate your new digs. Oh, can you do chocolate, peanut butter; you're not allergic to peanuts are you? I have Neapolitan if you'd rather."

"I'll happily share the chocolate, peanut butter."

"Okay, then, be right back." Marion scooped her plate and Jeanette's and headed to the kitchen.

There she dropped the silverware in the sink and set the plates down on the counter. She got six bowls out of the cupboard and pulled out six teaspoons and her great-grandma's antique, tin ice cream scoop. She carried the bowls, spoons, and scoop into the living room and sat them down on the table. She went back to the smaller freezer on the back porch and lifting the lid, she pulled out an ice cream carton. In the living room, she handed the ice cream carton to Gene and began scooping up the leftover food. Once she'd got all the leftovers into the kitchen, she took a moment to stash it in plastic containers and fridge the lot. To the living room and back twice more and she had all the dirty dishes in the kitchen. When she made it back to the table, Gene had dished up six bowls of ice cream.

"When are you going to settle, Sis? We'll be done by the time you stop," he asked.

"Let me just put the ice cream in the freezer," she remarked.

Gene grabbed her arm. "Sit down and eat. It won't hurt your ice cream to get a little melted. We nearly finished this one off for you anyway."

Marion sighed and sat back in her spot. She began eating her ice cream with gusto.

Jeanette was sharing some of hers with Jeremy, and he was happy, giggling with each small bite.

"This is really good ice cream, but I haven't seen the brand before?" Leon asked.

"It's Umpqua from Oregon. Marion's been a big fan ever since Mom and Dad took her to Portland after high school," Gene answered.

"Where do you get it around here?" Leon asked.

"Oh, at WinCo Foods," Marion replied.

Leon seemed shocked. "Is there a WinCo up here? I thought we only had them in the bigger cities in Utah."

"No, there's not, but Marion makes a special trip to the closest one in Ogden once a month just to buy her ice cream," Gene answered for Marion.

Marion let her brother know he'd pushed her buttons a little. "I do not. You know that I happen to hit WinCo when I'm in Ogden for other things, like oh, Smith and Edwards."

Her explanation pushed one of Gene's buttons. "Now, don't get on me for Smith and Edward's. You know they sell good stuff there."

"Yah, most of which you can get at R&R Hardware in Tremonton."

"Not the toys or the ammo."

"You can get the ammo and some of the toys there and, besides, like you need toys or ammo all the time."

Gene looked to Leon for some support. "Hey Leon, back a brother up here. Smith and Edwards is a fine institution."

"I have to admit that it's one reason I've been known to go to Ogden. After all, from Layton, it's the same distance to Smith and Edwards in Ogden as it is to AA Callister's in Salt Lake," Leon responded.

At that Jeanette spoke up. "Now you've dropped a fox amongst the chickens, Leon. Marion loves AA Callister's."

The discussion about the best western-gear and farm implements store heated up and the ice cream disappeared. Both Gene and Leon finished early and divided up what was left in the carton between them.

"So, do you like all ice cream flavors or just chocolate, peanut butter?" Leon asked.

"Auntie Marion only eats chocolate, peanut butter, even when her and Mom have their hen parties and eat the little containers of ice cream with the cartoons on them," Mick answered.

"Cartoons?" Leon asked.

"Ben & Jerry's," Gene supplied.

Leon smiled and said, "Oh. Makes sense."

"Where did you hear about Mommy and Marion's hen parties?" Gene asked Mick.

"When they shooed me back to bed when they're having one. Last time they were watching that movie where this guy has a big hat like President Lincoln, but his name is Darcy and that's a girl's name!"

Gene looked to heaven and shook his head. Marion and Jeanette laughed hysterically.

"You asked," Leon said.

"And, I deserve the answer I got," Gene replied. The men moved on to safer topics.

Marion and Jeanette sat quietly watching the men "solve the world's problems," then Jeanette nudged her and pointed to Nancy. Nancy was tuckered out. Her eyelids kept dropping and she'd stopped eating her ice cream.

"Poor little tyke. She's still got a grip on that spoon even though she's asleep in the chair," Jeanette whispered.

Marion then looked at Jeremy. He was sucking on his fist and looking around.

"Yah, but your little man has got his second wind. Probably all that sugary ice cream," she nudged her sister-in-law.

"But hopefully, he'll stay down all night when I put him down for bed," Jeanette laughed, quietly looking at Gene and pointed to Nancy.

Gene looked over to his little girl and then his wife. Quietly he said, "It looks like it's time we took someone home and put her to bed."

"Not me, Dad, right, I can stay up," Mick spoke up.

"Tell you what, Son, if you can stay awake once we've gotten home and Mom has put Nancy and Jeremy to bed, we'll talk."

Gene then addressed Marion and Leon. "Well, it's time I take my herd home. Marion, do you need me to stay and help you clean up? Jeannie can come get me when she's got the monsters in their beds."

"No, I can do it. It will help me relax after a long day. Besides, I never have a full load of dishes anymore," Marion said.

"Gene, if it's okay with you, I'll stay here and help Marion clean up," Leon interjected.

"Fine with me," he answered. "Jeanette and I have some parent-only stuff to do before we hit the sack, so come over when you are ready." He then looked to his sister.

Marion took the hint she saw in her brother's eyes. "Thanks, Leon. But, it's your day to celebrate, are you sure you want to clean up too?"

"I would. It will help me get the courage to face the home place. The grimy sink and kitchenette in the shop can't hold a candle to your kitchen. I hope that cleaning up here will give me the inspiration I need to have in order to make it through the next few days of heavy cleaning."

Gene stood up. "Okay, we'll leave you to it." He gently pulled the spoon out of Nancy's hand and lifted her up in his arm so her head rested on his shoulder as she slept. He then reached down and put Nancy's bowl and spoon into his own bowl adding his spoon before picking them up. "Ok, Mick, let's go. Take your bowl and spoon into the kitchen."

Jeanette bundled Jeremy up into her arms. She went to reach for her bowl, but Marion stopped her. "Leave that, Jeanette, I'll get the rest."

Jeanette headed to the kitchen with Marion and Leon following, each with a stack of dishes. Marion and Leon set theirs by the sink and the group met back up at the back door where Gene was holding up Mick's jacket for him to put his arms in.

"Hey buddy, carry your sister's coat will ya. Today was hot, but the storm really cooled things down," he said as Jeanette was putting Jeremy's jacket on him.

Gene then held up the baby carrier so Jeanette could strap Jeremy in. The group hugged before they left.

"So do you want to wash or dry?" Marion asked, turning to Leon.

"I better wash as I don't know where anything really goes."

"Sounds good." She moved to the sink and turned on the water to heat up. "Soap's here; I'll get the rest of the dishes and the high chair."

Chapter Seventeen

Leon put the stopper in the sink and squirted dish soap into the water as it began filling. The sky was nearly fully dark as he looked out the window above the sink. The clouds made it darker than usual. He could see his truck clearly, because the barn lights attached to the garage and the barn had both come on. Lightning struck every now and then but most of the rain had passed through while they'd ate.

He used the water sprayer to make suds and began loading the sink with the glasses. He'd wash them and the silverware first followed by the plates and the bowls. He'd tackle the serving dishes and grill pan last. He looked over his shoulder and spotted Marion bringing in the high chair. She took off the tray, sat it on the counter then reached into a drawer and pulled out a dishrag. She pushed close to him to dunk the dishrag in the hot, soapy water then spun away back into the living room. The sink had finished filling when she got back so she dropped the dishrag into the hot water and swished it around a bit before wringing it mostly out and used it to wipe down the high chair tray. She repeated the actions on the high chair itself.

"Do you want me to wait for that dishrag or get another?" Leon asked.

Marion turned pink with a blush. "Oh sorry. You can get another." She opened the drawer and then backed away so he could get into it.

Leon smiled, thinking he rattled her. Good. He couldn't resist teasing her. "Don't share your chores much, do you?"

"Nope. Not since Mom died. It's just me, me, and me around here."

"So, would you have really made Mick help you with the barn today?"

"Probably not. The smell would have made him sick and then I would have felt bad and had to clean him up, too. Now, if I hadn't have finished, I would have had Jeanette bring him down tomorrow and he and I would do a few wheelbarrow loads with a shovel. But, I wasn't looking forward to it. And, I think the kid knew that."

"Yeah, he's a smart one. Like his dad, seems to me."

"You're right. He's a lot like Dad, too. That little guy is one hundred percent Sullivan male."

They got back to doing dishes and cleaning up.

Leon filled the other sink with hot water for rinsing and began stacking clean glasses in the dish rack after their rinsing. From the other room, he heard the tabletop snap closed when Marion took the leaf out and then heard her running the vacuum. He was moving on to silverware as Marion went in the bathroom, washed her hands, and then came back into the kitchen where she began drying.

Leon looked at Marion now and then as they worked. He felt they worked together well doing this just like they did packing and unpacking her stuff. *But, she's never still*, he thought. Marion moved all around the kitchen as she dried and put items in the cupboards and drawers. Leon got the last serving bowl into the rinse water and then drained the soapy sink. "Time for some fresh soapy water. How do I clean your grill pan?"

"You just wash it in hot soapy water, I already wiped off most of the grease. It's enamel-coated aluminum. You could even throw it in the dishwasher, if I had one. Gene bought it for me for Christmas. I'd wanted a cast-iron, two-burner one so I could grill steaks or fry pancakes in bulk, and Gene thought this one would be easier on maintenance."

"Well it's a good pan. My steak was cooked perfectly."

"Thank you. I'll tell the chef."

He fished the last serving bowl out of the rinse water and placed it in the rack. He picked up the cold grill pan from the stove and plunked it in the new, hot soapy water to give the soap time to soak off the remaining grease, as the other sink filled with fresh, hot water. He wrung out his dishrag and used it to wipe down the stove. He rotated the grill pan in the sink to soak the other half, turned off the water tap, and re-soaked and wrung the dishrag to wipe down the counters in the kitchen. It took a couple of trips to the sink and back to re-soak the cloth to get all the counters clean. By the time he was done, the grill pan was ready to be cleaned. He noticed Marion had finished drying off the last serving dish and was standing near just looking at him. He looked her in the eye and then turned back to the pan. When he had it clean, he rinsed it and set it in the dish rack, then pulled the sink's stoppers. Marion reached up to get the grill pan with her towel, but he intercepted her.

"Let's let it air dry." *Time to make my move*, he thought.

Leon took the towel from Marion's hand and folded it neatly over the oven handle to dry then took both of her hands in his and turned them palm up as if to inspect them.

"You know, I look at your hands, and I can't believe how soft and finely shaped they are for as hard as you work them," he observed. He ran his thumbs up and down her palms. "Sorry that mine are a bit wrinkled from the water."

"They're fine." Marion's voice was a bit breathless. "What are you doing?"

"Should be obvious. I'm holding your hands."

"Why?"

"I want to. I've wanted to for a while, but didn't know how to approach you. You've been treating me like a dear family friend all day."

"Well, isn't that what you are? A neighbor? Gene's friend?"

"I'd hoped I could be your friend too, then when I saw you at the well today it all changed."

"You mean when you came by today as I was heading back into the barn?"

"No, I mean when I saw you dump a couple of buckets of cold water over your head."

"You saw that?"

"I did and didn't know what to do. It seemed to be a private moment and I didn't think you'd like me to interrupt you."

"I don't know what to say."

"Well, you didn't see me so I backed out and was going home, but then I changed my mind, came back, and beeped at you."

"I am so embarrassed."

"Don't be. You don't think I've dunked my head under a pump or sprayed myself in the face with the hose after a long day haying or being on the tractor? I totally understand, it just surprised me to see you doing it." Leon looked up from her hands to look Marion in the eye. He needed to see her face to judge her reaction to his words. "Actually, I realized today, as I was changing the locks at the Gorham place so it can become the Packer place, that it didn't look as promising as it did when you were there with me. I felt like I needed to see you there to recapture my plans for it."

"You didn't seem to *see* me there when we were there. You looked at everything else *but* me that day."

"I'm sorry about that. I was trying to keep a safe distance after Monte teased me that I could get you and your farm for the price of myself if I just tried hard enough. I didn't want someone else's farm and I didn't want to be Mr. Marion that day. Sorry."

"Mr. Marion?"

"I know. It's stupid when I say it out loud. I thought you were incredibly sexy when I met you that morning, but I saw this place as a burden that came with you, that I'd be a prized bull that you'd brought home. Then, today, standing on my own farmland for the first time, I realized that part of the reason I actually bought the place was to be near you and I've only just met you. Right now, being here with you, I feel like my life's coming together. It feels different than how I felt earlier at my shop. When I was out in my shop this morning, I got excited and then I felt lonely. It's mine, but I was all alone there."

Leon shook his head. "Sorry, none of this is making sense, what I mean is… I mean…," then he gave up trying to verbalize his feelings and kissed Marion full on the lips. He could tell he surprised her, but she pulled her hands away from his hands and placed them around his neck so she could pull herself to him.

He tilted his head for better access and opened his mouth against her lips. Her lips opened in response. He tasted the chocolate ice cream and Marion. His hands dropped to her hips and pulled her closer against him. Then he lifted her up onto the counter behind her so he could stand between her knees and get even closer. When he realized he was trying to get his hands under her shirt, he stopped the kiss and looked at her, unable to hide his shock over how he'd acted.

Marion's lips were red and roughed up by his afternoon stubble. Her eyes were sparkling but she looked a bit dazed. He couldn't help but kiss her again. Then he lifted her off the counter and stepped back a step until he was resting against the other counter. "Sorry that I lost control like that."

"I can see why you stopped talking." Marion was breathing deeply like she was out of breath. She looked at him, as if considering her words, and then said, "So, you were trying to ignore me, and think only of your farm, but you felt this great chemistry between us and had to do something about it. Did I get that right?"

She sounded like she was getting angry, and Leon wasn't sure what to say. "I am not sure how to answer you."

"How 'bout, 'I didn't see you as a woman until I saw you wet to the skin today, Marion.'" Anger definitely came through her words that time.

Leon felt more shock and horror at her words. "I didn't mean that at all. I thought you were sexy carrying a box in one hand and bantering with George at work the first time I saw you. You're a very beautiful woman."

Marion sounded sarcastic. "Uh huh."

Leon felt his own temper prick at that point. "Damn it, woman." He pulled her back into his arms and kissed her again, this time fiercely almost as if to dominate her. She met him equally but soon passion overcame their anger. Leon softened the kiss and gentled his grip on her. When he could pull away, he pulled her back at a different angle and tucked her head under his chin as he rested it on her hair. "What I should have said is, that while I was on a quest to find the perfect bit of land to start a legacy on, a beautiful woman came into work one day. Then I ran into her again on yet another harmless errand, but that time she needed my help. She ended up leading me to my dream farm but, when I had the farm in my hands, it didn't feel like a dream without her." He shook his head and continued, "You surprised me. I didn't expect to find my dream woman here, or ever, and not this soon. I didn't want to acknowledge my feelings so I pretended not to have them."

Marion sighed and tried to pull away. "You don't want me. You want a perfect wife for your farm." Then she succeeded in pulling away, and burst into tears as she exclaimed, "And I never wanted to be a farmer's wife!"

Marion ran out of the kitchen. Leon watched her go, very unsure of what to do or say. By the time he'd moved to follow her down the hall, she'd ducked into her bedroom and shut the door. *Damn. What do I do now?* he wondered. Leon did not have a habit of entering females' bedrooms, even with their permission. He quietly turned the door handle. Marion hadn't locked him out. Nervous about invading her territory, but worried that he needed to do something to fix the situation, Leon entered her room.

Marion had flung herself across the bed and was quietly crying into her pillow. He crossed the room and sat down next to her on the bed. He must have startled her, because she lifted her head and exclaimed, "What are you doing in here? Get out!"

"Marion, I know I've upset you. I don't know how to fix it. I know it's too soon, we barely know each other, but this thing between us isn't going away. Call it chemistry or sparks, or whatever, but I feel like you set sparks off in my heart."

She actually snorted at him. "Yeah, right. You just think I'm hot and convenient."

"No, I don't. And, to prove it to you, I'm going to leave you alone. I should have done something else tonight, courted you, or asked you out for another date, or something. I am sorry that I messed up so bad. If you want to talk about it, you know where to find me." *If she never gives us a chance, I can't leave her without trying one more time*, he thought to himself. Even though she looked skeptically at him, she didn't pull away when he leaned down to her. "I think there's something between us that we ought to grow, but if not, goodbye." And kissed her gently. She kissed him back just like she'd done before, and she matched the tenderness he'd tried to give her with the kiss.

He held eye contact with her as he stood up. Then he walked to her bedroom door and out of it, closing it after him hoping he could live with whatever decision she made. As he walked down her hall, through her kitchen, and out to his truck, he didn't want to look back. He was focused on heading straight for Gene and Jeanette's. Leon planned. If Marion got out of bed and flew out after him, he wouldn't see her and he wasn't looking back. He succeeded. He didn't look back.

The kitchen light was on at Gene's, but all the other house lights were off. He felt relief reading the note he saw in the kitchen.

Leon, we have an early morning, so we hit the sack. There's bedding down on your cot by your gear and fresh towels in the bathroom. We'll be up around six. – Gene.

Good. He had time to take a long shower and sleep on it before having to face her brother.

He remembered a line, in the shower, from one of his mom's favorite 80s songs that went like "I never took the smile from anybody's face before." The name of the song came to him; it was the same as the band—"In a Big Country" by Big Country. After the shower he went looking through the music on his phone for that song. He found it and a black mood overcame him. *How can such an upbeat song have such bleak lyrics?* he wondered. I'll *never hear it again without thinking of how I made Marion reject me.* "Stay alive." Sure.

Chapter Eighteen

Marion worried that she wouldn't be able to sleep after
Leon left, but she cried a bit more and the next thing she
knew she waking up because she had to go to the bathroom,
and it was morning. She rubbed at the tender spot on the
side of her neck where her left earring had dug in while she
slept and stood up. She looked at the clock with bleary
eyes. The red digits showed 4:30.

When she came out of the bathroom, she was wide
awake. *There's no way I can go back to sleep now*, she
thought. During the night, her subconscious mind had
worked a few things out. The last dream she'd had had
overtaken her and helped awaken her. In the dream, she
wore a wedding gown and was riding in an old-fashioned,
open carriage sitting next to her groom. She could still feel
an overriding sense of the happiness she'd felt being that
bride. In her dream, the carriage had been going down a
modern city street and when they'd stopped, the groom had
swooped her up in his arms and carried her down out of the
carriage and into a hotel suite. He'd sat her on the bed, and
taken off her shoes and was rubbing her arches, because he
knew the shoes were pinching her feet. She didn't know
how he knew that, but he did. Then the groom knelt over
her on the bed and kissed her amazingly. After the kiss, she
finally saw the groom's face and it was Leon and being
married to him felt right.

He had told her goodbye last night. *I think he meant
it*, she thought. She totally rejected him. She didn't give
him any hope. That felt wrong. She had to fix it. She didn't
know whether or not she could be a farm wife, but that was

a separate issue from how she felt about Leon. Marion rushed into her kitchen. Opening a cupboard, she pulled out a plastic container that held four leftover, sweet rolls that she'd made two mornings before. She couldn't go empty-handed so the sweet treats would work as a peace offering. She then grabbed her truck key and rushed out the door.

She made it to Gene's in record time and parked behind Leon's truck. She didn't worry about waking the house. If anybody was up, then they'd be in the kitchen and she'd explain her presence on her way downstairs. If everyone were still asleep, she'd be downstairs before they heard her. She was grateful they'd talked about Leon's sleeping arrangements so she could find him without waking the family.

The house seemed quiet. Gene never locked the side door into the kitchen, so Marion went right in. The kitchen was dark. She stopped to listen to see if she could hear any voices, or water running, to signify if someone was up. Nothing. She quietly made her way down the stairs that emptied into the basement utility area where the furnace and water heater were as well as Gene's freezers. A few steps brought her to the rec room. The furnace room light illuminated the room slightly.

Leon had set up his cot in front of the couch. He looked like he had a rough night. The bedding was tangled around him, and his leg was bent at an awkward angle. She was glad he was wearing pajamas as she didn't think she could face a bare chest or underwear right now... *Duh, stupid*, it occurred to her that he probably did it for the kids. At that moment, Leon shifted on his back, frowned, and put his arm over his eyes palm up. Marion felt a wave of tenderness for him wash over her. During the night she'd realized that, while she didn't love him just yet, she did care about him and wanted him to be happy. What she saw as evidence of his unhappy state brought tears to her eyes.

She blinked them away and knelt down by the side of his cot. His upset was all her fault.

She leaned over and laid her head on his chest with her hand resting near her ear.

"I am so sorry," she said, quietly. She stayed like that for a few moments as she listened to his breathing and heartbeat and tried to think of what she should do.

It was dim in the room, so Marion didn't see Leon's arm move but she felt his hand clasp her hand in his warm one on his chest. She lifted her head and saw that he was looking up at her but there were shadowed lines running down his chin like he was frowning at her.

"I am so sorry about last night. Please forgive me," she repeated.

His voice was rough from sleep, but quiet. "Done. Why are you here?"

Here was her chance, but she didn't know what to say. Then she thought of their first kiss in her kitchen. Leon had seemed to not have the words then, so he'd kissed her. She leaned over, giving him time to turn away, and kissed him softly. She pulled back and looked him in the eyes, but he gave her no clue of his thoughts and didn't say anything. So, she kissed him again. She put heart and soul into the kiss; she wanted to give him the kiss from her dream.

At first he didn't respond, but she stopped kissing for a second to say, "Please?" against his mouth. Then kissed him again. She cupped his cheek too. Finally, he began kissing her back. Then he started really kissing her back. She gave herself over to the kiss and her feelings.

Leon pulled her on top of him on the cot without breaking the kiss, and then he wrapped his arms around her hugging her tightly as the kiss deepened again. When they ran out air, Leon stopped the kiss and Marion laid her head down in his shoulder. They were both breathing hard, but Leon kept a grip on her.

"My heavens, woman you are something else," he said, after a moment.

Marion felt a little anxiety at his words. "A good something or a bad something?"

"Oh, definitely good, or can't you tell. I have never been so happy and embarrassed at the same time."

Marion wasn't sure what he meant until it hit her. "I am so sorry! I totally forgot about the morning blood flow down there. I'll get off." She couldn't seem to get leverage to get off the cot, but kept trying and her failure to escape further embarrassed her.

Leon's chest began to rumble and then he started laughing quietly. "If you don't stop wiggling you'll get me off, and then I promise that I will get you off as part of my revenge."

Marion froze, not sure what to do. Leon solved their problem. He held her tightly and rolled them both off the cot onto the floor. He used speed to add to the momentum, and though he landed on top of her briefly, he immediately braced his weight on his knees and elbows so as not to crush her. On the floor, he cupped her face with his hands and kissed her for all that he was worth, again.

"Stay here, I'll be right back. I am going to take a very quick and very cold shower, and then you and I are going to have a serious discussion," he said.

Marion smiled and held still as he put all his weight on his hands and knees so he could raise himself up. Once he'd stood up, astride her, she tried not to look up or giggle.

He noticed.

"Better close your eyes now or you will have a hard time looking me in the eye ever again," he said, stepping to the side and then down to the bathroom.

She lay on the carpet where Leon had left her and felt the hardness of the floor under her head. *He said I have to stay here, so I am sure he won't care if I get more comfortable,* she thought. She reached up to the cot and pulled down his pillow and quilt. She tucked the pillow under her head and arranged the quilt around herself. It was warm and smelled like Leon so she snuggled up within it and relaxed on her side to wait for him.

She was feeling warm and happy when Leon came back. She looked up at him where he stood over her. Before she could speak, he crouched down over her and opened up the quilt, then proceeded to lie next to her on the floor.

"Are you comfy?" he asked, once he got settled.

"Yuh huh."

He sighed. "Do you think you and I can really have a serious conversation like this?"

"Well, you told me to stay here, then I got cold, and this floor is cement under the carpet. Had you let me, I'd have gotten up on the couch or gone upstairs to the kitchen."

"That's really being serious," he said, sarcastically as he turned on his side facing her and threw an arm around her. He looked her in the eye. "Fine, let's take a nap instead, since you killed my sleep last night."

Marion wondered if he'd really fall asleep. It was nice lying by him, but she didn't think she could handle the hard floor for much longer.

"I'm sorry, I'll be serious. Can we please get up?" she asked. Leon didn't move. *Oh now, he's playing possum.* Marion wiggled closer to him on the pillow so she was touching noses with him. "I am being serious now. If you won't hate me, I'd like to get up and go home and shower and talk seriously after. I haven't even brushed my teeth or combed my hair yet this morning."

Leon's eyes popped open. "Ok. Let's go over to your house so you can get ready to go to Layton with me."

"I'm not going to Layton with you today. I have things to do."

"Like what? I know for a fact that you'd cleared today so you could go to town to look at new trucks."

"Fine, so how are we going to have a serious conversation if I go to Layton with you?"

"Easy, I am going to lock you in my truck so you are a captive audience as we hammer out some details."

"Oh, so I can piss you off and you, or I, can drive the truck off the road in our upset?"

"It'd be me driving us off the road. I don't think you can drive my truck."

"Stop trying to get my goat. You said you wanted a serious conversation. Besides, we can take my truck, and I'll drive."

"So you *will* go to Layton with me?"

"Depends. Why should I go with you?"

"To meet my parents. I am picking up their RV today."

Marion felt a panic over meeting his parents. "I hardly know you and now you want me to meet your parents?" She tried to get up.

Leon grabbed her middle and kept her still. He pushed her on to her back, and leaned over her. "I wish the light was on in here so I could see your face clearly to know if you meant that."

Marion felt sulky. "I did mean that."

"Why? Were you lying this morning?"

"Lying about what?"

"Didn't you beg me to forgive you, right before you kissed me like I was water and you were a desert this morning? Was that all a lie?"

"Now I need the light on so I can see *your* face. NO, I wasn't lying. I did mean it. But, maybe you are right. We do need a serious conversation so we both know what the other really means."

"So you really wanted my forgiveness, for what I'm not sure, and meant it when you kissed me but, again, what you meant is a bit cloudy."

"Now, who's not being serious?"

"I am serious, Marion. What do you want from me?"

The conversation was starting to prick both their tempers. Marion felt hers start to bubble up within her. "I don't know what I want from you. What are *your* intentions?"

"My intentions, as in if your father were standing here with a shotgun?"

"Yes, I think so. What is your end goal for us?"

"Damn, I don't know yet for sure. Marriage and babies probably."

"That's why I am not sure I should go with you to Layton to meet your parents. I could definitely marry you, but having your babies is another story."

Gene's voice interrupted them as he flipped on the overhead light. "What the hell is going on here? Marion, what are you doing here? Why are you and Leon in the same blanket and who the hell is having babies and talking of getting married around here?"

Marion couldn't tell who'd gotten to her feet sooner. Both she and Leon made it to their feet fast, but Marion got the quilt and Leon got the pillow. Marion spoke first.

"Gene, good morning. Did we wake you?"

"Did you wake me… no, the running water from the bathroom down here woke me, because I wanted to see how Leon fared after I abandoned him at your house last night. Then I heard voices and the words 'meet your parents' and got a bit curious."

Leon spoke and held up his free hand in a conciliatory manner.

"Look, Gene, nothing happened, I promise."

"Oh yeah, then why are you looking freshly showered, while she's mussed up and wearing last night's outfit and I found you snuggling together in the same bedding?" Gene answered him.

Marion's hold on her temper snapped at this moment. She flung the blanket on the cot, and swiped up her forgotten sweet rolls from the floor at Leon's side and turned to address her brother.

"Nothing happened, last night or this morning. Leon and I had a misunderstanding last night, and I felt bad about it this morning so I came over to see if we could talk about it and brought him some sweet rolls as a peace offering. And, I didn't sleep very well; in fact, what sleep I got, was in my clothes as you see me and so I want a shower and a meal before talking to you anymore." She turned back to Leon and dropped the plastic container on the cot. "There. Sweet rolls, probably dried out and definitely banged up. When you are done here, you can come find me at home, but give me a good half hour." Then she turned to Gene. "Count to ten before you speak to him. He and I will probably go to Layton later today. You and I can talk about me after Leon and I have reached an agreement." She made to make it past Gene and make a grand exit.

Leon caught up with her at the stairs. He spun her around and embraced her. Forehead to forehead he spoke softly, "I'll be over there as soon as Gene's done. Please have a little hope for us, please?"

Marion nodded.

He kissed her gently.

They were breaking apart when Gene came near them.

"*That's* what I'm talking about. Knock it off," he said, exasperatedly.

Leon spoke to Marion, ignoring Gene for the moment. "Drive safe, Marion." and she went up the stairs. "Gene, you and I need to have a heart to heart, but you have some wrong ideas in your head that we need to exorcise first," she heard him say, when she reached the top of the stairs.

Chapter Nineteen

As she drove home from Gene's, Marion was torn between wanting to run so she didn't have to analyze her feelings about Leon and wanting to stay with him now and forever. She knew it was too soon to love him, but she felt like there was something wrong. Marion felt cut off, like she'd left a piece of herself back at Gene's with Leon. She admitted to herself that it was also nice for Leon to stand up to Gene for her. Lately she'd gotten tired of trying to make Gene understand about how she was feeling stifled on the farm. Her brother was just like her dad… Both saw things their way and in black and white. She sighed, thinking if she *did* leave the farm, Gene would never understand why she doesn't love it here or how she could leave it.

She made it home without incident and was grateful to peel out of her clothes and hop into a warm shower. She could go to Layton today as she had finished up the only real chores she had when she got home that morning. Everything else could wait another day. She felt too rushed to wash her hair and had bundled it up on her head, so her shower was quick, but effective. She dithered over what to wear, and decided on what Jeanette called her 'uniform' of jeans and a nice shirt. Needing all the help she could get, Marion put on her red shirt. It was her favorite shirt and made of a soft cotton-silk blend in dark, rich red that went well with her skin and hair. She would add her mother's garnet earrings and her dad's belt to the ensemble to give herself some much needed parental support.

Marion went to the tall bureau to look for the earrings and looked at her hair in the mirror. She wasn't sure what to do with her hair. It was too hot to wear hanging down and she'd braided it the night before. Undecided, she left her long hair hanging in its freshly brushed state and put in the earrings, then tucked her shirt into her jeans. Her dad's belt was hanging in the closet. He'd made it in school and tooled the leather himself for the grade. As expected at the time, it spelled his name 'Eugene' across the back. He'd given it to her as a teenager. He'd said he'd never be as skinny as he was in high school and he'd be most grateful if she'd wear it out.

She began pulling her shirt out of her waistband. She didn't usually like tucking her shirts in. She felt self-conscious showing off her waist and butt like that. She ran her hands down the shirt to smooth it when she heard Leon's voice behind her,

"I like it tucked in, but I like hiding your assets from everyone else besides me even better."

She turned around. "You scared me."

"Sorry, I didn't mean to, but when I called out, you didn't answer. I would have waited in the kitchen except your door was open, so I figured you were covered."

"You're lucky this time. What if I was still getting dressed or getting undressed? I do live alone, you know."

"Then I would have enjoyed the show until you spotted me and threw me out."

"You sure are cocky."

"Can't help it. I'm a happy man. I have my farm and the woman I want likes to kiss me. Today can only get better."

"Well, we're never going to get going if you don't get out of here so I can do my hair."

"Going? So you *are* going to Layton with me?"

"I thought about it and I better."

"Why?"

Marion looked at herself in the mirror again. *Better 'fess up, girl. Remember what Mom said, 'truth always.' If there's a doubt, tell the truth.* She turned back to face Leon.

"Because you're right, we do need to talk, but when I ask myself what are *my* intentions, the answer scares me."

That brought Leon to stand directly in front of her. "So, what is your answer, and why does it scare you?"

Her nervousness made her fidgety and she didn't know what to do with her hands.

"So, Marion, what are your intentions?" Leon pressed.

"I think I better marry you," Marion replied, knowing she had to say it.

Leon seemed to pretend to consider her answer, but sounded serious when he said, "I like the words, but your tone worries me. So here goes, why *ought* you to marry me?"

"Because seeing you hurt makes me hurt, and knowing that I may have hurt you last night ate me up inside so much so that I invaded a strange man's bedroom to kiss him senseless in an effort to ease the hurt I'd caused him."

"I like that answer, but there's one of the points we hit this morning at Gene's that worries me. How exactly did you hurt me last night? You know, what should I forgive you for from last night? Be specific, please."

"I don't know how to say it, but I'm sorry for rejecting you last night. We should explore the feelings we have for each other and see where they take us," she sighed.

"That's what I forgave you for. Thank you for saying it out loud. I needed to hear it." Leon closed the remaining gap between them and gave her a hug. "Will you spend today with me? I don't know where 'we' are headed, but I don't want to be apart from you for even a day."

"Yes. Let me do my hair and then we can go."

"Good. It's way too soon to say this, but I think I could really love you, lady."

"That's what worries me. I think I could love you too, and I am not sure what to do."

"That's the other point we hit this morning." Leon looked up at the ceiling and then back down to her. "How about this... how about we just date for a while, and see how we feel, and decide in say, oh, I don't know, a month? No pressure to marry me or to even be totally serious, just dating for a few weeks to see how you feel. Okay?"

Marion bit her lower lip between her teeth as she thought. "Well, that should work, but I still have some worries that you should probably know about."

"Do you want to talk about them today?"

"Not really."

"Will they make you uncomfortable when you meet my family?"

"I don't think so."

"Ok, so, how about we shelve any more of your worries until after today and until you're ready to talk about them?" He paused as if a thought struck him. "There aren't any deal-breakers in your worries are there?"

"Deal-breakers? What do you mean?"

"I mean, would any of your worries affect you marrying me at some future date? Is there anything floating around in that amazingly smart head of yours that would make you say 'no' if I asked you to marry me?" he asked.

"No. I don't think so. But...."

He cut her off by actually placing a finger on her lips. "Then, no buts. I think we can work through anything else."

Marion wouldn't be shushed though. She moved his finger down and said, "Ok, but there's one worry that I think you really need to know."

"It can wait."

Her worries and his unwillingness to hear them caused her voice to strengthen. "No it really, can't, I mean you just bought a farm."

That got his attention. "What about my farm?"

"It's not your farm in particular, or even mine. I have had this worry lately that maybe I don't want to live on a farm."

Leon's eyes widened and he got very quiet as he stared at her. His silence made her more nervous.

"Uh oh. Did I just hit one of *your* deal-breakers?" she asked.

"I don't know. I am confused, though. I caught you doing one of the most God-awful jobs there is to do on any farm yesterday and you did it well and with good spirits. Hence, my confusion."

"Well, I could have mucked out the barn due to stubbornness, not love for my farm."

"You are that stubborn? So, maybe you're just too independent to want to marry me and this is a ploy."

"Do you really think that?"

He shook his head. "Of course not. I just have to consider other options for what you said to help me deal with the idea that my dream woman may not want to live with me on my farm."

Marion's heart twisted at the worry lines that appeared on Leon's face with that statement. "Well, I am not sure about it. Not wanting to live on a farm, I mean. It's been bothering me, and you need to know about it. But, can we live together with me feeling unsettled like this? I mean, I am pretty sure I can be your dream woman and live with you. Is that enough?"

"Live with me with the where and occupations in question?"

"Yes, for now, until I know."

"Okay. Maybe. But... I am still processing this and this is by no means our final conversation about this topic... what would you do if you didn't farm?"

"I'd get a job and move to town."

"Which town?"

"Whatever one where I could get a job to support me."

"What if I could support *us*?"

"But, we'd lived and worked on a farm…."

"Yes.

"That's a good question. I don't know. I don't know if it's the farm, the farm work, or this farm."

"So, and this is a temporary answer, could you live with me on *my* farm if I could support us and you didn't have to help me like you help Gene?"

"If I had a house that I could make my own too, I think, maybe I could. I mean, I don't know if I could live on any farm, but I do know I want my own house. Living in Mom's is too hard some days."

"Well that settles it for now. I need a house too. So, let's date awhile while you work on your concerns and I work out something that will allow you to feather a nest with me."

"Do you want to talk about babies now? That's the last topic from this morning that we haven't covered," she asked.

"Do you?"

"Only to tell you this. I think I would *love* to have your babies, and I always thought I'd have a houseful—like we'd have to drive a Chevy Suburban to hold them all. My doubt about babies is whether or not I want them to grow up on a farm."

He seemed to relax after hearing her explanation. "Well, I can probably help your worries on that point. I grew up in a household where the dad was an engineer and the mom was an artist. The kids could, if they chose, work on Grandpa's farm as much or as little as they wanted. So far, I am the ONLY farmer in this generation and I have thirty-four cousins. Does that reassure you that I will never force any of our babies to stay on the farm? I can't say that I wouldn't make them help with farm chores, but I don't expect that my kids will have to help me on the farm for it to be financially successful."

"That does help. See, for me to quit this farm, I'd have to sell the sheep and then Gene and I would have to sell one of the houses."

"Now, that's a decision I think we can definitely keep at bay for another day. In the meantime, can you handle dating me exclusively and being with me as much as possible between your farm work, my farm work, and my day job?"

"Yes, I think so."

"Good. See, a serious conversation and we survived it. Now, let's get on to why I really came in here." Leon swooped down and captured her mouth for a scorching kiss. "Good morning, Marion." He let her go and then moved to leave the bedroom. "I'll be in the kitchen waiting for you. Do you want eggs and bacon or pancakes?"

"Can we do Cream of Wheat?"

He smiled. "Sure can. Mush coming up." At the door, he stopped. "That kiss, that good morning, that's how I think I want to start every morning for the rest of my life by the way." And walked down to the kitchen.

Chapter Twenty

Leon could not stop smiling as he rifled Marion's kitchen for breakfast provisions. Joy lit his face when he found a fresh loaf of homemade bread in a bag in her old-fashioned breadbox. *I love homemade bread. It will make great toast. Bless that woman*, he thought. He found a large container of Cream of Wheat farina in the cupboard, and spotted some fresh strawberries in the fridge. There was plenty of milk and butter for the mush too. He pulled out the strawberries and inspected them. They looked like homegrown and were fresh and washed. He pulled the green top from one and popped it in his mouth. The strawberry tasted as good as he felt. He wondered where Marion had the strawberry patch around the property. He hadn't looked close enough at the huge garden out back.

A movement out the kitchen sink window caught his eye. He sighed. Gene's truck was pulling in behind Marion's truck. Gene was alone. No Jeanette or kids with him meant breakfast would have to wait. Leon put the milk back in the fridge and slid the empty saucepan for the mush back on the counter. He rested with his hips against the sink and arms folded waiting for Gene to appear.

He didn't have to wait long. He couldn't tell whether Gene was pissed off or, if so, how much. Gene came in the back door and into the kitchen. His head moved to scan the room and stopped when he'd seen Leon. He came further into the kitchen, but stopped level with the fridge. He'd left about eight feet between them and had cornered Leon by blocking the opening between the bar and the wall of cabinets that held the fridge and stove. The thought that Gene, at least, wasn't backed into a corner crossed Leon's mind. That thought brought a twitch to Leon's mouth, which caused Gene's eyes to open wider.

"So, what are your intentions towards my sister?" Gene finally asked.

Leon couldn't help but jab as he responded, "What do you think they are? Did I slink away after our chat today or did I come find my lady, who happens to be your sister?"

"It's rude to answer a question with another question."

"I know. That's why I did it. And, like I told you not an hour ago, my intentions are totally honorable."

"Yet, you were not specific then, and here you are again, alone with my sister having not declared yourself."

Leon's patience ended. "Dammit, Gene. I've known of her existence for a total of two or three months, since you sent her into my job for parts. I've only spent time with her on a handful of occasions. Of course, I haven't 'declared myself,' she and I are still figuring out what we want to do ourselves."

"So how come I found you and her wrapped up together in a blanket in my basement this morning? You wouldn't answer that question earlier, but I want an answer."

"Fine. I kissed her last night and she freaked out and ran to her bedroom crying. She let me know I pushed her too far *emotionally*, let's be clear about that, and so I left and went to your house. I figured I'd ruined any chances I had with starting something with her. Then *your sister* thought better of it this morning and came to find me to apologize. I accepted her apology and the details and anything else we do or did from that point on *is none of your damn business*."

"Well, dammit, she's my baby sister. I don't want to see her hurt."

"Hell, Gene. Do you really think I want to hurt her? I went to bed last night thinking that maybe I only bought the Gorham place to be close to her."

"It galls me to think of you taking advantage of her."

"Gene, you're killing me. Would you rather it be someone else who fell for your little sister? Am I some sort of monster?"

Gene's shoulders dropped like the tension had left them. "No, I'm worried because it *is* you. I think you could take her anywhere, anytime, to do anything, and she'd go willingly. You got the jump on me."

"I understand. Believe it or not, I've been where you are, except my baby sister is all of twenty right now and the next guy will probably be aiming to marry her, not some teenager I can scare the holy shit out of."

"So you plan to marry Marion?"

"Criminy, Gene, isn't that horse dead? Yes, I *hope* to marry Marion if things work out. And, if she didn't have some sizable concerns that I'm not sure how to fix and we'd known each other a bit longer, I'd take her shopping and put a rock on her third finger later today. In fact, if I wasn't worried about getting on God's bad side, and I was only after a good time, I could have locked you out of your own basement this morning and had my way with her. Would you rather drag us in front of a bishop right now and get us married? Is that what you want to hear?"

Before Gene could respond, Marion came into the room. "Gene, just what are you doing here? I thought I told you to get it out with Leon before he came over here."

Gene held up his hands and backed away from Leon to face Marion. "Now, Mare."

"Don't 'now Mare', me. I heard a bit of that conversation and I'd thank you to stick your big nose out of what could be my love life." Marion shook her finger at her brother as she got in his face. "Dammit, Gene. What Leon and I do is none of your business and I expect you to give us the privacy that I give, and gave, you and Jeanette!"

Leon looked at the two siblings and figured that while Marion was royally ticked off, Gene seemed to have calmed down.

Marion asked Gene, "Can't you see me as an adult after all this time?"

Leon looked at Gene and wondered if he should step in between the two and be a peacemaker. He couldn't help but feel like this situation was probably his fault. He moved to stand closer to Gene and faced Marion.

"Are you okay leaving us alone for a bit?" he asked Gene.

Gene looked at him and shook his head. "I guess so." He turned to Marion. "Sorry, hon. I just worry about you."

Marion seemed angry still, but tried to be nice. "Fine. Just don't overdo it. I am a grown woman."

"I know. But with Mom and Dad gone, you and Jeanette are my girls. I sometimes can't fight the need to watch over you."

"I know. Just try, okay?"

"Okay."

Gene turned to Leon.

Leon wondered what he'd say.

"I am not going to apologize to you. I hope you understand that I mean it when I say I will protect her with my life. I'm her family and you better not hurt her," Gene said.

Leon nodded. "I can accept that. She's safe with me, Gene."

Gene turned to leave. "I hope so, I really hope so, for both your sakes."

When Gene had gone, Marion stood by the end of the kitchen and just looked at him.

"So, do you still want mush?" Leon asked.

"I think I've lost my appetite," Marion shrugged.

Leon came over to her and pulled her into his arms to hug her. "Sorry that I yelled at your brother in your house."

"Don't be; he shouldn't have come after you."

"Maybe he should have. He got me thinking about my behavior. I am pretty sure I would have reacted the same way had some guy done to my baby sister what I've done to you over the past twenty-four hours. I should have had more control or something."

Marion looked up at him and smiled. "Am I complaining?"

"No, but maybe you ought to." Leon looked at her and calculated what he knew about her with what he'd witnessed, and asked, "So, did you catch all or just most of Gene's and my discussion?"

"Oh, all. I figured he'd make his way here. I also figured he needed to get it out of his system, and I'm all for 'lancing the boil quick'… some things just get worse if you let them linger. I am sorry that I didn't step in sooner. I don't know what he said to you at his house, but I'm sorry he tried to give you the third degree here."

"Well, honey, if I am honest with myself, maybe he should have. I know they're just excuses, but when I tell myself I lost control over myself last night due to tiredness, the stress over the farm sale, or just plain lust, I have to question it. I've never been so forward with a woman in my life. I probably would have stripped you down this morning and truly 'got you off.' It was a near thing, nearer than I've been since I was engaged."

"I heard two points in that that I'd like to discuss, but before I get to the main one, when in the hell were you engaged and why is this the first I've heard of it?"

"Whoa, we're not engaged, so I'm not sure I have to disclose any prior engagements yet."

"You brought it up."

"You're right, I was just hoping to get out of my mistake... I was engaged when I was twenty-two to a gal I'd dated off and on in high school. When I look back at it now, it was habit and hormones more than love. Luckily, she'd been dating my cousin behind my back and decided to elope with him. If not, I'd probably have married her and been divorced by now. But, at the time, hearing that she'd jilted me didn't really bother me, which taught me an important lesson about love—that I wasn't in love, not really. I tell you this to contrast how I've been feeling since I've met you. It's come on quick and strong and all the feelings I've had have shown me that I never really loved before, because I wasn't as tore up, obsessed with, or worried about anyone like I am about you already."

"I can accept that. Now, I won't usually give you tit for tat, but in this case I will. I've never been engaged. Never has anyone asked me to marry them. The last time I dated seriously was in high school though that boyfriend's mom only recently accepted that I won't marry her son. Life got in my way, so my love life has truly been a desert these past few years; a date here and there, but nothing too serious."

"Though that's too bad for you, and I wonder what the guys you dated were thinking, I'm glad. I have the feeling that any fellow getting as close to you as I have would have snatched you away. I am glad I got here first."

Marion leaned up to kiss him at that moment. She pulled back before he could deepen it.

"About the other thing... the jumping my bones stuff. No. You can't. I won't until we're married. Which leads me to part of my 'why not' for that. I feel like my 'why not' is the same as your 'why not', so I ask, when you said 'bishop' does that mean you are LDS?"

Leon smiled. "I wondered when, or if, you were going to ask me about religion."

"That's not an answer."

"I know, but I figure that you and Gene are LDS. I spotted the garment lines under both Gene's and Jeanette's clothing, signifying that they're not only LDS, but married in the temple, right?"

"Yes, but that's still not an answer."

"You won't let it go, will you?"

"Probably not. See, I can handle any religion in my man. I think that a difference in religion is something that any couple can find a way to live with. But, I don't want ugly discussions about where the kids go to church. So, since you mentioned babies, and you know I want babies, you should know that I'd like my babies to grow up LDS. So, are you LDS? If not, are you okay if our babies will be?"

"Wow, now that is a serious statement."

"You told me to be serious. And, still you haven't answered me. You know enough to know what garments are, so are you ex-LDS, is that it?"

Leon was having too much fun teasing Marion, but he noticed that her cheeks were pink. He realized he was probably pushing too far and leveled with her. "Sorry, Marion. I couldn't help but tease you a bit. To answer your question, I was LDS when I was younger and I am full-LDS now. I have no problem with having our babies raised LDS, and I called my bishop yesterday and started the process to have my church records transferred up here to the Stone Ward. I wasn't going to bring up religion yet because you haven't said whether or not you'd marry me, so there didn't seem to be any point to talk about what we'd do on Sundays or whether you'd like me to take you to the temple when I marry you."

"Thank you for answering my question. In our few days together, Sundays and church haven't come up, but God and church is why I won't have sex with you unless, or until, we're married. As for the temple, I'm not sure I can marry you for time, let alone for eternity."

"But you're okay kissing me like that?"

"Well, no. I… um… lost control a bit myself. That's part of why I freaked out last night. I got too hot too fast and it overwhelmed me a bit. Sorry."

Leon had to hug her and hold her close again. "Don't be sorry. It's not a bad thing for my dream woman to tell me that I turn her on and make her lose control. That's a good thing. We just need to devise a way to be around each other all the time without one or the other of us throwing the other down and having their way with them. Are you sure you don't just wanna run off and get married today?"

"Look who's getting too serious too fast. But, I think we can devise a way. I think I better just keep my lips off you."

"Nah, I don't think I can live with that. How 'bout 'lips only'? No roaming hands or fingers and no lying down together? Will that work?"

"I think so, but I feel silly in these modern times acting this way. If we were in a movie, we'd have 'done it' last night, and the movie would be over."

"Yeah, but this is real life, and you and I have bigger problems that can't be solved in a ninety-minute movie. Plus, I think you and I are old enough to exert a little self-control. Small sacrifices for a bigger reward, right?"

"Yes, please, but I have to say again, Leon, you are too sexy for my state of mind sometimes, so if I back away from you, know it's to keep your virtue intact."

Her statement made Leon laugh out loud. "My virtue should be fine," he snickered. "Not that I've ever heard it called that for a guy. I'll try harder to keep you safe. It will help me, though, if you can give me a little reassurance… I know we're still working through this but, on a scale of one-to-ten, what are the chances of you saying 'yes' were I to ask you to marry me, not today, of course, but down the road."

"Serious this time, for serious, how likely would I be to marry you?" Marion seemed to think for a moment. "Last week I had a ten percent chance of marrying anyone before I was forty. Last night, I was sure I wouldn't marry anyone if I couldn't marry you. But today, in the cold light of day and realizing how serious you are, I think there's an eighty to ninety percent chance I'd marry you."

"So your worries make you ten to twenty percent doubtful?"

"I think so. If it helps, right now there's a one hundred percent chance that I won't marry anyone other than you. If I don't marry you, I feel like I probably won't marry anyone."

"I like the idea of you *not* marrying anyone else. But, I'd rather you marry me and let us be happy for a long, long time. What you said gives me the hope that I need to give you time to worry about your concerns while I think about options, like how we could live farm and non-farm."

"So, can we just relax and have fun the rest of today? This heavy stuff makes me tired."

"Sure can. But, don't you still need to buy a new truck sometime today?"

Marion smiled. "Nope. That is totally shelved for now. See, if I don't marry you, I'll have to leave here and I won't be able to afford a new truck."

"Wow. You've already decided that?"

Marion leaned up. "Now that we've gotten through to the core issues that would keep us apart or break us up, I realize that I care for you a lot you already, and if I couldn't marry you, there's no way that I could stay here and see you all the time if we weren't together. This county's not big enough for the two of us if I can't be with you," she said, quietly.

When she got through speaking, Leon saw tears gather in her eyes. *Damn, that Big Country song is coming back to me. It would take a big country to hold us with enough distance to keep each other out of sight if we weren't together*, he thought to himself. "Ah, Mare. Don't cry. I think I care for you already, too. I know this came on a bit fast, so let's just try and have some faith. We can find our own way." He took a breath to keep his own tears at bay and to clear the thickening in his throat. "I never thought I'd find someone to really love or someone who'd love me for me, and now that I've found you, I have to change my thinking. If what I'm beginning to feel is real, there's got to be a way for us to be happy. Give us time... trust me?"

"I already do."

Chapter Twenty-One

Marion found she really loved just being with Leon. He was funny and smart and flatteringly curious about her. He also matched her in candor. She bubbled over with happiness. She looked down at their hands clasped together on his leg. Leon was her kind of western guy. If he was in a truck with his woman, she was sitting next to him, not on the passenger seat. Of course, he'd chosen an automatic-transmission truck with a bench to facilitate such a plan.

Most times when she'd look at him, he'd be looking at her. She caught him doing it again and said, "If you don't keep your eyes on the road, we'll crash."

"I can't help it. I like looking at you. Besides, I can feel you staring at me and I am compelled to meet those looks."

"You are totally full of it."

"You know it, sister. Better be prepared to fight fire with fire."

"You are way too frisky this morning."

"That's your fault. You woke me up this morning. If you hadn't have rescued me, I guarantee I would have been more like a grizzly bear woke up too early. I don't think I slept at all last night for tossing and turning over you."

"I am sorry about that."

"I know. Don't feel bad. It was my guilt. I meant to ask you out for another date, but you looked so good wielding that dishtowel that I had to kiss you and then hormones won out."

"Well, you are a good kisser. Makes me wonder how many girls you've dated besides your ex-fiancé."

"Believe it or not, there haven't been that many girls. I am a natural-born kisser."

"And if I believe that?" Marion laughed.

"Well, you are no slouch at kissing either. How many farm boys did you waylay in the fields?"

"Good point. We won't discuss who's kissed who."

"Oh, so it must have been a lot, then."

"You know it wasn't. I only kissed my boyfriend in high school and that was years ago. But, you are right. Who we did what with before doesn't matter. It's who we do things with now that does."

"Are you saying you want to 'do it'?"

"You are such a tease. I don't think I can survive you," Marion sighed.

Their banter continued as they went south on the freeway.

Soon enough they made it to Leon's parents' house. He pulled into the drive next to a large, camp trailer and Marion stared at the house and yard. She decided it was no surprise that Leon could afford to buy a farm based on his parents' house. It was all brick and had the garage in the front to help hide its size, but she bet it had to be thirty-five hundred square feet. She looked around at the other houses and decided Leon's parents lived in a tract neighborhood of nice houses with big yards from in the late 1990s. Marion knew she could never afford a place like this.

Leon pulled in and parked. He opened his door and held his hand out to Marion to help her get out of his side of the truck.

"Well, we're here. What do you think?"

"It's huge, but very nice." Marion said, wondering if his parents were rich. Or, what they would think of a country bumpkin like herself. Her nerves made her blurt out, "How big was the farm that was here?"

Her last remark seemed to get his attention. "Farm?"

"You know, the one that was here before a developer came in and took it out to build all these houses."

"Wow. Um, as far as I know this was a tiny farm that went out of business in the 80s and the grandkids sold to a builder. What put the venom in your tone?"

Marion felt embarrassed but couldn't seem to calm her temper. "I don't know what's wrong with me right now... I hate it when somebody sells the land to subdivide for houses, but that's a bias I have. It's none of my business what happened to make these houses. Your parents' home is beautiful. I'm sorry I was so negative. I'll work on it."

"Believe me, I understand. I guess I am just used to it, having lived here most of my life. Besides, homes have to go somewhere and folks seem to like newer homes... I didn't really think about my parents' house this way. Does it bother you that something like this happened to my Grandparents' farm and that's where I got the capital to buy my farm?"

"I don't know. I don't know what to think. I've just now realized that I've always looked at the houses coming in all along the Wasatch front eating up farmland as a bad thing. I've always worried about where our food would come from if we build houses on all the fields without considering where everyone could otherwise live. So, I guess I am biased against the idea, but will try to live with it."

"Well, I am sorry that it upset you this morning. I don't know what the solution is. Sometimes a farmer just can't make it and the houses do sell. Until both those trends stop, I don't see housing developments stopping."

"Thank you. I guess I need to consider what you've done and judge you by your actions."

"That suits me just fine. But, I have to admit, had I not found the Gorham place, I would have had to buy a house like this in Tremonton or I'd be homeless when Eric's grandma sold her place. So I'm no paragon about this issue."

So, can we talk about something more pleasant and go in and see your folks?"

"Sure can, but first..." Leon pulled her over to him and kissed her gently, but thoroughly. "Smile. Today is a good day. Keep positive." And then he took her into his childhood house.

They found his parents in the kitchen making pancakes. His mother noticed them first.

"Hey, hon, looks who's here and who's with him," she said to his father.

Leon introduced everyone. "Mom, Dad, this is Marion Sullivan. Marion, this is my mom, Susan, and my dad, Kent."

Marion felt nervous standing on the edge of the kitchen, but came forward and smiled and shook hands. Leon must have noticed her nervousness because he took her hand in his and held it.

"As you can see, we're a little late with breakfast. Kent and I were getting the RV ready and time got away from us. Have you kids eaten yet?" Susan asked.

"No, we'd love a bite," Leon answered.

Marion nodded her agreement to Leon's words, too shy to speak.

Kent spoke as he turned back from the griddle. "We've got a few more cakes to cook, why don't you take Marion on a tour of the place, Leon, and we'll holler when brunch is ready?"

"Will do. Come on, Marion." And tugged her out of the kitchen.

Out in the hall, he pulled her against him. "What's wrong? You're all stiff and quiet."

Marion felt an illogical urge to burst into tears, she started to speak.

"I'm okay, it's just...," she managed to get out, and the tears came. She ducked her head and covered her face with her hands as she began sobbing quietly.

Leon came near her instantly and pulled her into his arms and held her.

"Shush, baby. Let it out. It'll be okay," he repeated it over and over as she cried.

Marion knew she was soaking Leon's shirt, and she was grateful of his arms around her and his gentle pats on her shoulder, but she couldn't seem to stop the tears. A few minutes passed and then his mother's voice brought her out of it.

Susan came down the hall and stopped next to Leon. "Hey, Leon, there you are, breakfast's... what's wrong?"

"Don't know," Leon answered.

Marion pulled away and took a couple of breaths. When she could speak she said, "Susan, I am so sorry. I had a bad night and seeing you and Kent in the kitchen cooking like that reminded me of my parents and our big Saturday breakfasts and I lost it." She stopped speaking as she tried to control her breathing.

Leon seemed aware of her problem and explained to his Mom, "Marion's mom passed last January, and her dad died just a few years ago."

"I am so sorry, honey. Take all the time you need," she told Marion, seeming to understand. To her son she said, "We'll be in the kitchen when you're ready."

Leon nodded to his mom and then turned back to Marion. She was wiping the tears off her face with her hands.

"Come downstairs with me?" he asked.

"Okay." She said in a broken sob, hoping she wouldn't start hyperventilating.

Leon held her hand as he led her back towards the kitchen. Before they got there, he turned down an adjoining hall, passed two doors, and then went down some carpeted stairs into the basement.

Marion took note of the basement as he led her to a door at one end. She saw plush carpet, wood trim, and pocket lights--high quality finishes. The basement was not the typical half-finished basement she was used to but a nice downstairs. They passed the large sitting area by the TV that took up the center of the space. The leather sectional could fit eight. The TV was huge, probably ninety inches, and hanging on the wall.

She was feeling better as Leon opened the door and pulled her into what looked like a suite. Behind the door, a large full bathroom opened on the right while a large walk-in closet was on the left. A short hallway between them led to a spacious bedroom. He pulled her into the bathroom and turned on its lights as he entered. He stood her in front of the sink as he went to a linen cupboard between the vanity and the commode that faced the tub/shower. He pulled out a washcloth and a towel and handed them to her as he sat on the edge of the tub.

Marion fingered the washcloth and stared at him.

"Can I hang out here, or do you need to use the facilities?" he asked.

"You can stay. I'll just wash my face." The warm water felt good on her eyelids and cheeks. She longed for her moisturizer and thought of asking Susan for some. Marion sat the washrag down and picked up the towel. As she dried her cheeks she looked at Leon in the mirror. He smiled at her and she smiled back. "Thank you. I feel better. Sorry I lost it. I haven't been around happy parents like yours in a while."

"I'm glad you're doing better." He stood up and clasped her hands. "I'm sorry you don't have your parents anymore."

"Thank you. I was also thinking how much I miss being able to talk about you to Mom. I think she'd really like you and I was wondering what she'd say or whether she'd approve."

"I'd hope she'd approve of me. Of course, Gene will give you a reading that you can trust."

"Yeah, but he doesn't see me as a grown woman. Mom has been there and she knew me a bit better than my older brother."

"What about your dad?"

Marion smiled. "He'd love you. In fact, he'd have driven us down here today to meet your parents. He'd be all for mingling with the in-laws. I'm sure he's up there looking down on us and rooting for us to get married ASAP."

"I like your dad more and more," Leon said, smiling.

"Oh, knock it off. You are such a tease."

"Can't help it. You are fun to tease. And, I'd rather you giggle, laugh, or get mad at me than look at me with your eyes huge with tears. I'll let you in on a secret. I can handle most female tears, but not yours. I think I'd give you anything you asked of me if you were teary when you asked."

"I'll keep that in mind. But, the truth is I hate to cry and I was hoping you'd never see me cry again. I am a red-nosed, puffy-eyed, ugly crier."

"Well, I don't mind how you look… it makes my heart ache and hurt for you though, so I'd like your permission to do what it takes to keep you from crying ever again… if that's even possible. My mom and sister have worked hard to convince me that women need to cry now and then."

"That's mostly true. But, I have to admit that I'm not at my best today. You have caught me in a weak moment." Marion stood straighter and hoped to change the subject. "I'm ready to tour your house or have breakfast or whatever. I promise to stay dry-eyed the rest of today."

"Let's take today as it happens. As for a tour or breakfast or whatever… how 'bout this?" Leon asked, as he kissed her sweetly.

"Let me show you around. Then, we'll eat," he said, after ending the kiss.

"Good."

He started the tour where they were. This suite was intended to be a second master bedroom or mother-in-law area, but Leon, as oldest had called dibs on it and had used it for his very own as soon as they moved in. His parents now used it as a guest room. Back in the open area of the downstairs, there were sliding glass doors to the outside on the other end of the TV area, followed by two other bedrooms and another bathroom through another opening much like Leon's old bedroom suite.

Back upstairs, he showed her the living room just off the front entrance and the den/office where his parents each had a desk and workstation. A formal dining room followed the office and, after it, another bathroom marked an intersection in the halls where they'd come upstairs. The two other doors in this hall led to two bedrooms, one of which was his parents' master suite. They then followed the arm back to the main hall that led them to the open concept, kitchen/great room.

Leon's parents were sitting at the table in the breakfast nook, and had put all the breakfast foods away, just in case it took Leon and Marion too long to come to eat. Marion followed Leon's lead and let him keep hold of her hand as they went to sit down at the table. Susan stayed sitting and chatting with them as Kent got up to warm the food and brought it over when it was ready.

"I am so glad you found a place, Leon. Instead of having you take the RV up with your truck, your Dad and I would like to drive the RV up today and look around your place. Then, we'll head over to Logan to see Aunt Kathy," Susan said.

"That suits me. Marion, are you okay hanging out with us all day?" Leon replied.

"That would be fun," Marion nodded.

Susan then spent the rest of the morning politely, but effectively, grilling Marion about her life, her dreams, and her intentions towards Leon. Kent and Leon participated in the conversation and, every so often, one or both would steer Susan back into neutral territory.

Marion was glad to have Leon there to take care of her with his parents. He seemed to know when his mom had cut too close or gotten too deep, because he jumped right in and helped his mom know when to back off. Marion appreciated how respectful and gentle he was with his mom. He was honest, yet remained kind to her. Her mom always told her she would know if a guy would treat her right by how he treated his own mother.

Leon also sat right next to Marion so they could hold hands under the table. Kent noticed this and asked them, "So are you guys going to hold hands for the rest of your life?"

"If we can, Dad," Leon answered.

"Definitely," Marion agreed.

When the meal was over, Leon offered to help clean up with Marion.

"How about you and Mom clean up so I can get to know Marion a little better?" Kent said, overruling him.

It was much easier for Marion to talk to Kent. He seemed to be interested in her as a person, and was fascinated to hear that she'd been an engineering major.

"Would you go back and finish your degree if you had the chance?" he asked.

Marion noticed Leon had turned around from the sink to watch her as she answered. "I don't know. That was a while ago, and I've found that I use my engineering skills a lot around the farm."

"Like how? Kent asked.

"Well, when the upper stock yards flooded out when one of our ditches burst, Dad had me and Gene rebuild them," she answered. "He gave us total control and even allowed us to design them and move them if we wanted. Gene and I spent a few days going over things and we played with Great Grandpa's survey equipment and re-sited them. I made a plan. Then Gene helped me build it and even worked with me to grade the ground for better drainage and rebuild the ditch. He also helped me build a new bridge over the ditch. It was great fun planning things out and then doing the work to build them."

"So, I take it you were doing civil engineering at USU?"

"I was. But I was thinking of switching to chemical and heading out to the oil fields. I had a wild idea that I could work out in the North Sea or up in Alaska."

"Wow. That would be hard with all those rough necks."

"Yeah, but I figured I could handle it. Farming's a pretty masculine career too. I will say that I probably would have ended up in mechanical engineering. Gene says there's no machine I can't fix."

"I asked Monte if I would never have met you if Gene hadn't have been busy that first day, and he told me that you are the tractor repairman in the family, so it was more likely that I'd have never met Gene. He also said that you help George sometimes more than he helps you," Leon piped in.

Marion turned pink with a blush.

"You shouldn't be embarrassed, Marion. Knowing how things work is not a gender-specific skill and you should be proud of it. That's part of why I've loved working as an engineer all these years; I enjoy the work so it's a vocation for me, not a job," Kent remarked.

Marion thought about what he said. "You are right. That's how farming was to my dad and is to Gene." She looked over to Leon and met his gaze as she continued, "That's one thing that Leon and I have been discussing… whether or not farming is the job for me. I've been doing it out of necessity, and lately have been feeling like I need a change."

Marion watched Kent look over at his wife and son. She noted that Susan met his look and then looked at Leon. Marion noted the family communication going on and wondered if they would include her.

"So, is that why you and Leon haven't spoken about how serious you are?" Kent asked, turning back to Marion.

Marion looked to Leon. He seemed interested in her answer. *Honesty is still the best way*, she thought to herself. "Well, yes, kinda. Now, I know I am a stranger to you both, but I think I could love your son. So, much so that I don't want him hurt…" She paused for courage and then continued. "The problem is, unlike Leon, I never wanted to farm. Never did I even expect that I'd have to stay on my parents' farm. And, now that he has his farm, I have to be very sure that I can be happy there too, before I marry him."

"That's part of why I was late getting down here today. Marion and I are working through some things," Leon added.

Susan chimed in, "Well that's understandable." She continued, "Love is one thing, but blending two lives together can be tough." She then looked Marion in the eye. "Though, there are always problems in a marriage, it's worth it to stick to it and get through them." She ended by giving a loving look to Kent. "I wasn't sure I wanted to marry an engineer and move to Utah from Colorado, but my mom told me never to look back, and I haven't. We've been very happy all these years."

"Thank you for that," Marion responded. She looked to Leon, "That's my hope… but, I need a little time to get things square in my mind."

***

Leon divided his time between watching the road, his parents' progress with the RV as they drove in front of him, and Marion. He was worried. Marion was still sitting next to him and was holding his hand, but she was quiet. She seemed to be staring into space. He figured she was lost in thought. He couldn't blame her. He'd tried to help her as his mom gave her the third degree almost as bad as Gene had given him earlier. His mom had just used a nicer tone, then his dad brought up her first choice of careers that fell through. She had to deal with that on top of the emotionally trying, prior night and that morning.

"Penny for your thoughts?"

Marion turned to look at him and stroked her fingers up and down his hand. "Just thinking about things. Being with you all day today makes me think I could marry you. But, I am still trying to imagine what it'd be like to live on *your*, or maybe *our* farm instead of Mom and Dad's or Gene's. I need to chew through it in my mind to see if I can handle that."

"Okay, sounds good. I'll leave you to it. But, remember that I haven't even taken you on a real date yet." He then changed the subject, "Holler if you need to stop. Otherwise, I think Dad's plan is to head straight to my place and drop off the RV."

"That works. Let's talk dinner to your parents and about our first real date when we get to your place."

"Good idea. Thank you for doing this with me today."

"It was a good day. It's good to meet your folks. Helps me see what your life was like. I like learning about you."

He smiled. "You're beautiful in and out, Mare."

"Thank you, handsome guy."

Chapter Twenty-Two

"Hey Leon, it looks like Bishop Morley has dropped in to see you," Marion called out from her position at the front of the RV. They were working to hook it up now that Leon had the rest of his new farm's utilities switched to his name.

The past two weeks' activities ran through Leon's head as he watched a truck approach. He had taken a week off work from TT and he and Marion had now dated a few times. He'd camped out in the RV while Marion stayed at her place, but each evening they did something together. Their official dates consisted of a nice dinner at a local restaurant, a movie, and two long drives and didn't seem like enough, but he hoped they would count as honorable courtship activities to Marion's spiritual advisor and old family friend.

Leon moved up to the front of the RV to stand next to Marion as the truck came up the drive. "Bishop drives a black truck a lot like yours, but for the color."

"I wonder why he's here. Did Gene tell him about you?" Marion speculated.

"Well, I did have my bishop send your bishop my membership papers as soon as I had the right address for this place. I'm just glad we're in the same church ward so folks can speculate about who you're dating instead of wondering about the crazy guy who bought the Gorham place."

"Ha, ha. I've been notoriously single for years and you're a looker. There's no chance they'd even care about you buying this place… 'Marion's got a man' will be the topic du jour for months."

Leon leaned down and kissed her quick. "I am happy to be your man no matter what anybody says."

Marion sighed and said as she waved to Bishop as he was pulling in, "Of course, Bishop saw you do that. So you get to explain our relationship to him. I won't."

"So, I can tell him the baby's due in six months and he needs to marry us ASAP?" he teased.

She pinched him in retaliation, so Leon was rubbing the tender pinched spot on his arm and laughing at her as Bishop got out of the truck.

Leon took stock of the bishop as he sauntered up to them. He was a tall, strong guy wearing jeans, a button down western shirt, and work boots. His truck had a sign, indicating he was probably in some trade, not a farmer. Leon squinted and saw 'construction' on the sign. The bishop lived way out here, but does construction. He found that interesting.

He also noticed the bishop had a direct way of looking at and speaking to a person. He wasted no time approaching them.

"Hey Marion! Is this fellow, Leon Packer?" he said, immediately.

"Sure is, Bishop." Marion answered. "Meet Leon. Leon, this is Bishop Norm Morley. He's the spiritual leader of our LDS flock out here in the sticks north of Snowville."

Leon held out his hand. "Good to meet you, Bishop." It was neat to him that Marion followed the Mormon tradition of calling the current bishop by his title instead of Brother or by name out of respect for his position. *I think I'll like this ward*, Leon thought. "Did you get my church records?"

"Sure did. But, I was headed out this way anyway to meet the guy who actually bought the Gorham place. Bill Metzler told me someone had, and I was a mite curious," the bishop answered. The bishop then looked Marion in the eye with his direct stare. "And, I pull up here and see Little Miss Marion and a stranger kissing in front of an RV." He turned the stare to Leon. "That makes me even more curious."

Leon spoke. "You caught us, Bishop." He looked down to Marion. "If it were up to me, I'd ask you to give us the pre-marriage interview right now and help us set up the temple ceremony next week, but Mare here has some reservations about marrying me."

Marion shook her head and sighed. "Put it all out there, why don't ya."

"Sorry, honey, but I can't lie to my new spiritual advisor. I am not rushing you, but he needs to know our situation… in case I convince you to marry me on the fly. I need him to understand why he might need to marry us quick-like," Leon answered her.

Marion appealed to Bishop Morley. "Please don't take him too seriously. Yes, Leon and I are working through some things, but I haven't agreed to marry him, yet." She looked sideways at Leon. "He promised to give me a few weeks to date him, but here he is spilling the beans to you."

Bishop laughed. "You two seem perfect for each other. Don't worry, Marion. I think I have an idea why Leon spoke the way he did. When, or if, you guys need me to marry you, or you are ready to talk pre-temple marriage, just let me know. In the meantime, how's things?"

Leon and Marion chatted with the bishop as they showed him around the Gorham place. Leon knew he was being scrutinized. *Marion told me she's known the bishop all of her life, and that he was good friends with her father. He's certainly going to review my status as a husband candidate for her on behalf of her dead father*, he thought.

The bishop seemed to approve of Leon's choice to buy the farm. "Leon," he said. "I am glad you were able to buy this place. It has good bones and needs a family to take care of it." Bishop then looked to Marion. "I know you never knew old Mr. Gorham but he was born and raised here, and was a good man. I think he felt bad when his son didn't take on the farming spirit but, at least, the son supported his mother until her death."

He turned back to Leon. "Now, Leon, I am dying to see the inside of the house. Did you get a key to the lock? It was in great shape when Mrs. Gorham died and I'm curious how it's held up."

"You just can't keep your hands off houses, can you, Bishop," Marion replied.

"Marion, you know me so well," he laughed. "I do love houses, old ones, new ones, and even ugly ones. I enjoy keeping them going and seeing them turned into homes. It's why I got into construction in the first place." He looked over to Leon. "Of course, my two brothers split our farm, so Dad wasn't upset when I gave up my share of the land to build houses. It saved him from doing the hard math to divide everything by three."

It was fun watching Bishop look at the old Gorham house. He did love houses. Leon also watched Marion's reaction knowing he was pretty sure that he'd do whatever she wanted him to do with the place. He'd love to see it fixed up but, if she wanted it knocked down for a new place in order to marry him, he'd do that, too.

Bishop pulled out a penlight and shone it all around. "Are you going to knock this place down?" he asked Leon.

"I don't know, Bishop. I feel like it was great and still has potential. But, I don't know if it can be updated and well-used; I'm a tractor guy, not a house guy."

Bishop turned back and looked at him. "Well, it sure seems solid. Do you want my crew and me to go through it and tell you what it needs? I'd tell you what I'd do to it if it was my place. I could even give you an idea of the costs so you could decide."

Leon looked to Marion. "I'd like that but, Bishop, part of my agreement with Marion is where she wants to live, whether she can live here on my farm. She hasn't yet told me whether she wants a new house or would take this one if it can be saved."

Marion cocked her head. "Well you two sure know how to pressure a girl... all right. I've always liked this house. I like the tall ceilings and wood everywhere. It could be small if Leon wants a bakers' dozen kids but, if it can be saved, I am all for saving old houses.

"I look at houses the way Gene does," she addressed Bishop. "You know he would have lived in the old homestead had it not burned down. But, I like his new place too."

"Well, Marion," Bishop replied. "This place is older than your current place and it's probably only been partially updated to power and central heating. In fact, I think Mrs. Gorham still used the old wood and coal stoves to keep warm in the winter."

Leon spoke up at that point. "I think you're right. Half of the coal stoves are still here and there's no furnace in the basement. But, there is a hot water heater down there and electric heaters along the living room baseboards."

"That's what I thought. So, do you think you'd like to consider saving it?"

"I'd like to know what all it needs and have an idea of what it costs so I can budget a living situation," Leon said.

"I agree... if this place can be saved, I could live here," Marion added.

Leon noticed the bishop smiled at that and seemed to purposely head into the rest of the house to give them privacy. Leon took the opportunity to hold Marion back. "Do you mean it? If I can fix this place up, you'd live here?"

Marion nodded. "I think so. I've never had my own place, but I've always figured I could live anywhere, and there are good things about this place. Besides it faces east and west so I can have sunshine in the kitchen during breakfast, and have western sunshine in the living room in the winter."

"Mare, do you mean it? Could you really live here on my farm?"

"I think so, Leon. I like it a lot. But today, and seeing inside this place, has shown me the variables I need to consider when I think about my worries. I'll need to sleep on it, but I've learned a lot today… I know I can deal with your family, that I can spend 24/7 with you, and I think I can live here on your farm in this house. What I don't know is what I would, or should, do with myself. I know that I can't be just a wife and mother on a farm… I'd have to *do* something too. Work or farm, or something, and that's what's unsettling. I don't know what I'll *do* with myself while you are at work or are out in the fields. Do you understand?"

"I think I do. So, for now, let's stick to our plan. We'll keep dating, etc., while you think on these things, and when you know, let me know."

"Will do." She leaned closer to him and said, "I learned something else here. I love you, Leon."

"You do? Wow! You mean it?"

"I do. It came on fast, but I felt it for sure when we were talking to Bishop outside. I love you, honey."

Leon had no words, so he showed her how he felt by taking her in his arms and kissing her tenderly.

The bishop's loud clearing of his throat startled them out of the kiss. He came back into the room asking, "Are you sure you two don't want me to call the temple right now and set up a sealing date?"

Leon responded for them. "Sorry, Bishop. Marion just decided that she loves me, so we're one step closer, but not quite there yet."

"Marion, I think you need to come talk to me on Sunday after services. Whatever is keeping you from marrying this man seems like a problem we need to discuss," the bishop said.

The bishop's statement caught Leon by surprise. He wondered whether he should have shared something so personal with a stranger. The only thing he could do was hope that she really meant it and that she wasn't just caught up in the excitement of fixing the house instead. Marion's reply to Bishop interrupted his thinking.

Marion nodded. "Okay, Bishop. I do need to talk to somebody about it." She nudged Leon. "Somebody besides Leon that is. He's a bit set in what he wants, while I am still working out what I want."

Leon relaxed a bit, reassured by her words. He resolved to focus on the idea that Marion loved him. It seemed clear, based on the interaction between Bishop and Marion, that she was very close to the man and was okay sharing their courtship with him. He realized he was staring at her when Bishop spoke.

"Okay, you two. Now, let's go through the house, if you can see where we're going with all the windows boarded up, and I'll tell you what I saw on my tour... I will say, Leon, that this place is definitely salvageable. Some of the structure needs beefing up and a few boards replaced but, if you want to, this place can definitely be updated."

"That's great news, Bishop," Leon replied, looking at Marion. "Ready to take the tour?"

"Sure am."

"Do I need to go get my big flashlight?" Leon asked the bishop.

"Yes, do that. And I'll get my Maglite from the truck. After the tour I'll tell you what I think you need to do to protect this place while you decide what to tackle first."

Leon and Marion said in chorus, "Sounds good."

Chapter Twenty-Three

"Hey Jeanette! Glad I caught you," Marion spoke into her phone. "I've got Leon's mom in on the plan. She'll get his dad, brother, and sister there. Do you think you and Gene can do the same with the kids? I think you guys can all hide upstairs in the lodge and surprise him when we get there. I think everyone will love playing in the pools and the waterslide's amazing this time of year."

"I'm sure we can. But, are you sure 'an everybody included' family party is how you want to surprise Leon for his birthday?" Jeanette responded.

"I think it will be best. Leon's very close to his family. His mom was excited with the idea, too. So I am going to trust her instincts in this."

"So, even though you're not engaged, you are okay mixing the families?" Jeanette questioned.

Marion mulled over her response for a few seconds.

"Mare, are you there? Did I lose you?"

"No, Jeannie, I'm just thinking about what you said… maybe it's not appropriate, right now, to mix the families. We're just dating after all. Heck, maybe I should back out and let the Packers plan Leon's birthday. Maybe I shouldn't even be there." Marion couldn't keep the tremor from her voice.

"Oh, Mare! I didn't mean to imply that it wasn't appropriate for you to go. I just wonder whether Gene and I should bring the kids to Leon's birthday party, especially as you'll meet his siblings for the first time there."

"I hadn't thought about it like that. I got so excited to think that I could surprise Leon for his birthday, I forgot about how it could affect his folks or his brother and sister. I guess I am too used to doing everything with him. He's so taken with your kids, and I got fixated on seeing him in the pool with Mick and Nancy. Sorry. I'll regroup and get back to you."

"I'm sorry to burst your bubble, Marion. I really am."

Marion heard Jeanette's sigh.

"No, it's okay, Jeanette. I may have got a bit impulsive with this one. Let me think on it and call his mom back, then I'll call you back."

"Sounds good, Mare. I'll support you either way. It may be fine."

"If you say so. Bye."

"Bye, too."

Marion sat the phone down and left her house. She needed space and time. With little thought, she grabbed her old Stetson and a bottle of water and headed out the garage. She passed her truck, the garden, and the stock barn. Her steps increased in speed and her feet found the dirt road that wound its way up to the cattle's stock yard and ended at the base of the hills bordering the Sullivan land.

As she walked, Marion's thoughts rushed through her head. In the mix, she worried once again whether she should just marry Leon and settle down. *He's certainly willing and I do love him*, she thought.

She could easily live with Leon she knew. Marion was constantly surprised at how well they suited. But, she still wasn't totally sure about her feelings. *Could I be settling for Leon, just because he's the first man I've really liked who's been interested in me?*

It was much easier when she was with Leon. When they were together she felt like the peas to his carrots. It felt right and natural to be with him. They enjoyed things like buying groceries together as much as dressing up in their best clothes for a nice dinner on the town.

It had been a month since Leon got his farm and they started spending most of their free time together. As she walked, Marion thought about the short time she'd known Leon, and couldn't help compare her situation with the courtships in her family. Her great-grandparents had met one spring and only waited until September to get married, because great Grandpa had to wait until the next church conference for his next church ordination so he could marry great Grandma in the Salt Lake Temple. They'd spent an idyllic summer courting and then after the conference had used the families' pooled gas vouchers to drive the two-plus hours to Salt Lake to get married in the middle of World War II.

No matter how quickly the relationship developed, Marion felt like she knew Leon well enough to bet her life on him. She definitely loved him, she just didn't know if she *should.* Her thoughts continued like this for another half hour when Marion reached the stockyards and turned south. The road narrowed here, and the grass between the two wheel ruts got taller as she went down to her land's southern boundary. It took thirty more minutes, but Marion made it to her destination.

Here, in a rocky, sheltered corner of the Sullivan land was a tiny spring under a rocky outcrop that fed a large cottonwood tree before emptying out into a tiny meadow. The first Sullivan had camped here in this shady spot with good water while deciding where to place his permanent homestead. The tiny cabin he'd constructed was long gone and the original trees had died and others grown, but generations of Sullivans kept the spring maintained and Marion's parents had planted a soft pasture grass in the meadow making it into a great picnic spot. Gene even joked that Marion had been conceived out here one spring afternoon.

Marion didn't know, or care, whether Gene was right but she'd always felt the most at peace here. From a little child, she'd often find her way here in the good weather to play her childhood games or to think through a teenaged problem. She spent hours here when her father died, and didn't cry over her mother's death until the snows melted enough for her to spend a day here bawling.

She felt a good cry coming on. Emotions overwhelmed her and Marion fell to her hands and knees on the cool grass in the shade of the massive tree.

She cried out her feelings for what seemed like hours. At the end, she felt limp and drained. Sighing, she lay down and turned on her side resting with her head on her arm and her hat over her eyes, as she tried to summon peace.

Marion awoke some time later. Slowly, she realized she'd fallen asleep. The afternoon sun warmed her toes in her boots. A light breeze tickled the hair lying along her jaw. She reached up and moved her hat off her face where it shaded her eyes and looked around. The peace she'd fought for had overtaken her during her nap making her feel much better. She still wasn't sure what to do about Leon, but she wasn't worried about it anymore.

She rolled onto her back and stretched. She spent a moment watching the incredibly blue sky, above her head, through the cottonwood's leaves and upper branches. It sure was a perfect summer day.

She lay, trying to decide whether to get up or not, when Leon's voice startled her upright.

"Feel better?"

"What the heck, Leon! You scared me!"

Marion sat up and got her bearings. Leon was lounging against the tree within arm's length above where her head had lain.

"How did you find me here?" she asked, turning to face him.

"Well, it wasn't easy but Jeanette wondered if you'd come down here. So, I found my way here," he answered, calmly.

"What time is it?" Marion asked.

"About four. When did you come up here?"

"I'm not sure. I talked to your mom at one, so maybe one-thirty."

"You talked to my mom, huh?"

Leon's question made Marion realize what she'd said. "Um. Yeah," she said, as she blushed.

"Why? It wasn't about my birthday was it?"

"Damn it. How'd you know?"

"Hon, my birthday is next week and you and my mom are the most important women in my life. It wasn't hard to deduce that you'd be planning something together. Besides, very few things make you turn pink, so I figured you'd let something slip," Leon teased.

Marion smiled. "Well, I need to call your mom back. What I planned won't work, so maybe you'll need to plan your own birthday."

"I suppose I can do that. Before I do, why don't you come over here and tell me what made you so upset that you took off down here?" Leon patted the grassy spot next to him and looked at her expectantly.

Marion loved being near him, so it was easy for her to stand up and take the two steps to his side. He waited patiently for her to get comfortable and then pulled her into his arms for a quick hug. Then she settled down by him and slid her hand into his.

"So, what's wrong? I got off early and looked all over your spread for you. Then I found Jeanette at home and she told me you were probably upset and up here at the spring. She gave me no details, so what's up, Mare?" he asked.

"I don't want to talk to you about it."

"Why?"

"I'm embarrassed."

"With me? Really Mare? Come on, spill."

"Fine. Jeanette asked me whether it was inappropriate to include her, Gene, and the kids with your family for your birthday. In her words, 'we aren't even engaged.'"

"So, what upset you? Mixing both sides of the families or being engaged to me?"

Marion shook her head. "That's why I didn't want to talk about it. You don't get it."

"What? That having you, and your brother, and sister-in-law come to my party with my parents, sister, brother, and sister-in-law would mix two families prematurely? I understand that. I agree that could be awkward for both sides, and I can see we should talk about it a bit more before we do such a thing. What I don't understand is why such a normal question would send you to your sanctuary so upset that you cried yourself to sleep in the middle of the day." He motioned to the tear tracks on her cheeks to emphasize his words.

"You're right. Mixing the families wasn't what upset me. I should have thought of it first, but missed it. What upset me is the 'us'. Jeanette's right. We aren't engaged, and I don't know if we should be or not."

"We can be if you finally think it feels right."

"With that statement, we're back to where we've been since day one. I don't know whether I should marry you. So, I have no right to plan your birthday. Don't you see?" she sighed.

"I understand that that kind of thought would have upset you. Marion, there's no one else I'd rather spend my birthday with. I love my family and would be just fine celebrating with them and with your family too, but you are my first choice. I love you and I want to be with you. I know that much."

"Birthdays are big steps though. I've always thought it takes a fiancée, or wife, to trump a mother's birthday plans." Marion was so frustrated, she felt like pouting and it leaked into her tone.

Leon's tone turned comforting. "Mare, that's silly. My birthday is my problem. Sure, my mom and family are usually there, but I get final say on my birthday. I vote you. Okay?"

"Okay, I guess."

"So, what are we doing for my birthday?" Leon cajoled.

"I can't really tell you. Plus, I need to change it all up."

"I can talk to Mom and ask her about mixing in-laws prior to an engagement and get her take on it."

"That won't help. It doesn't seem right for me to meet your brother and sister and sister-in-law for the first time at the party I throw for you."

"Hey, I get a party?"

Marion playfully slugged Leon. "Knock it off. Be serious, will you. It's not quite proper."

"I get ya. So let's do this... you call Mom and ask her what she thinks and you two can plan the party. Meanwhile, I'll call Dad and arrange a Packer family get-together tomorrow after church so you can meet my side before the alleged birthday party. How does that sound?"

"Sounds good."

"Great. So tell me about this place. I noticed the big tree on one of my runs around here with Gene, but I didn't know anything about the spring until Jeanette told me where you'd probably taken refuge."

Marion told Leon all the family stories about the Sullivan spring and they stayed there, talking under the big cottonwood tree, until dusk. The last rays of the sun setting caught Marion's attention.

"Oh, Leon. We should get back. I need to call your mom and it's past time to feed the sheep."

"No problem, Mare. Jeanette lent me Gene's four-wheeler so we'll be back to your place in a jiffy."

"Wow. She must have been worried about me. Gene never lets anyone else drive his toy."

"Well, I was concerned, and from what you told me, I can see why Jeanette was worried. I hope that if you ever agree to marry me, you'll talk to me before taking a three mile hike the next time you get upset like this."

"When I decide to marry you, I'll probably trust you as well as love you just enough to do that, Mister."

Chapter Twenty-Four

Leon stopped by Tremonton Tractor late in the day. He'd left his parents and siblings with Marion and her siblings, camping out at the hot springs family water park north of Brigham City, Utah in order to do an errand at work. He went through the shop hoping to find George.

"George? George, you in here?"

"Leon, I'm back here," George said.

Leon heard his voice faintly from the open storage area at the rear of the shop and followed the sound. He found George amongst the stacks of tractor parts near the back.

"George, can I help you, buddy?"

"Nah, Leon. I got it. Just give me a second."

Leon waited for George who appeared after a minute from between two large stacks of boxes with a small box.

"Let me put this part up front so it's ready for Monday. I'll be right back," he nodded to Leon as he passed him by.

"I'll wait patiently. I can't wait to hear what you and Monte heard," Leon answered.

"You won't believe it, man," George stated, as he stepped out of sight.

Leon fidgeted and shifted his weight between foot to foot as he waited. Images of earlier in the day floated through his head. Marion had followed through with her birthday plans for him but instead of hijacking him, and having both families surprise him with a cake when they arrived at the water park, Marion and his mom pushed through with the same party minus only Leon's surprise.

He'd spent the morning swimming in the mineral water and regular swimming pools, going down the waterslides, and having big-time fun with his family, and

Marion's, in the water. They'd grilled burgers and hotdogs at lunch in the campground and picnicked. Then, while the kids napped, the adults sat in the shade drinking cold drinks and getting to know everybody.

Leon was shocked that everyone got along so well, and Marion surprised him when she took it all in stride in a total turn-around from her earlier worries. She told him that, because both families were relatively small, they could mesh easily in one-on-one contacts. She also said they could get along because they had so much in common.

His sister and sister-in-law fit right in with Marion and Jeanette, while his brother and Gene really hit it off. He smiled picturing a moment when, while his mother and sister were watching Gene's kids, the three of them, him, Gene, and his brother, had snuck up on their girls in the pool and dunked them all. It started a terrific water fight and ended with the guys holding their girls close. He'd found himself in cool, chest-deep water holding Marion against him while his brother was kissing his very pregnant sister-in-law senseless on his left and Gene was lip-locked with Jeanette to his right.

He'd looked down to Marion, and she was looking up at him, so he decided to mimic the brothers and kissed her senseless too. They broke out of it when the cheers from the two couples, his sister, and his parents reached their ears. The rest of the pool patrons also joined in the teasing jeers. Gene told him later, that he'd timed him and Marion kissing for six and half minutes.

Leon couldn't wait to get back to the party. The family had rented two adjoining campgrounds with his parents', and Gene's RVs, in each and a scattering of tents between them. Marion had promised to set up her camp cot under the stars next to him on his old army cot. He was looking forward to talking to her after the rest of the clan had gone to sleep.

He'd only come into TT, because Monte had sent a cryptic text:

Hey L, Happy Bday! Come by the shop before 6 if U can. G got a letter from HQ that you won't believe.

George's re-entry into the shop storage area pulled Leon away from his thoughts of Marion and his family at the water park.

George waved a letter at Leon.

"Leon, I didn't win, but they want me to go to Racine!" he exclaimed.

"Wow, George, that's the annual prize notification letter right? Can I read it?"

"Sure can, man. This is all your fault. Thank you!"

George handed Leon the official notice from headquarters. He noticed it was printed on heavy paper. Leon read it quickly and felt true excitement for his friend and co-worker.

"Wow, George. This is amazing! You and Monte got Honorable Mention, and they want you for the Troubleshooters! That's is so cool! What are you going to do?" Leon asked.

"Well, my wife is over the moon. She has family in Minnesota, so Wisconsin will be a lot closer to home for her. And, of course, my parents are excited though they say they can use my brother for family projects from now on. Monte says he'll miss me, but he can't begrudge me such a golden opportunity."

"That sounds perfect, George. I told you they'd like you. You have real talent for their tractors," Leon clapped George on the shoulder. "My old buddy Eric is still back there. I'll get you his number. He can give you great advice if you need it."

"Thanks, Leon. That means a lot. I'd definitely like to look Eric up and ask him about things. I mean, this dream job is what he's been doing, right?"

"Yup, for the past few years."

George held up his hand to shake Leon's.

"Thanks, again Leon. I wouldn't have dared to try without your help. I don't know how I can repay you," he stated, choking up.

Leon felt like answering with emotion, but said, "Naw, George. I was just paying it forward. I've had my turn. This turn is yours, and it truly makes me happy to see you get something like this. I hope it takes you great places."

"Thanks, man. I'll miss you."

"Me, too. I'll have to see if Marion would be willing to take a road trip out there when you get settled."

"I'd like to see that. I mean, man, I think she likes you, but I don't know if you'll ever bridle that filly," George laughed.

"Thanks for the vote of confidence, George."

"Anytime, Leon."

Leon left soon after and called Monte from his truck as he drove back to the water park campground. Monte confirmed what George had told him, and explained he and George were going to Racine the next week to visit the manufacturing plant and get photographed for a write up in the next month's company magazine. Leon agreed to run TT that week and looked forward to a challenging week that would surely test all his work skills.

After Monte hung up, Leon mulled over the other thing Monte had talked about--his need for a new shop mechanic.

He arrived at the campground about seven, just in time to grab some Dutch oven chicken and dumplings Jeanette and his Mom had crafted. The family then tanked up on chocolate, cherry, upside down cake for his birthday cake and got the kids in bed by eight.

After dinner, Leon finally cleared some private time with Marion. He watched the dinner cleanup crew until he judged he could steal Marion away from it. He grabbed her arm as she took the last load of dishes into Gene's RV where Jeanette was running the dishwashing brigade.

"Hey Marion, do you have a minute?" he asked, and then poked his head through the RV door keeping hold of Marion. "Hey Jeanette, I need Marion, okay?"

Jeanette met his eye over his sister's head. "Sure can, Leon. We've got it here."

"Yeah, Leon. We can certainly give you and Marion some alone time. It is your birthday after all," his mom chimed in.

The group laughed while Marion looked at him questioningly.

He reassured her. "I have some news for you and wondered if you'd be okay going over to the pavilion and talking until lights out at ten?" he asked.

"Sure. I can do that."

Hand in hand they walked the one hundred or so yards down to the pavilion that separated the campground from the waterpark itself.

They skirted the picnic tables, in the open area on the ground level of the pavilion, to reach the nearest stair. There, they made their way to the upper, walled-in, dance hall level. This upper level was, mostly, a large wooden dance floor with built-in benches all around. Large, wooden shutters along the sides were tied up above the benches opening it to the outdoors and making for a cool breeze as night fell.

Leon tugged Marion along to a corner bench where they could have privacy, but see the families' camp in the distance. He sat down and she sat next to him, still holding his hand as was her habit.

"So, you know I made a quick run out to TT to talk to George. Well, he and Monte didn't win the annual prize, but did get Honorable Mention and will be going to Racine next week. Monte needs me to run the store and shop while their gone. So, I'll be staying in town for a week."

"That's great for them. And I am okay if you need to spend a week in town. You know me. I am pretty self-contained."

"Thank you for that. I am going to miss you though. I realized driving back here, that this will be the first time we've been apart for more than a couple of days since we started this whole dating thing."

"I didn't think of that. But, we should be okay, right? I mean I can still call and text you, and it's only for a week. Besides, I'll need to run into town at least once for groceries next week and can visit you."

"You're right. It should be fine. I just don't want to be apart from you that much." Leon's tone turned more serious. "In fact, it got me thinking that I am not sure I want to be very far from you at all."

"What are you saying, Leon?"

"I think you know what I am saying. But, I know you're not ready yet, so I won't say it, or ask *the* question. I just needed you to know that this change has caused me to re-think some things. But, that's only part of why I wanted to talk to you." He looked away for a minute gathering his thoughts, then continued, "Mare, there's more about this trip that will affect my job at TT. HQ wants George to come work for them. He's already agreed to go, so he won't be back after next week. Monte has a line on a promising mechanic who can start in a month, but he'll need some training. This kid is the son of one of Monte's good buddies, so the long-term plan is that the kid will also get to be GM someday. Monte has asked that I train him in the shop and then split the shop and General Manager duties with him for the next year while he decides which one of us will keep which job. Are you okay if I scale back some of my house plans in order to work hard at TT for the next few months?" he finished.

"Uh, I think so. I mean, won't your hours stay the same, basically full time during this?" Marion asked.

"Yes and no. Monte knows the farm will support me, but he knows I can use my TT job money, too. His alternate suggestion was to have me train the kid in the GM duties, bring on another part-time mechanic, and have me do around thirty hours a week as the full-time, or 'most' time, mechanic. That would allow me to work four days out of six and give me more time in Stone, but less money. What do you think about that?"

He watched Marion. She looked to be thinking on what he said.

"I think," she said. "If I were you, I'd do the thirty-hour thing. Monte knows that you aren't there for the next forty years, and it sounds like the kid might be. Heaven knows I'd love to see you out in Stone full time, but I know you can't quite afford that yet."

"Thanks, Marion. I am leaning that way myself, but it's good to talk through things with you. I need your input, you know. You are the most important person to me, and I am trying to do all I can to make it possible for you to marry me."

Marion's eyes filled with tears. "Oh, baby, I know. I feel so honored that you'd do all that for me. I am working on it. You are very special to me, too. I love you. I am sorry it's taking me so long to figure this out, but I feel better about you working less hours in Tremonton and more at home."

Leon couldn't help but kiss her.

After the kiss he said, "I am doing just fine keeping busy while you figure things out. I think the next few weeks will be a trial, but I think I'll find out real quick what won't work about Monte's plans as soon as he gets back and saddles me with the protégé."

Leon shifted so Marion could rest against his chest as they watched the sunset through the western side of the dancehall. He decided it had been a pretty good day and a darn fine birthday after all. *Here's hoping I'll be with Marion, but she'll be wearing my ring come the next one*, he prayed.

Chapter Twenty-Five

"Atzo, that's a great idea. When are Atzo Jr. and his girl getting married?" Marion asked, as she spoke with Atzo in the kitchen of her house.

"Next month, Miss Marion."

"I'm certain that Gene and I can have everything cleaned out and our equipment moved by then. You're sure just the five acres around the house and the barn will suffice?"

"Oh sure, even with his mother's and my help and the help of her parents, this five acres is the most they can afford until they expand the herd. Besides, that will leave the bulk of the farm to you and Gene, and we'll rent the rangeland from you from here on. They can always buy more land later. Now, are you sure that you can sell your home?"

"Oh, yes, Atzo. Even if I had never met Leon, I never expected to live here permanently. We always expected one of Gene's kids to live here. But, I am glad Atzo Jr. wants it. The sheep herd should grow back to the hundreds great-Grandpa had and stay here."

"Very good. We'll meet you at the bank to sign the papers next week then."

"Sounds good."

Atzo turned to leave and passed Leon coming into the house.

"Hello and goodbye, Mr. Leon," Atzo said.

"Going back to your herd, Atzo?"

"Yes, but only long enough to bed them down. I am going into town tonight to speak to my son and his fiancée. Miss Marion and Mr. Gene are going to sell him the sheep and this place so my grandchildren will have a bright future here."

"That's great news, Atzo. Please pass on my congratulations to him. I wish you guys every happiness here."

"Thank you. Now, if you don't mind an old man's advice, I hope you make Marion happy by marrying her and taking her home to your farm. I know that, though she believes that she is not a farmer, this land is in her blood and I feel that she will miss it if she leaves."

"I'll do my best. Thank you for the advice."

Atzo closed the door behind him and Marion looked to Leon and saw that he moved to stand by the sink looking out the window. *I hope he's okay with decision to sell*, she mused. She went deeper into the kitchen and said to his back, "How was work?"

Leon turned to look at her. "It was work. I sold a big tractor today and Monte is going to let me go with the delivery driver to Corinne when we deliver it."

"That's neat. Good for you...," Marion paused. Something seemed wrong with Leon's tone. "You seem a bit put out. Does Gene and me selling this place to Atzo Jr. bother you?"

"Not really, I'm just a little shocked. I mean, after dinner last night, you and Gene left me and Jeanette with the kids while you went out in the fields to talk, and when you came back, you told us about Atzo's offer. Then, here, not twenty-four hours later, you've accepted the offer and are selling your part of your parents' farm."

"But, you are okay if I sell out?"

"That depends."

"On what?"

"On whether or not this keeps you from marrying me or not."

"Well, it shouldn't. Besides you still haven't asked me yet." She smiled, hoping to soften his mood. "I still love you, you know. Selling my farm hasn't changed that. It seems freeing to me…"

The speed of Leon's reaction shocked her. He dropped down to one knee right there on the vinyl floor of the kitchen, grasped her hands.

"Marion, please marry me," he said.

"I don't know what to say."

"It should be easy, yes, no, or maybe. Any of those will work."

Marion blushed. Warning signals were going off in her head. "I don't like your tone. I want to say yes… this morning I would have said yes, but you look angry, not ecstatic right now."

"So, is that a yes?"

"It's a strong maybe."

Leon let go of her hands and stood up. "In my experience, maybes are often a 'no' when someone can't say 'no' or a 'not now.' Which is it for you?"

Marion saw anger in Leon's face and hurt caused her to lash back. "Well, it was a 'let me think about it,' but since you are being so nasty, it's now a 'not any time soon.'"

"Fine," he said, as he made to move past her out of the kitchen.

Marion moved with him and he stopped when he noticed her following him.

"What's wrong? Why are we fighting?" she asked.

"We're not fighting. I asked a question and you answered me. I'm going home now."

Marion felt despair. "We're over just like that?"

"I don't want to be, but you still need time to think about marrying me, something we've talked about for some time, yet you were able to decide whether or not to sell your childhood home and family legacy overnight. It seems clear that while you say you love me, you either don't want me or don't know what you want. I can't live with either, and since I am committed to my new farm, it seems best for me to leave."

Marion didn't notice the tears streaking her face. "Please, don't leave like this, I just need some time to make sure. I do *want* to marry you. I'm just not sure if I can or should."

"Well, I'm sorry, but that's not good enough. Goodbye, Marion."

Despair and futility swamped her. "Goodbye, Leon. I am sorry."

His "Me too." was quiet, but she heard it.

She moved to the window over the sink and watched him drive away. He didn't look up or back or wave, he just drove away.

And just like that it was over.

She sniffed. Marion began feeling the tears when they starting hitting her chin and dropping on to her hands clasped over her stomach. They were rolling down her cheeks in a steady stream. Then the sobs started and she fell down to the floor where she sat in the same spot Leon had knelt and wept.

Marion did not know how long she sat on the kitchen floor crying. She noticed when it got dark, dark enough that she needed a light turned on to clearly see her cellphone when it rang. She wanted to let it ring until she saw the name display. *Thank heavens it's Kim. Thank you, Heavenly Father for my best friend calling me when I need her.*

"Hello," she answered, hearing her best friend since kindergarten answer,

"Hey, Mare! Just calling to see how you are. It's not dinner time is it?"

"No, but you have great timing as always. I need you. Leon just broke up with me."

"What the hell happened? You sound upset. You two were going hot and heavy like gangbusters. What went wrong?"

"I did. I couldn't say yes to his marriage proposal."

"Well, why not? You love him, don't you?"

"Yes. More than I understood until now."

"So, why didn't you say 'yes,' now?"

"My doubts overwhelmed me... oh, I don't know why, but I don't know whether or not I can be married to him."

"What are your specific worries?"

"That I can't be a farmer's wife, that I can't stay out here in BFE any longer, that I'm not good enough for him."

"Oh, Mare, can you hear yourself? You're being silly. Have you talked to Leon about this? You promised me you would."

"No. I don't dare."

"Well, Marion that's your problem. You should dare. You should risk it all for him. From what you've told me, he's worth it."

"I don't know if I can."

"You better. Look Mare, I've known you all your life. This isn't like you. Grow your balls back and marry him. I mean it."

"I can't."

"You should."

"But..."

"No buts."

Marion heard Kim sigh through the phone, then she said, "Look, Mare, I don't want to argue with you, so let's just leave it at, I think you're making a big mistake, okay?"

"Okay."

"So what was your text about? You're selling the farm?"

Marion told Kim about the pending sale.

"That's great for you. Now you can try something else," Kim responded.

"Yeah, but I don't know what. I've only ever farmed and I don't know what kind of non-farming job I could get with one year of college engineering, and a summer's experience of waiting tables."

"You could always come out and live with me. There's always room for more staff at my hotel. You could hang out with me until the fall semester starts."

"Hey, that's not a bad idea. I can even afford the plane ticket to Oahu if I sell my truck."

"Well, I'd love to have you."

"I'll work on it and get back to you."

Chapter Twenty-Six

Leon was restless. His parents' RV was nice and comfy, but he felt caged up in it tonight. He knew he was restless and edgy because of breaking up with Marion. Ever since he'd left her place, Leon had been rehashing what happened. He realized he couldn't blame it all on his shock at her selling out. It was also her infernal wavering over "them." He steamed. Marion had to know that they were perfect for each other. What was her hesitation?

Leon thought some more. Then he realized his real problem. Damn, it was all his fault. A picture of Marion's prize ram popped into his head. She'd taken him with her on runs to deliver Atzo's supplies. On one, they reached the field where the sheep camp was about dark. The sheep were all bedded down and Marion had pointed out the members of her flock who were notable and restated why that the ram was not with them. She'd explained that she was keeping him healthy and happy at the home farm. When the ram wasn't with his harem, but near enough to smell them, he was moody, irritated, and downright mean. Marion had called it testosterone poisoning, and that for that reason the ram was usually without his ladies outside of breeding season.

Leon couldn't help but wonder whether he, too, was suffering from testosterone poisoning. *Could it be sexual frustration causing him to lash out at Marion? How dumb was that?* He hadn't had a big fight with his woman and broke it off because of hormones, had he? The shock of this line of thought struck him making him say out loud, "I've got to fix it."

He wondered how he could have been so arrogant and touchy with her. He realized he'd promised Marion time to think things over and then, when she finally made a crucial decision quicker than expected, he'd jumped her shit for it. *I am nuts. What a stupid, stupid way to act with her,* he thought.

Leon left the RV and went straight for his truck. He made it back to Marion's in about ten minutes, proving that he could go as fast on dirt roads as he could on pavement. Her truck was still in the drive and her kitchen light was on. He wasted no time getting into her house.

He was yelling her name before he got the kitchen door open.

"Marion?" he called out. "Marion, baby, where are you? I'm so sorry." He walked right past the kitchen and kept calling out through the front room and even went to her bedroom. The door was open, but she wasn't there, nor was she in her bathroom, the other bedrooms, the hall bath, or the back mudroom. He went back to the kitchen and debated on where to go looking for her when he noticed a movement out of the corner of his eye. He looked to his right and then down and saw Marion sitting on the floor by the sink staring at him.

Leon turned towards her and crouched down in front of her. "I am so sorry. Please forgive me. I had no right to treat you that way. I was wrong to mock you with a false proposal. Please forgive me." He stared at her face. She'd been crying hard. Her eyes were puffy and she hadn't even wiped the moisture off her cheeks. He looked down and noticed her phone on the floor next to her.

She didn't say anything. Her hands lay at her sides, palms up, but she made no movement towards him. As he stared into her eyes she turned her head and looked away. He noticed tears starting to fill up her lower eyelids and spill out onto her cheeks. "Please, honey, don't do this to me even though I deserve it."

She looked up at him. She didn't stop crying, but said quietly, "You broke my heart." That was all. She looked away from him, and then she folded her arms in her lap and dropped her head lower.

He watched as her chest started to shudder with her crying. "Oh, sweetheart." He didn't know what to do. Leon stayed there, crouched and watched Marion cry for some minutes. Desperate, he reached in to pull her up to her feet with the intention of putting her to bed. Marion resisted slightly, then allowed him to pull her to her feet. Once upright, she turned away and held her fist against her mouth as she began sobbing harder. Leon couldn't stand to see her crying so hard. He moved next to her, and tried to pull her into his arms. Marion flung his arm away and then leaned down over the sink, with her hands grasping the edge of the counter as she began to sob audibly louder. He tried again and this time, she collapsed against him.

Relief filled him as she began to cry in earnest against his neck. Unlike the day at his parents', he didn't try to soothe her, he just held her and let her cry it out hoping for her to let it out so they could talk and fix things. He was too worried that he'd crush their fragile truce with any words to speak.

Leon was prepared to stand there all night holding her, so he'd totally lost track of time by the time Marion's sobs quieted and her hiccups started. As they continued, he realized she wasn't hiccupping at all; she was hyperventilating. It had been a long time since he'd seen anyone hyperventilate and he didn't know what to do.

He tried to remember what caused hyperventilation and remembered that it happened sometimes during a panic attack. He thought about getting her a paper bag to breathe in, but couldn't remember if that worked. Marion started to sway like she was going to faint as her breathing worsened. Panicked, and working on instinct, he swung her up in his arms and carried her over to the living room couch. He sat her down and then had her lower her face towards her lap while he pulled out his cell phone called Gene.

Gene answered on the second ring. "Hey, Leon. What's up?"

"Gene, I need help. I'm over at Marion's and she's hyperventilating. She can't get her breath and it's freaking us out. What do I do?"

"Oh, damn. She's having a panic attack. Listen, you've got to get her moving. She's got too much oxygen and exercise will help even though you don't think it will. If not, get a paper bag and make her breathe in more carbon dioxide. If you can, also try to get her to breathe deep from down in her gut. She should breathe in and out through her nose with her 'outs' being longer than her 'ins'. Got that? I'll be right down."

"Got it. Be fast, Gene." Leon disconnected the call and looked at Marion. She wasn't improving, but she was now over breathing at a constant rate. "Okay, honey. You know you're hyperventilating, let's get you moving."

He tried to make her stand up, but Marion resisted. Brokenly she said, "I… *puff*… can't… *puff*… get… *puff*… my… *puff*… breath."

"I know honey, that's why you need to get moving and concentrate on your breathing." Leon was past his limit. He forced her to her feet and half carried and half lifted her out the front door of the living room and down the front porch steps. He started walking and pulling her along with him. "Breathe through your nose—breathe down deep in your gut. Try to breathe out more than you breathe in. Come on, move."

He kept up a litany in a forceful voice as he matched his tone with his grip on her hand. He began walking at a fast clip with her in circles around her house. They made it around the third time when Gene came barreling in the drive.

Gene was out of his truck as soon as he killed the engine. He ran over to them and began talking as he walked with them around and around the house.

"Leon, what happened? Marion, you'll be okay, keep moving and breathing through your nose like Mom taught you."

Marion answered before Leon could. "Go... *puff* away..., *puff* ... Gene."

"This is all my fault," Leon said. "We had a fight because I was stupid and I came over here to try to fix it, and she started sobbing and then this happened."

Gene was clearly pissed. "Why the hell did you do that? Haven't you done enough to stress her out? Hell, on one day you tell her you'll wait as long as it takes for her to decide whether or not she can marry you, while on another, you're pressuring her to run off an marry you that moment."

"I said I was stupid, Gene."

"Ah. Damn, I know..."

"Go away... *puff* Gene," Marion repeated.

"Good, Marion, you're doing better, see," Gene responded.

"I... mean... *puff*... it... *puff*. It's not... *puff*... your business... *puff*."

Gene looked at Leon and Marion, clearly torn. "I think I should stay here and help Leon help you."

Marion was adamant. "Go!" *puff... puff*.

Gene appealed to Leon. "Do you need help?"

Leon sighed. "I guess not. She's breathing better already. Maybe you need to leave, Gene, so that we can talk this through. Thank you for telling me how to help her, though."

"Okay, I'm going, but I'll be a call away if *either* of you need me." Gene went back to his truck and pulled out.

Leon kept walking with Marion. A few more laps and she was breathing better.

"That's it, keep breathing like that," he praised her.

"Go away… *puff*… Leon. I don't want to talk… *puff*… to you," Marion was able to say.

"I know. But, I can't leave you yet." He resolved to stay as long as possible. *He had to fix this. Lord, please help me make this right.*

Once Marion was breathing normally, she yanked her hand away and sped up her walking as she headed into the house. Leon had to work to catch her. But, at the kitchen door, he caught her.

"Go away, we're done," she said, spinning around to face him.

"No, we're not, I was stupid. We need to talk." He moved up on her, which caused her to back into her kitchen.

He followed her in and closed the door behind him.

"Like you were willing to talk to me about my selling this house?" she asked.

"Yes, you're right, I should have let you talk about that. We also need to talk about how I haven't been honoring my promise to let you think on your worries before pressuring you to marry me."

"How about you explain that bullshit proposal, then," she shot back.

Leon didn't know what to say.

"Well?" she asked, again.

"It was totally wrong. I shouldn't have done it. I don't know why I did it, so I don't know how to fix it or take it back. You mean everything to me, so I don't know why I dishonored you like that. I am sorry, and I would undo it if I could."

Marion didn't seem mollified. Her tone proved it. "I think you did it, because you don't care about my issues and just want me to marry you so you have your nice perfect life all wrapped up with a big, red bow. You don't care how I feel or what I want, not really. You've got your farm and now you need a woman to populate it for you. Either that or you want sex and you know that marriage is the only way you'd get it from me." She looked at him expectantly.

Leon felt despair return. "You're right, Marion. I've been telling you I care about your concerns, but I haven't acted accordingly. But, you're wrong about the sex thing. Love is not sex, but sex can enhance love. I do love you, and I am deeply attracted to you, but I want it all with you, not just sex. I want you to want to marry me, to be happy to live wherever I live and support me in what I do. I'd also hope you could be confident that I'd put us somewhere where you could be happy and that I'd support you in your pursuits."

He paused, then said, "When I came out here today, after work, I was going to tell you that I got a big bonus on the tractor deal. I was going to use it to pay for a couple of years of engineering for you at USU. Eric's grandma is going on a mission for the church and she asked if I could stay at her house for the next two years while she's in Russia. You see, I thought that we could live in Tremonton for two years and you could commute to Logan each day for school. I'd keep my tractor job and let Bill keep renting the farm. I figured we'd figure out what to do with the farm after you'd decided whether engineering is your calling. Then, I got here and realized that you'd gone ahead with your own plans, without talking to me, and that upset and distracted me." Leon rubbed his hand over his eyes and didn't see Marion come up to him.

She reached up and pulled his hand away so she could look into his eyes.

"You'd be willing to let me go back to school, really?" she asked.

"Really. Seeing you talk engineering with Dad, knowing how good you are at engineering, and talking about vocations, made it clear to me that while you can be a farmer, it's a job for you, not a dream job. How can I make you do something you hate, just because I love it?"

"So why did you lose it over me wanting to sell my farm, then? Selling this place would only make things easier for you. Plus, you had to know that I'd get cash as my part of the sale."

Leon thought for a minute before answering. "I was jealous and scared. Jealous that you obviously talked all about the farm sale with Gene and Atzo, and even did it without consulting me. I felt like I should have had a say, so I guess I was hurt, too. Then, I figured selling out would give you a nest egg so you could take off and leave me. I don't want you to leave me. So, I guess, I lashed out at you wanting to hurt and punish you."

"Do you want me to keep the farm?"

"Hell, no. I want you free of whatever hold this place has over you."

"Would you sell the Gorham place and move to Scotland to support me on my oil rig in the North Sea? You'd have to live in Aberdeen."

The truth hit Leon at that moment. Marion *was* more important to him than his farm or his job. He was able to look her in the eye and say with absolute certainty, "Yes, Marion. I would sell my farm, my truck, and my tractors and go where you need to go. They farm in Scotland, I could work there."

Marion's eyes widened. "You really mean that, don't you? These past few weeks, my biggest worry was that if I couldn't farm, I'd have to give you up. Losing you terrifies me."

Before Leon could speak, she dropped a bombshell; "It's good that I'm not going to Scotland, then. You also don't need to pay any tuition just yet. You'll just have to hang out here for a few months, while I go to Hawaii to get my head straightened out."

Leon was shocked. "What do you mean, you're going to Hawaii? When were you going to tell me about that?"

"Oh hey, don't get mad about me not telling you about Hawaii. I made that decision after you broke up with me. And, since you were done with me, I didn't figure I'd ever have to tell you about it."

"It's been two hours since I left here earlier. How in the hell did you decide to go to Hawaii in the time it took me to get back here?"

"It was easy. You broke my heart and then left, without looking back I might add, and then my best friend in the world, who happens to be in her third year at BYU-Hawaii calls me out of the blue. She hears that my world is shattered and offers me a bunk with her and the possibility of a few months' work on Oahu to clear my head of you. I know that Gene and Jeanette can clear this place out for me, and you were done with me, so I agreed to join her in Hawaii. I called Delta as soon as she hung up and maxed my emergency credit card with non-refundable, fly-now, open-ended-return airfare, and I am going to Hawaii, tomorrow. I was getting ready to scrape up the remnants of my life and call Jeanette over here to explain things to her and get her to help me pack, when you returned and tried to kill me with your apology."

It took Leon a few minutes to process her explanation. When done, he asked the most relevant question first. "Tomorrow? You're leaving for Hawaii, tomorrow?"

"Yes. And though I despise love games, this is unfortunately a test for you. I need to get out of here. And, I need some space from you, too. I love you, but I can't think around you and I need to get some things settled in my mind and heart. So, I'm asking you to wait for me. Give me a few months in Hawaii, and then I'll be able to answer you once and for all. Can you do that?"

Leon had to share his greatest fear. "What are the chances that I'll lose you?"

Marion answered in her typical honest way. "You won't lose me. There's no chance of that. I'll be back."

"Okay. I'll hold you to that. So what do I do until you go?"

"You can come with me up to Gene and Jeanette's while I explain."

"Okay. And tomorrow, I'll take you to the airport."

Chapter Twenty-Seven

"Leon, I am grateful that we were able to let the high school kids work on your house these past few weeks," Bishop Morley said as he looked around at the crew as they worked. "It seems like a positive experience for both you and them."

Leon grunted as he worked to fill yet another wheelbarrow with dirt from his basement. "I agree, Bishop. I don't think I could have accomplished a tenth of what those kids have done in twice as much time. But, none of us could have done spit if you hadn't agreed to take on this project."

"Well, Leon. I've always had a soft spot for Marion. She needs to be in Hawaii for some reason and I want to support her. She's been a good friend to my daughter over the years, and I couldn't leave you in a lurch. Besides, I always liked this old house and didn't want to see it torn down."

"Yeah. It seems meant to be. I thought almost those exact same words the day the realtor let me walk through it. It has good bones that I felt deserved the chance to be a home again. But, I have to be honest, had I realized how much work it was going to be to update this place and get it up and going, I'd have probably balked and brought in a pre-fabbed job."

"Well, that would have been okay too."

Just then, one of the kids called the bishop on the walkie-talkie radio.

"Okay, foreman, one of your lost sheep needs you," Leon remarked. He paused for a moment to wipe the sweat off his forehead as he watched Bishop walk away talking on the radio. Leon rested for a minute from his labors and considered that he *was* glad that Bishop was helping him update the place. Doing the work had showed Leon that he could never do it on his own. Leon also admitted the work was good in another way; it tired him out so he could sleep nights. For the umpteenth time today, he wished Marion were there. Oh well, she wasn't, and he couldn't take care of her yet without a house anyway. Forcefully he told himself to go back to work, while feeling grateful that there were things that he was qualified to do to update his new, old house. Leon had planned that having his own place would require him to do all sorts of jobs, but "skilled laborer" had never been one of his job titles before.

As he shoveled more dirt to dig down his crawl space into a basement, Leon tallied all the work the crew and he and accomplished since July.

When Marion left, he'd been distraught. In desperation he'd tracked down Bishop Morley for some spiritual advice. Bishop not only helped Leon find a new way to think of his and Marion's predicament, but proved to be a practical man when he had the idea or inspiration to get him serious about what could be done to make the old, Gorham place livable.

Bishop had told Leon that he should put a roof on and paint the Gorham house to protect it from the elements and then take as long as he needed to work on the fixes it needed inside and below. He'd sent Leon home from their counseling session determined to succeed with two main tasks to accomplish: First, rip off the plywood and paint the outside boards and second, rip off shingles so he could sheet and shingle the roof. He smiled thinking about how they'd talked about those two things. "But, Bishop, I'm not a roofer," Leon had said.

"Son, I think that anybody can use a hammer and crowbar to rip off shingles. You're not afraid of heights are you?"

"No, but…."

"No buts, Leon. I'll come over in the morning and test the roof to ensure it can hold your weight and then you can get to it. I'll even bring a dumpster with me. You have shovels, a wheelbarrow, a good claw hammer, a crowbar?"

"Well, yes."

"Then plan on it. If you can get the roof down to the slats, me and my sons can be there in two days to sheet and paper it. I'll also bring you one of my large roof tarps so it will be okay even in the rain until we get shingles back on."

Leon admitted that Bishop had browbeat him into doing this work at first, but now thanked his good fortune that Bishop continued helping and now acted as general contractor on this job. Leon had also learned to trust the bishop. Each time he couldn't even figure out what exactly to do about the next item, Bishop would show up with a crew, supplies, and a permit.

The bishop got Leon working immediately. The hard work gave Leon what he needed, a reason to get out of bed each day and a way to wear him out and make him too tired to moon over Marion at night. Bishop also helped Leon decide about whether to quit the tractor shop and move out to the farm or put that decision off. Leon was grateful Monte understood his situation and agreed to let him be the part-time mechanic on Saturdays and whenever the new kid was off. The extra money from those TT hours helped and the work kept his tractor skills strong.

That first day of the house job, Leon had started on the roof tearing shingles off as he was instructed. From the roof, he'd watched the bishop bring in a well digger rig and crew to dig a couple of test holes around the place to check the water table and percolation rates for a new septic system. The bishop hadn't mentioned it that day, but it was clear that he was working to help Leon meet all his goals for the house, including digging down the floor in the "basement" so a man could stand up comfortably.

Leon had worked hard and persisted and got the roof down to the bare boards in two and a half days. The bishop was as good as his word and let Leon help him, and his two oldest sons, re-sheet the roof with a layer of three-quarter inch plywood. Then, they papered and shingled it. He also let Leon pay for the supplies but donated the labor to what he termed Leon's "good cause."

The bishop brought over his foundation specialist the next day and, while Leon was taking down the plywood covering the windows and doors, the foundation guy attacked the coal chute and chipped out enough blocks to make a serviceable, if rough, entrance into the cellar from the outside.

While Leon installed the old storm windows to protect the windows from any construction damage, the bishop taught his youngest son how to frame-in a doorway by helping him build a doorframe for the new door hole in the foundation.

That night, the bishop had sat Leon down and gave him an updated list of what he needed to do with the house that included approximate timeframes and costs. They'd sat at the tiny table in the machine shop's kitchenette and hammered out a plan with a timeline and budget. The next week, the bishop started bringing in the crew of handpicked, high school kids from the area where he'd taught house-building skills in his tech classes that past school year.

Leon could still hear how the bishop had explained to the kids. "The school district doesn't have the money to build a new house this year, but they did agree to help the kids buy their own tools and help me get some supplies for you." Leon knew he'd never understand how the bishop found the time to run a successful home construction outfit, teach a shop class at the high school each term, and teach his children and these kids all summer.

Only later did Bishop explain part of how he could accomplish so much when he explained, "I'm trying to teach my oldest son how to run a job site. My final exam is to leave him alone on a job to see how he handles it."

This reverie, thinking about the start of his house project, got Leon through his last day of basement digging. He was happy to take the last load of dirt in the wheelbarrow out and stand by the cottonwood tree drinking a cold bottle of water. Now that he'd dug down three feet everywhere, there was sufficient clearance for him to stand comfortably even after they added more footings and blocks to reinforce the foundation before pouring a cement floor. He looked over to the house and saw that the framers were finished installing the last beam. He was very grateful the bishop was helping with the structural fixes.

From where he stood, Leon could also see the fireplace guys working on the stovepipe connections on the roof and some of the high school kids who were working inside fitting the replacement boards in the framing. He sat down on the dry grass in the shade and rolled his shoulders and back to stretch them.

He hadn't sat long before he saw Gene's truck coming up the dusty lane from the east. It slowed down at his lane and pulled in. It was Gene driving. Leon stood up and met him at his truck.

"Hey, Leon."

"Hey, Gene. How's things?"

"Fine. Fine. Jeanette sent me down here to see if she could bring your crew lunch."

"Maybe. Let me find out." Leon pulled out his walkie-talkie and called the bishop. "Hey Bishop, did you cover lunch today? Okay. Jeanette Sullivan would like to feed the crew. That all right? Roger. I'll tell him. Off." He looked to Gene. "The bishop says that's fine. Can she do about one o'clock?"

"Sure can. I'll tell her. Then, I have a favor, Leon."

"Shoot."

"I need your help at the old house. I need to pack up the rest of Marion's stuff so Atzo's son can move in."

Leon spoke casually to cover his upset. "Okay. When?"

"Tonight after dark if you can."

"Okay. Do you need boxes?"

"No, just packing help and some strong arms to help me carry stuff to my truck and then into my house."

"Can you use another truck?"

"If you're willing."

Gene looked at him as if he'd say more, so Leon asked him, "Spit it out, Gene. What is it?"

"You know. It's Marion. I don't know what to do."

"About what? She's fine. Probably working hard, getting tan, and eating all the pineapple she can hold."

"Well, it's about you too. Have you heard from her at all?"

"You know I haven't. I would have told you. Hasn't she called or written you guys?"

"No more than a few words every couple of weeks. Like you said, if I'd heard anything I would have told you… that is unless you don't want me to."

"So that's it… Gene, do you want me to give up on your sister?"

"Of course not. I just had a thought this morning, that maybe you needed space or was done with her."

Leon shook his head and looked heavenward. "Gene, you know that if Marion didn't tell you about our last conversation before she left, that I'm not about to. I will say this though. If I thought there was no chance of your sister ever coming back here, I'd tell you. Just like I would if I was sure she'd never agree to marry me. I know you'll be second to know that she's agreed to marry me; second after the bishop."

"So, you think she'll marry you, eventually?"

"Honestly, Gene, I don't know. I have to keep hoping, but I don't know for sure. I think that you and I both know that when Marion makes a decision about marrying me she'll let us both know; of course, I hope she'd tell me first."

Both men smiled at Leon's half joke.

"Thanks, Leon. I guess I needed to hear that you still have hope. It's killing me that she had to run off all the way to Hawaii," Gene said.

"Well, Gene, if it helps, I think she'd have gone anywhere, but here, to try to figure out what she wanted. I agree that Hawaii was a bit far, but she could have easily gone to Vegas or the coast or even back East." Bitterness crept into his tone, "Anywhere away from me."

"Now, Leon, you have to know that's not true. I could tell she hated leaving you. She just needed to get away from the farm."

"I try, every day, to hope that you are right."

The bishop came over to them at that moment. He nodded to Leon and looked at Gene. "Hey, Gene. Good to see ya, but I need you to leave Leon alone. I'm working him hard." He winked to soften the censure.

"Leon, don't think about Marion right now. You have a house to work on," he told Leon.

"How do you know we were talking about Marion?" Leon responded.

"Well, besides the fact that you were talking to her brother, you have that wrinkled brow you get when you speak of her." He turned back to Gene. "Now Gene, have a little faith in your baby sister. She's just getting a new perspective. Treat this like a learning experience for you. Think about how you are going to handle it when your Nancy feels like moving to Salt Lake to go to the U." He then addressed both men. "Okay boys. Home with you, Gene. Back to work, Leon."

"Okay Bishop. Bye, Leon. I'll be at the house when you get there," Gene said.

"See you, Gene," Leon said, and followed the bishop back up to the Gorham house.

"Leon, I looked over your basement. It looks good," the bishop said. "I think I'll call my foundation guys in tomorrow and the cement truck the next day. I ordered the cement already so I'll have the final bill when they're done. You still okay with the ten thousand dollars for the basement foundations and concrete?"

"Yes I am. That money I have covered easy from my house budget. I will be glad to see the dirt walls below the existing foundation blocked in and the foundations for the posts poured, let alone the floor."

"Good, good. Do your shoulders feel up to running the compactor? I think that's a job you could handle and it would probably take you the rest of the day to compact the soil now that you've dug down."

"I think so."

"Good, come help me get it off the truck and I'll get you started."

Leon had been working to compact the basement soil for an hour when Jeanette arrived with lunch. He sat with everyone else on the ground, under the huge cottonwood tree, eating thick roast beef sandwiches, pickles, fresh tomatoes, and chips. They drank frosty lemonade and finished off with homemade strawberry shortcake.

Jeanette went around and gathered everyone's used plastic wear and paper plates in a big garbage sack after lunch. She stopped to sit by Leon for a minute as he was still finishing his strawberry dessert.

"These from your garden, Jeanette?" Leon asked.

"Yes. Picked 'em yesterday."

"They're good. Thank you. You're a good cook."

"Thank you," she stopped, then continued, "Leon, I'm taking the kids over to the old house when I get back. I'll pack all the stuff we need to store in boxes so you and Gene will just have to move them."

"I appreciate that, Jeanette."

"I figured. I don't know why Gene thought it would be good for you to pack her things. Sorry that he's a bit insensitive."

"It's no big deal. I feel a bit unsure about what to do about it, myself."

"I know. I'm sorry." She laid a gentle hand on his arm. "If it helps, I'm praying she comes to her senses and gets her tail back here, and soon."

"Me too, Jeanette, me too."

Chapter Twenty-Eight

"Marion, that bikini looks killer hot on you. You have such a great figure. Plus, that red and pink flower print is really pretty," Kim observed, as she peeked into the beach boutique shop's dressing room where Marion was standing in front of a mirror.

"It makes me almost wish that our hotel dressed the waitresses in bikini tops and grass skirts like the one I stayed at in Waikiki." Marion responded.

"You don't mean that. I think those girls get pawed. And I disagree with jobs that hire you because you "look right" on principle. Though I must say, you've got the right hair and curves to wear the grass skirt but, frankly, I think you're too big for the coconuts."

"Oh, sure, follow up a good point about principles with a coconut crack, Kimmie." Marion turned around and changed the subject. "So, can I buy the matching boy-short bottoms instead of the French cut?" She turned around so Kim could see how the shorts looked.

"I think so. They make your bootic look cute, and seem to be more modest, even though they are totally tight."

"That's what I was thinking."

Kim passed Marion a lava-lava. "I think you should buy the sarong too. It will help you knock the socks of Leon when he sees you in it, especially if you only wear it long enough to drop it and show off the shorts."

"Hey Kim, you know the rules. Don't bring up his name while I'm here."

"I have to," Kim persisted. "You're pretending he doesn't exist but I've caught you staring off into space one too many times. You can never run far enough from your problems, hon. It's time you faced facts. Now, I'm not saying that I wouldn't love for you to stay here and be my roomie, but I don't think that coming here to be with me is making you as happy as you wanted."

Marion finished tying on the lava-lava. It rode just right on her middle, and showed her belly button perfectly. She looked at the bikini top and considered how it looked under the white, cotton cover-up that she had knotted closed in front. Then she turned back to her best friend.

"Kim, you may be right. I was just thinking how I could pair the white, cover-up blouse with this and look totally modest, but then undo two knots and knock Leon on his butt," she sighed. "I am still so obsessed with him."

"Ah, Marion. Come on, admit it. I think you really love him."

"I don't know if I can say that out loud here. I mean, I told him I loved him and I thought I was tired of the farm but, standing here with you, I feel scared. Could I have run all the way here to Hawaii, because I was scared of marrying him?"

"You wouldn't be the first woman to run away because someone got too close... but I still think you should stay here the full three months like you planned. I think you need to be absolutely sure that a different lifestyle won't fix your problem. Besides, I know that you work as hard here with me cleaning hotel rooms, waitressing and escorting tourists around as you do on your ranch."

"Kimmie, what would you do?"

"I don't honestly know. I mean, I have a year left of school at BYU-Hawaii, and have saved enough from tips and work to take a year off after that. I was planning on staying here for that year and getting a killer nest egg before I go back to the mainland. But, I have never had a man profess his undying love for me... so I cannot say that I *wouldn't* throw it all down to roll the dice with a handsome man who loved me, especially if I loved him back. Isn't that what life's all about?"

Chapter Twenty-Nine

"Holy cow, Leon, you've done so much around here! WOW." Gene remarked as he came in the back door into Leon's newly remodeled kitchen. He held Jeremy in his arms and Jeanette followed on his heels carrying a box with Mick and Nancy following her.

"Thanks, Gene. But I was just labor on this. The bishop and his crew did most the work."

"Well, it looks great. The wood floors glow under their new finish, those pendant lights are great and it's great that you kept the old wood stove in place."

Leon watched Gene start his walk-through of the house. He turned back to Jeanette.

"What's in the box?"

Jeanette sat the box down on the new counter next to the new sink. "Oh, just some staples. When the bishop told me that the electrical was done and you finally had a fridge in here, Gene and I wanted to help you fill it as partial thanks for you watching our kids on and off these past few weeks."

Leon went over and looked in the box. He saw milk, cheese, various fruits and vegetables on top and white freezer wrapped packages of what were probably meat on the bottom. "Gee, Jeanette, that's neat. I haven't been to town in a week and was running low on everything."

"Yeah, Gene told me, we're glad to help."

Mick came up and tugged on Leon's shirt hem. "Hey Leon, I told Nancy about your window in the shower upstairs and she didn't believe me. Can ya take her up there and show her?"

Leon smiled, and glanced up to see that Jeanette was smiling too. He said, "Sure thing, sport. Let me stash the groceries your mom brought me and then I'll take you and her on the whole tour."

He looked at Jeanette. "I've let Mick and Nancy play downstairs in the basement, but only Mick was around when we got the upstairs bath going. Can I include you in the kiddie tour, or do you want to find your husband and baby."

"I'll go with you. Gene will probably be stuck on the finishes and I would love to hear about why you did what you did."

"Okay."

Leon slid the box down the counter, past his new farmhouse sink and dishwasher to the fridge. He opened the lower door to the freezer first and then the upper fridge door. He started putting the food away when Nancy came over and tugged on his shirt.

"Me help," she said.

"Sure thing, cutie," he said, and moved the box to the floor. He moved over and then watched over Nancy as she handed him the carrots, and then took out one of the paper-wrapped meat packages and put it on the freezer shelf she could just reach. He and she continued working until the box was empty.

When done, Nancy reached up to take his hand and started walking to the hall.

"Come on, Leon. Come on Mommy," she said.

Mick grabbed his mom's hand and said, "I've got Mommy. You take Leon. Let's show Mommy the neat basement first."

Leon enjoyed taking Jeanette and the older kids on the first tour he'd given anyone of his new house.

They started in the kitchen where he'd shown off the cabinets the bishop had helped him refinish and the tile countertops the bishop's daughter had installed for practice.

You know, Leon. Marion would love the cobalt blue color you picked," Jeanette remarked about the tiles.

"You think so? I guessed on so many things, but I loved the blue and with all the wood tones from the floors and paneling, I figured the kitchen could handle the strong color."

"You've got a good eye."

They continued through the hall past the stove and paused at the bedrooms.

"I figured the little room could be an office, so I painted it white. Because the bedroom faces south, I painted it light blue to cool it down," he said.

Nancy pulled Leon over to the closet, and said, "My play closet." And pointed to the door.

Leon obediently opened it and explained to Jeanette, "Inside this closet, there's an access door down to the basement where the old water heater was. When we boarded it off downstairs to make the furnace room, it made a little square box at the bottom of the closet that Nancy was using as a cubby hole for her dolls to sleep in."

Jeanette peeked in. "It makes a great dolly bed, and can hold stuff you don't want folks to know you have."

"You got it."

They moved down the hall to the front room. "Oh, Leon," Jeanette said. "I am so glad you kept that lovely front door. The wood looks amazing." She turned and looked at the new tile where the antique coal stove from upstairs now sat. "The bishop told me you were able to save one of the old coal stoves and convert it to wood, is this it?"

"Yup. It seemed like just the thing for down here, and since the furnace is on the back end of the house, we figured it would be neat in the winter to have a small fire in here for ambiance as well as extra warmth."

"That's a great idea." Jeanette turned and looked out the big windows on either side of the door and turned back to him. "I can just see a huge Christmas tree in here, with a fire going and a couch or some chairs... this will make a great, family, gathering place for you."

Leon moved to stand on the southern end of the room by the stairs. "Yeah, and my aunt said I could have Great Grandma's old, upright piano. I figured it could go here where I'm standing."

"That's perfect. What a great idea." She looked down at her son. "Then, I'll bring Mick over and give him piano lessons."

"Anytime."

Gene came down the stairs at that moment. "Hey Leon, I love how you updated the stairs and found new spindles to match the banister."

"That was another one of the bishop's pet projects. One of his shop students wants to be a carpenter so he and the bishop devised a jig for the spindles and made them all in the high school wood shop."

"That's great," Gene said. "I am glad the bishop is keeping those shop skills alive." Gene then looked to Jeanette. "I'll be back in the kitchen." He held Jeremy up a bit and said, "Someone needs a new diaper." and headed down the hall and into the bathroom.

"While Gene is busy, let's do upstairs and then the basement?" Leon asked.

He took his group up the stairs and through the first bedroom.

"I wasn't sure I wanted to keep the set-up of going through one room to get to the other, but ultimately the bishop convinced me that we couldn't lose that much space to a hall up here... as you can see, we got the spray-foam insulation done in here, but not the drywall," he said.

"That makes sense. You'll keep in the heat or the cool, and then can finish it when you can," Jeanette said.

"Well, I hope I picked the right bedroom to finish. I decided to finish the back bedroom because I like its view of the hills. I ran out of money up here mid-bathroom, so we got the tub/shower in, and the plumbing ready, but I can install the sink and set the toilet in an afternoon."

"That makes sense," Jeanette continued. "That bedroom should be cooler in the summer as it faces east."

"That's my hope too, though it's too hot now, so I've been staying downstairs in the kitchen on my cot. It's cooler there and I don't need to run my new A/C."

They ended the upstairs tour with the bathroom and Leon held Nancy up so she could look out the window in the shower.

"I like the tile in here too, Leon. The dark blue and green accents really set off those crisp, white, subway tiles and go with the marble floor," Jeanette observed.

"Mommy, why does he have a window in the shower?" Mick asked.

Jeanette looked to Leon and said, "I bet because that's the only window in here and he wanted to keep it, right?"

"That's right." Leon told Mick. "I put in a special window and framed it with marble so it can get wet."

"And you can watch Bill plowing as you shower," Mick said.

"You got it, champ."

Leon led the group back downstairs and then down into the basement.

"I can see why you let the kids run around down here. With it being open like this, they can go crazy," Jeanette remarked.

"You got it. It's also cooler down here in the afternoon and, once we got the posts in and the final support beam up, it was the one place in the house where me and kids could stay out of everybody's way."

Jeanette wandered over to the new door that replaced the old coal chute. "Does this go outside?"

"Sure does. It opens into a dug-down stairwell just north of the front steps."

"That makes is really convenient to store stuff down here."

"My thoughts exactly. The bishop went so far as to make it a four-foot wide opening so I can move in bigger stuff if needed. One day Gene brought the kid's bikes down through it and we did circles around and around."

"Well, Leon, I don't know whether or not my sister-in-law will come back to herself or not, but if she makes it back to you, she will love what you did with your house."

"That's my hope."

Chapter Thirty

"Bishop, it's Marion. Yeah, I'm back from Hawaii. Actually, I'm at the airport. If I can get to Ogden, can you help get me home? Okay. Call my cell phone if you need to. Thanks, Bishop!"

Marion wheeled her suitcase down the terminal and out past the baggage claim. She hopped on the Trax, light-rail train that would take her into Salt Lake City, where she could catch the larger commuter train to Ogden. *I'm glad I got on the early flight*, she thought to herself. With the time zone changes, had she been any later, she'd have had to stay overnight in Salt Lake.

She could feel her skin and hair drying out in the hot, desert air of Utah. She'd bought a big tube of lotion, lip balm, and a large bottle of water in the airport as she'd left the gate. Knowing it will be dryer in Utah than in Oahu was one thing and experiencing it was totally another.

She made it on the second-to-last FrontRunner train heading to Ogden that night. The bishop, having said he'd be in Tremonton with friends tonight, told her all she had to do was tell him when the train would reach Ogden and he'd be there. Marion clicked the text out and sent it. She laid her head back on the seat enjoying the air conditioning in the train car. She knew she'd be jet-lagged for a bit with the four-hour time zone difference between Mountain and island time. She missed Leon and hoped he would still be where she could find him once she made it home.

The bishop met her in Ogden and they chatted the whole way to the dirt road that led to her lane and Leon's.

Marion got out of the car with her suitcase, stood on the gravel road, off Leon's lane, and leaned over to hear the bishop.

"Are you sure you'll be okay walking from here?" he asked, from the car window.

"Leon should be sleeping in the house, right?"

"Should be, but I don't know for sure. Today's his day off."

"Don't worry, Bishop. Worst case scenario is that he's not here and I call Gene or Jeanette to come get me."

"Okay, Marion. Let me know what happens. If the best happens, I can marry you any time you guys get the license. I can even work to get you a temple ceremony time next week, but you need to let me know tomorrow so I can set it up."

"You're pretty hopeful, Bishop," Marion smiled.

"I know you two. I also know that Leon worked hard to let you go, because he hoped you'd come back. You are back for good?"

"Yes, I am. That's why I'm back early in fact. This is where I need to be. I know that now."

"Okay, honey. Keep me posted."

"Will do. Thank you again for coming and getting me."

"My pleasure. It's the least that I can do for you and Leon. You two deserve to be very happy."

Marion looked around and started walking down Leon's lane. She'd asked the bishop to drop her off up on the state line road a bit away from Leon's house so she'd have a chance of not waking him up. The sodium light from Leon's new barn light and power pole, attached to the shop, gave everything a yellowish color and allowed Marion to see the house and driveway quite well. Leon's truck sat in its usual spot by the shop, but his parents' RV was gone. *That makes sense*, she thought. *The bishop said he'd be sleeping in the house, so he doesn't need the RV anymore.*

The rocks in the gravel roadbed soon got too tricky for her suitcase's wheels, so she hefted it by the handle and then made her way carefully over to the house. She looked around curiously. She could see that the house had been worked on. It had been painted, had a new screen door on the front door, new roof, new trim, and generally looked habitable. She liked it.

The bishop had told her about how he and Leon were working to get it livable as economically as possible. He'd also told her a bit about what they'd done. She knew Leon was doing it for himself, but she hoped that part of this was for her. Leon *did* say he'd make them a nest they could feather together. She hoped he still felt that way.

Marion thought about what she knew of Leon's plans. The bishop said they had most of the house finished and that Leon would keep working on the remaining drywall and the upstairs bathroom through the fall and winter. Jeanette had said that the new, TT general manager wasn't working out so Monte had hired a new mechanic and asked Leon to work at the tractor dealer four days a week for now. *That should help Leon's nest egg stay strong*, she thought.

She wasn't sure how to enter the house, but the bishop had told her that Leon was close to his budget for this year, so they'd stopped work for now. Leon could move in because they had made good progress downstairs. She went around back to the kitchen thinking she could get something to eat if Leon was sleeping. That gave her pause, she hadn't thought out where she would sleep. Since Leon's parents' RV was gone, and Atzo Jr. had her house, she may have to take the shop cot. Then she thought of her truck. Maybe she could sleep in it. But, she wasn't sure where Gene had parked it and she had no keys with her anyway.

She reached the back porch pushing aside her sleeping arrangement worries until she was tired, or found

Leon. If necessary she would sleep in the back of his truck. The back porch had a new set of three cement stairs with a wider stoop. Marion was glad to see that Leon had kept the old screen door and inner door, but fixed them up. She'd always liked the back door with the window that matched the inside door with the window for the hall. She wondered if he kept the wood floors and that big, old wood stove.

Marion climbed the stoop steps and set her suitcase down at the top. Carefully, she eased open the screen door, expecting its springy chain to creak. But it had a new hydraulic arm that was very quiet. She saw that Leon had installed a new deadbolt and replaced the door handle in the solid door. Gingerly, she turned the handle. It turned. *Great. It's not locked. He must be inside*, she thought. She turned the handle again and gently pushed it open. She poked her head into the kitchen. There was a tiny glowing green nightlight plugged in next to the old, wood stove that gave some light. Marion moved into the kitchen slowly to allow her eyes to adjust. She was getting ready to take another step when a set of arms grabbed her firmly around her upper chest and whirled her into the kitchen as it lit up.

She'd got out half a scream before she heard, Leon's voice.

"My God! Marion!" he exclaimed, and the arms that held her tightly suddenly released her.

She stumbled against the cold wood stove after losing her balance. She blinked rapidly trying to adjust her sight from her night vision to the bright light from the new pendant lights hanging from the tall ceiling.

She got her balance and looked over to see Leon was looking at her. She noticed he was wearing a thin, white, holey T-shirt and some baggy cotton pajamas that had been hacked off at the knee. She said, "Leon, I…" But couldn't say anything more as he moved quickly to embrace her. He held her tightly and as she returned his embrace, she felt him shuddering.

They stood there each holding the other tightly for a time.

Leon let go of her and fell to his knees at her feet. He grabbed her around the waist and put his face against her stomach as he knelt there. She clasped his shoulder with one hand and rested the other on his neck rubbing the soft hairs there as tears of joy ran down her cheeks and emotion stopped her throat.

Leon's shoulders continued to tremble and she felt his arms continue to shudder as he held on to her. After a moment, he looked up at her and she saw what was causing him to shake; he was crying. No sounds came, but tears were running down his cheeks.

"Oh Leon, honey. I am so sorry I ever left you. I love you. I've come back. Please, don't cry."

"You're really here? You're real?" His voice was rough.

She pulled his arms from around her waist and pulled on them to make him stand up as she said, "I am. I'm here. I love you. I don't ever want to be apart from you again."

"Marry me."

"Yes. When?"

He stood up and hugged her tightly again.

She rested her head between his shoulder and neck.

"Now? Today," he answered, finally.

She pulled back a bit. "Good, I'll text the bishop. He should be home by now. He dropped me off about twenty minutes ago."

"Do it quick."

"Okay."

Marion pulled her phone out of her pocket and typed out a quick message.

Leon pulled it out of her hand when she hit send and set it on the counter. He pulled her close again, and went to kiss her.

"The door's open and my suitcase is out on the step."

"So?"

And then he did kiss her. She kissed him back, and Marion knew she was home to stay.

When the kiss was over, Marion asked, "Can I stay here tonight?"

Leon laughed. "Yes, if you want my cot or the floor. I'll take whichever you don't use with my sleeping bag. I don't have a bed yet."

"So, do you want to sneak into Gene's house and get mine? That way you can keep your cot, but I can have my comfy bed."

"Actually, we can sneak into his garage and get it."

"Oh, no! My mattress will be full of mice."

"No, it won't. It's only been in the garage since this morning, and it's wrapped in plastic besides. Gene wants me to store your stuff here in the house and he was bringing it over tomorrow."

"Why is my stuff your problem?"

"That's kinda your fault. I did what you asked and didn't tell Gene about your plan to use Hawaii to decide farm or non-farm. His putting your stuff in my house is his way of ensuring that you spoke to me one last time."

"He thinks I abandoned you, doesn't he."

"That's my fault. Mare, I missed you. Sometimes I couldn't hide it. I tried to be strong and keep hope that you'd be back but, sometimes, I wondered whether I could compete with Hawaii. I don't ever want to be a burden to you."

Tears filled her eyes. "Oh, baby, you could never burden me; you're my salvation. I was overwhelmed by my baggage over the farm when I should have been courageous and married you weeks ago. You're my heart."

She saw Leon smile and swallow, but he didn't speak. Instead, he held her close to his chest. After a few minutes he said, "I love you more than life. I had to let you go, because I couldn't bear to cage you if you didn't want to stay, but living without you would have killed me had Bishop not come up with the plan to use this house to distract me. I still feel like I'm asleep and you are some cruel figment of a dream."

Marion pinched his arm. "Wake up, I'm here and I'm real... I'm also real hungry and very jet-lagged. So, if I stick by you like glue for the next few days, will that help you believe that I'm back to stay?"

"Maybe if you stay with me for a year, I may be okay. As for food, it's two in the morning, let's raid Gene's fridge when we go get your bed."

"Deal."

"By the way, has the bishop answered your text?"

"Oh, I didn't look." Marion grabbed her cellphone, "I left it on silent, but that's okay as I would rather listen to and watch you right now." But she looked down; there was a response text. Marion smiled hugely as she read it.

"Well?" Leon asked.

"It says: 'Ogden or Salt Lake? I'll call the temple tomorrow and be by for breakfast around ten.'" She looked at him. "The bishop knows I don't want to get married in Brigham or Logan, so which do you prefer, Ogden or Salt Lake?"

"Well, Grandpa and Grandma were married in Salt Lake, so can we go there?" he answered.

"Suits me just fine. My great-grandparents were married there too. I'll text him." Marion typed out the text, and then asked, "Can you take me shopping for a dress tomorrow?"

"Sure. I can look for a tux and maybe a ring?"

"I don't need a ring, since you won't wear one due to your job."

"Okay, but you have to explain that to Gene."

"Leave my brother to me, sweetie. I love you, Leon."

"Ditto, my heart."

Epilogue

"Bye, everybody!" Marion and Leon spoke in unison to the happy crowd of friends and family who were gathered on the LDS temple grounds in Salt Lake City. Leon's Mom's protégé had taken down her camera now that the last picture was taken. The good wishes and hugs were done and folks were heading to their vehicles to go home.

Leon looked down at her and smiled and then gave her a quick kiss. "I love you, Mrs. Packer."

"I love you, too, Mr. Packer," Marion answered back, smiling. He pulled her over to the curb and handed her up into the open-topped carriage he'd hired to take them to the hotel.

"I am glad you were okay with us *not* having a wedding breakfast/dinner or a reception. We've got the rest of our day to start our honeymoon. No more good wishes or friends and family wanting hugs or pictures," he said, once they were settled.

Marion snuggled into his side as he raised his arm over her shoulders. "I agree. I figured we don't need three crockpots, two irons or one-towel wedding gifts."

"You don't miss the money do you?"

"Not really, but I noticed that you got envelopes from a few die-hards. I just want to *not* feel guilty about no wedding party. Mom always said you should have a wedding get-together because there are some folks you only see at weddings and funerals and, while weddings allow everyone to be happy together, there are usually more funerals. But, I am glad we skipped it. I'm glad we're done doing what other people want."

"That's a good way to put it. It was our wedding, but it seemed like we did lots of stuff for folks besides us."

"Yup. I learned that at my parents' funerals. Some things are for the others and I wanted today to be for us."

"That's reason number nine-hundred and fifty-two why I love you, lady." He gave her a long, lingering kiss.

They sat enjoying the bright, autumn sunshine shining through the trees along the wide, city streets. Marion found the clip clopping of the horse's hooves on the asphalt soothing. The carriage would take them the five blocks from Temple Square to the hotel, and it was nice way to travel the few blocks.

"Penny for your thoughts?" Leon asked.

"Just thinking that I am glad we took the train down last night and stayed in the hotel. It's nice taking a carriage ride back instead of walking."

"Better than a limo?"

"Much better. It's too pretty a day to stay indoors. Besides, we're showing folks something good to see."

"I agree. If I wasn't looking at my lovely bride, I could have waved at six different sets of folks who waved at us in the last block."

Marion laughed.

Soon enough, they reached the hotel. Marion felt a moment of déjà vu taking her back to her wedding dream, as Leon got out of the carriage first. Unlike her dream, he didn't carry her out of it, but he did help her down and then they walked into the lobby hand in hand. She turned pink as most of the hotel patrons stood up and clapped at them. *Clearly, I am a bride because of my silky, white dress and pink-rose bouquet, and Leon makes a uber-handsome groom in his black tuxedo*, she thought to herself. Leon joined her in smiling and waving as they made their way to the elevators.

"So, how was the room last night?" she asked.

"Wonderful, but lonely. It was weird staying in the bridal suite by myself and it killed me that Jeanette wouldn't let me see you last night. I will say that you'll love the tub."

"I can't wait."

Gene and Jeanette had gifted them a five-night stay at the high-rise hotel in a bridal suite. When she and Leon had asked for two regular rooms for the night before the wedding, the hotel let Leon have the bridal suite for that night at the regular rate and gave Marion a room on the same floor. On their way to the temple, Leon had left the hotel early with Gene, Mick and Jeremy. Jeanette and Nancy had squired Marion. Leon had told her "good night" at check in and she didn't see him again until they met in the rooms in the temple prior to their wedding.

"I'm glad Jeanette and your mom were with me in the bride's room at the temple. Did your uncle and aunt do okay with Mick, Nancy and Jeremy outside?" she asked.

"Yes, and my teenaged cousins helped because Jeremy was squirmy."

"It was neat for Gene and your dad to be the witnesses." She stroked his cheek. "You looked handsome in your temple whites."

"As you did, and do, in the dress you are wearing. I must say I am dying to get you out of it though. It's been a long summer keeping my hands off you, Mrs."

Marion laughed. "Only if I get to peel you out of that tux, Mister. It shocked me how handsome you look in the black. Your blond looks blonder and the white shirt makes your skin look so tan."

"Why thank you, my lady. Glad that I can please you."

"Oh knock it off. When are we ever going to dress like this again?"

"Hopefully never. You can't believe how tight and stuffy this thing is."

The elevator doors chimed. Leon looked at her and, before she knew what he was about to do, he swung her up over his shoulder with her head hanging down his back and her toes dangling behind her.

"Hey, this isn't how you're supposed to carry me over the threshold!" she cried.

"Well, it's the only way I can keep your feet off the ground and slide the card in the door lock. I'll fix it at the threshold, okay?"

"Okay, just don't drop me. I don't think I can handle the fall from this high."

"Ha, ha, wifey... here we are."

Leon swiped the card and opened the door. He paused for a moment putting his foot in the door to keep it open as he pocketed the keycard.

"Hold on, here we go, Mrs. Packer." With that he swung her off his shoulder and caught her under her knees and behind her back in a smooth motion. He proceeded into the room with great ceremony, raised her up and dropped her onto the waiting, king-sized bed.

Marion felt another déjà vu moment from her dream, but Leon didn't take off her shoes, instead he leaned her back against the covers and gave her the long lingering kiss she remembered. When he was satisfied for a moment, he leaned up on his arms and asked, "So, Mrs. Packer are you ready?"

She shook her head. "I've got something for you first."

"Oh fine." And Leon rolled to her side acting wounded.

She leaned over him. "Hey, buck up, sweetie. You'll like this." She scooted off the bed. She paused by the ice bucket on the bureau and took it with her into the bathroom.

In the bathroom, she located her small suitcase. She was glad Jeanette stashed it in there like she asked. She filled the ice bucket with cool water and then dropped her bouquet into it not wanting the flowers to wilt just yet. Then, Marion carefully removed her wedding dress, stockings and shoes, stripping down to bare skin. She stashed her underthings in her case and hung her dress in the waiting garment bag hanging on the back of the door. She hurriedly pulled out the red bikini Kim had helped her pick out in Hawaii. She wiggled into the bottoms and tied the front tie to the top. She tied the lava-lava around her hips. Then she pulled one of the roses out of her bouquet and tucked it into the hair above her ear. She evaluated herself in the mirror and decided to skip the cover-up and go as she was. She took a deep breath and relished the anticipation of the start of her honeymoon with her groom and opened the bathroom door.

Leon's eyes found her the minute she appeared and didn't leave her as she made her way slowly to him. He'd taken off his tuxedo jacket, shoes and socks, and was laying sideways on the bed leaning up on one elbow. He'd also undone his black bowtie and its ends were hanging down against his chest betraying the deep breaths he was taking.

He kept staring at her, his mouth hanging slightly open. Marion stopped at the edge of the bed and stood staring back at him.

"Well? I bought this bikini for you back on Oahu… It's kind of my wedding present to you," she said, when she couldn't stand the wait anymore.

Leon's voice was thick with emotion. "It's amazing. You're amazing. He sat up and pulled her so she was standing between his knees. "Now, I can give you your gift." He held her around her waist with his left hand as he reached into his trouser pocket with his right. One-handed, he pulled out a pink silken bag. He let go of her for a minute as he opened the ribbon drawstring and upended the bag over his palm. A sparkling gemstone and gold ring fell out. He pocketed the empty bag and then gently pulled her left hand forward. He looked up into her eyes as he slid the ring onto her third finger. "I know the family wondered why we didn't exchange rings after the temple ceremony. But, I wanted to surprise you with this. I know you know that I can't wear a ring, but I wanted you to have one." He held her hand up so she could see the ring.

Marion looked at it. Oval cut garnets were offset with diamonds across the ring. "Oh, it's beautiful! Garnets and diamonds?"

"Yes. I asked Jeanette what were the red stones in your earrings that first night I kissed you and she told me about your mom's garnets. Then Mom helped me design a ring and I had it made in Layton just for you."

"How did you know my size? It fits perfectly."

"When Jeanette packed your remaining stuff from the old house, she showed me the rings in your jewelry box. Most of them just fit my left pinkie, so I had the jeweler use that for the size."

She leaned down and grasped his cheeks and kissed him in thanks. "I love you, Leon. Now and forever."

"Ditto, baby. Now can I take this off?" he asked, as he tugged on the center tie of her bikini top.

"As soon as I can get this off you," she replied, as she tugged on his shirtfront.

About Virginia Babcock:

Virginia Babcock has always loved romantic fiction, and now writes her own stories of love and life in the real world. Virginia lives in northern Utah where she works full-time when she's not writing books. Her husband and cat keep her constantly entertained the rest of the time.

Social Media Links:

Facebook:
https://www.facebook.com/VirginiaBabcockBooks/

If you enjoyed this story, check out the other books by Virginia Babcock:

September Summer

FBI agent, Mitch Harper, is trying to keep a domestic terrorist, Michael Gooding, from blowing up any more U.S. targets in the summer of 2001. The FBI's computers are breached, so Gooding knows the names of the active agents and all of their travel plans for the next six months. Gooding has set three of his planned ten bombs. Mitch and his team are desperately trying to stop Gooding from setting off the rest. His only weakness is beautiful women, but he knows the identity of all the female FBI agents.

Jenny Johnson is doing all she can to manage her college class load while working full time for the IRS to pay the bills. Because she's a federal employee who happens to have a summer itinerary that matches Michael Gooding's known plans, the FBI taps her as bait, hoping to catch Gooding in time.

Jenny is the woman Mitch has always wanted. Mitch looks like the man of Jenny's dreams, despite his bossy, perfectionist attitude. As the next bombing date approaches, Jenny pushes Mitch's buttons as he tries to remain professional and train her to survive the mission. Will the FBI be able to corner Gooding in time? What will happen to Jenny? This is no time for love to interrupt a mission.

http://bookgoodies.com/a/B00WZSRG20

Reva's River

Robert Leland has been through a rough couple of years. First, his wife divorced him after she had an affair with the senior partner in her law firm, then he was tortured nearly to death after the mobsters he was staking out found out about his FBI undercover assignment. His injuries have cost him more than his cover, and it will take years for him to regain his physical abilities. In the meantime, his FBI boss wants him out of the team—there's no room in the DC mob taskforce for an undercover who can't walk.

Reva Findstein needed a change. Her family had deserted her for Israel and were now happily embracing their Jewish history while she languished in the old Maryland neighborhood. Only her DC FBI career had kept her occupied through her long, lonely days lately. Now, after nearly 20 years, she wondered whether she should quit the FBI and find something else. Then, Reva's boss takes on a special case. They need to transition a new agent for their terrorist team. He's in bad shape after running afoul of the mobsters he was investigating.

Can Reva help Robert regain his humanity? Will helping Robert give Reva something to live for after all these years? Sparks fly, but can these two overcome years of baggage and physical and mental anguish in order to grab a second chance at love?

http://bookgoodies.com/a/B015EJRGOO

Rock Hound Falling

Lexie is a young woman trying to exert her independence from her well-meaning, but overbearing brothers. She's an engineer in a family of engineers. This summer, she's trying a new tack--taking her turn to herd the family's cows high in the mountains. She's hiking there to meet her oldest brother before she starts this two-week endeavor.

On her hike, Lexie spots some rock climbers scaling her brother's favorite cliff. To her horror, she sees one fall. Knowing she's probably the only help for the fallen climber, Lexie rushes to his aid. He's survived the fall, but has grievous injuries. Lexie has no choice but to use her engineering skills to find a way to get the climber to help.

http://bookgoodies.com/a/B01I5DX6MW

www.ingramcontent.com/pod-product-compliance
Lightning Source LLC
Chambersburg PA
CBHW052033020726
47501CB00004B/1386